Mother Death
Paul O'Neill

Dear Shannon,

Thank you so much for giving me your time. I hope you enjoy it.

May your shadow never grow less

Paul O'Neill

First edition – January 2024

Copyright © 2024 by the author.

All rights reserved. No part of this publication may be reproduced without the written permission of the copyright owner except for review purposes.

This is a work of fiction. All names, characters, places, and events are the imaginings of the author, used in a fictitious manner. Any resemblance to living persons or actual events is coincidental.

No A.I. was used in the creation of this tale or the cover art. The cover was created by the author using stock images and Photoshop.

Dedication

For Susan Catherine Margaret O'Neill
You are nothing like the mother in this book.
You were never selfish.
Not once.

Contents

One	1
Two	8
Three	12
Four	17
Five	24
Six	29
Seven	35
Eight	39
Nine	49
Ten	55
Eleven	59
Twelve	64
Thirteen	68
Fourteen	74
Fifteen	82
Sixteen	86

Seventeen	91
Eighteen	96
Nineteen	102
Twenty	108
Twenty-one	112
Twenty-two	119
Twenty-three	124
Twenty-four	131
Twenty-five	135
Twenty-six	140
Twenty-seven	146
Twenty-eight	150
Twenty-nine	158
Thirty	165
Thirty-one	168
Thirty-two	172
Thirty-three	176
Thirty-four	181
Thirty-five	183
Thirty-six	190
Thirty-seven	200
Thirty-eight	208
Thirty-nine	213

Forty	217
Forty-one	222
Forty-two	230
Forty-three	235
Forty-four	242
Forty-five	250
Forty-six	254
Forty-seven	256
Forty-eight	262
Forty-nine	269
Fifty	275
Fifty-one	281
Fifty-two	289
Epilogue	301
Afterword	304
Into the Drinking Dark – Bonus Short Story	306
About the Author	311

One

Dottie Matheson waited in the shadows, leaning against one of the four metal pillars that held up the centre of the circus tent. Her son walked through a curtain and onto the circular stage. The scent of heavy latex and trampled mud was strong as she moved her hand back and forth along her stomach.

The last dregs of the Kirkcaldy crowd queued in the narrow entranceway while circus hands yelled back and forth to find space for them among the three hundred or so already packed into the cheap plastic seats that looked down on the stage. Signs saying *No Kids Allowed* were taped everywhere.

Megadeth blared over the speakers as the light tech tried to spotlight Harold. Her son always had a stroppy, almighty look about him, like he'd just taken a delivery from a chippy and they'd gotten his order all wrong.

The June wind gusted beneath a tent flap behind her, cooling her bare shoulders. The daylight peeking in robbed some of the mystical darkness they tried to create. Harold's act was more of a night-time thing.

"Hold on to your hats," boomed a voice that tried far too hard to sound spooky, "for now rises to the stage, the one, the only, the heart-stopping, faint-making, best friend of death, Scotland's finest – Harold the Impossible."

She shook her head, watching as the crowd clapped like a bunch of bored seals. She'd told them to cool it with the intro. Keep it short and intriguing. The way the workers looked down on her just because she was a woman made her want to kick them all in the nuts.

Silence rippled through the crowd. This moment always made rats scurry inside her stomach. Lose them in these early seconds and they'd throw whatever they could get their hands on. Since it was strictly over-eighteens, that would mean a bottle of half-empty booze.

The light found Harold, flaring off his pale skin and the messy, crow-feather-like hair that fell over each side of his face. The rest of him was covered in black, cape and all. This Poundstretcher version of Dracula was all they could afford, but she knew it wouldn't always be like this. One day, her Harold would fly.

Despite the stage being below the seats, he still managed to peer down his pointy nose at the crowd. She resisted the urge to get his attention, to get him moving. He turned his head and nodded at a stagehand. Gothic music started playing, followed by rising white plumes of smoke from a smoke machine.

The music exploded like someone turned the dial all the way up. She felt its bass in her belly as the crowd winced as one, covering their ears. The slow, violin-led instrumental returned to a friendlier level. Great start.

It didn't phase Harold. Nothing phased him when he was on stage. At home, he moped around like nothing could cheer him up. Here, he breathed in the adoration like it was pre-ordained. Like he was born to be worshipped.

"Good afternoon, ladies and gentlemen," said Harold, hands held out to the crowd.

"Wrong town, pal," yelled a lad from somewhere in the back. "No ladies about here."

The music built slowly towards its crescendo. Harold glanced at Dottie, his eyes holding nothing but contempt at the crappy attempt to throw him off. She nodded, willing him to get on with it. He acted like he'd heard it all a million times before, but this was only his tenth official show, and the first with the circus.

She eyed the crowd. It was against Circus Nightmare's wishes to take videos, but you couldn't stop the hordes of young folk pointing their mobile phones at the stage. It was like they preferred to watch life filtered through a screen instead of experience it.

All it would take is one video.

This could be his shot.

The music went quiet.

"Death is not for the faint of heart," said Harold. "Our fascination with it is centuries old. We ask, what's on the other side of that door? What does it feel like? What I'm about to do has never been done before. If you are squeamish, I suggest you leave. This is not a trick."

He stepped to the side of the circular stage. The circle of light followed him, lighting up his metal contraption. Its black paint shone fierce. Light gleamed off it, grabbing the eye. Some of the crowd gasped. It was just the reaction she'd planned for.

Harold's machine was twice his size and made of interlocking bars of metal. It looked like a fierce robot terrier that would come to life, snapping him up in its sharp jaws. A thin set of steps ran up its middle between the rows of spikes.

Dottie surveyed the crowd. Hot blood rose up her neck when she saw a man pointing at the stage, chatting to his two small daughters.

Moist stones scraped under her cowboy boots as she marched over to the row where they sat. She shimmied down the row, muttering apologies.

She tapped the father on the shoulder. The tart smell of cider hit her when he spoke. "What? What is it?"

She opened her mouth to speak. White pain twisted in her stomach. She barely resisted the urge to double over.

"Trying to watch something here, doll," he said.

"Get your bairns out of here," she said. "Over eighteen's only, chump."

Anger pulsed in the man's eyes. "Paid our money."

She leaned in. Her blond hair flicked angrily at him as if striking out on its own. "I will twist your nipples and kick your arse if you don't shift it. Or do you want me to stop the show and shine the spotlight on your ugly mush?"

She braced for action, her thin, ropey muscles tensed. Harold continued to talk about life and death on the stage as the music ramped up again.

The oldest of the two girls set down her phone and let out an exasperated sigh. "Let's just go, Dad. Don't wanna watch this boring bastard, anyways."

"Thank you," said Dottie.

She made her way back down the aisle, listening to hushed comments.

"What's the hold up?"

"Shut up and get on with it, man. Shaggy looking bastard."

"Nah, don't go. My cousin seen it last week at the pub. Gonna be well gnarly. Trust me."

Harold's reputation was growing. A few shaky videos from shows in bowling clubs and pubs around Fife had appeared online, but he just needed a few more to push him to the next level, to show they meant business.

She made her way back to the cool shadows by the stage, watching the father and his daughters stomp out.

Harold whipped his cape off with a flourish just as the violins started their frantic build. The contraption wobbled as he set his black shoe on the first step, staring at the crowd with hungry eyes. He wanted to eat every tense moment so much that Dottie wanted to throttle him. It was enough to kill the whole act.

He hauled himself up, holding on to a pole, leaning back like Gene Kelly singing in the rain. Pamela came onto the stage in her tiny, shimmering silver outfit. She kept her head down, staring at the floor as the horny males in the crowd wolf whistled. Dottie had been against adding Pamela to the act tonight, but she provided a moment's break as she wheeled the contraption around the stage, doing her best to show the crowd that it wasn't booby-trapped. After she was done, she wiggled her way off the stage.

"Come on, son," Dottie said to herself. "She's there for the crowd to ogle, not you."

The thick air in the tent changed as the crowd murmured in electric excitement. The sight of people holding their hands over their mouths, leaning forward in their seats made her feel like a little girl sitting a horse for the first time. A fresh billow of smoke rushed from each side of the stage, covering the floor. The candy floss taste of it filled Dottie's mouth.

Harold ascended the steps of his machine. He turned back to the crowd slowly as if nervous, playing them just right. He gave them a scrunched-up smile and a sorrowful nod like he regretted what was about to happen.

When he reached the top step, he turned and faced the crowd, raising his arms out to each side, holding them high. His splayed fingers almost touched the tips of the sharp jaws that hung over him. Something about the pose struck Dottie as religious – like he made an offer of himself to whatever God he prayed to. God wouldn't like to see this.

People pointed their phones, trying to be sly about it, the light from their screens shining on marvelled faces. Let them take their videos. Let them spread the word.

Harold closed his eyes, leaned his head back as if convening with a deity, his fingers held out in supplication. He closed his fists. It was the signal.

Metal spikes dropped. They made a wet, plunging noise which echoed around the tent. One went through his skull, coming out his jaw before re-entering his chest. One impaled his shoulder, taking half the arm with it.

The music cut. All Dottie could hear was the *drip, dripping* of Harold's blood on the floor.

Someone near her turned and puked. The stench of stale carrots drifted to her as she stared at her mangled son, waiting for the pandemonium to begin. The muggy wind whistled through the bottom of the tent behind her.

A man screamed and stood, his plastic seat scraping beneath him. That broke the spell. The rest of the crowd followed, calling for help, kicking away from their seats like a mutant spider was on the stage coming to eat them all.

They swarmed the exit, stomping and climbing over each other, all human decency forgotten in wild panic. She hoped they filled their phones with decent footage to share with their friends.

Pamela stumbled over to her, mascara running down each puffy cheek. "W-What happened? Don't just stand there. Do something!"

"Calm down, missy," said Dottie, shaking her off. A wave of dizziness hit her and she almost reached out a hand to steady herself on Pamela's shoulder.

"He's dead. I-I pushed the button. You told me he'd be safe, but he's fucking mutilated and—"

Dottie grabbed her by both arms, holding her tight. "Calm it. Wait until they're all out. I'll show you what's what."

The tent's entrance thronged with the last of the stampeding crowd. The shaking spotlights shone on the stage, illuminating her son's corpse and the flow of dark blood that escaped him.

She looked at her watch, then rubbed at her stomach, waiting for the panic to end.

Two

When the last of the crowd escaped through the tunnelled entryway, Dottie walked onto the stage. She gagged as she stepped in her son's pooling blood, trying her best to avoid looking at the eye that dangled from its nerve ending. The wheels of his death device squelched through his blood when she pushed it towards a side curtain and through to the backstage area. It was heavy work with his body still impaled, still dripping in the claws of the contraption.

Pamela ran in front of her. "Where you going? He needs an ambulance."

"Ambulance won't save him now, hen. Step back."

"What?"

Dottie glared at the girl. She was pretty in an innocent piggy kind of way. The kind of girl who'd laugh off the advances of men for years to come. The worry etched on her face was that of a dear old friend, not someone they'd hired only yesterday.

The chalky scent of sawdust was cloying in the small, erected space. Dottie listened to check if anyone was coming, then leaned over and pulled a lever on Harold's device. The spikes shot up with a noise like scraping knives. The body of her son tumbled out, landing face first on the floor by Pamela's dolly shoes.

Pamela's balled fists leapt up to her mouth. A shrill whimper eeked out of her.

"Grab me a bucket, doll," said Dottie.

"Just watched your son die and you want me to—"

"Thought you said you weren't flappable when you took this job? Trot on and find me a mop and bucket, or you can forget about getting any money from me."

A tear slid down the side of Pamela's face. She didn't move, only stood there with her eyes wide and wobbly.

"Look," said Dottie, setting her hand on Pamela's shoulder, "he's fine. Will explain it all in a wee bit. I'm gonna fix him up, make him brand new, but we need to clear the mess before someone rocks up and starts asking questions."

"What? I... Eh?"

"You're an eloquent one. Bucket. Mop. Answers later."

Dottie knelt beside her ruined son, lifting his head onto her lap. The pole had sunk in above his eyebrow. His eye swayed loose from a blood slick optic nerve. He smelled like he'd been dead for days already. It was a smell she was getting far too used to.

She swept a lock of thick black hair from his forehead and closed her eyes. A fiery wave curled inside the pit of her stomach, shooting through her chest, down her arm, out her hand. She set her hand on his forehead.

His wounds began to heal.

To Dottie, it looked like thousands of tiny spiders slung their grey webs, stitching the wounds together. A sound like fingers swishing in a tub of thick jelly made a shudder rip up her spine.

Harold's eyeball was tugged slowly back into its socket. He sat up, almost head-butting her, clutching in breath like he'd been submerged underwater.

"Welcome back, sunshine," said Dottie.

Once his breathing settled from a pounding gallop to a trot, he stared at her like she'd just stuck her finger in the middle of his soup. He stood and wiped his hands on his tattered clothes.

He stared at the contraption that had killed him countless times – a vicious device they'd both dreamed up.

"Really felt that one," he said, his voice fuzzy like he'd been on the sauce all day. "How was the crowd?"

Dottie pushed herself up. The space spun around her, making her blink. She leaned her hand on the chipboard wall. "Like a stampede of wild horses. They—"

Something thudded behind them, making fright dance along the back of Dottie's ears.

"She's a fainter, then," said Harold. "Perfect choice for this type of gig."

"Give her a break. She was great. Right concerned about you when I wheeled your heavy arse back here."

"Maybe tell the next one what they're getting into beforehand."

Pamela groaned and shoved herself back to her feet, rubbing her eyes.

"I dunno," said Dottie, "think this one's sticking around. Got grit. Now she knows your secret, we'll be quite the team. You alright there, Pam?"

"Pamela," said Pamela, dragging a mop and bucket over on squeaky wheels. "Hate Pam."

"See? Gritty as fuck this one."

Harold made a tutting noise like a stroppy horse and walked over to the death machine, tracing his finger along its surface. An ache swelled inside her. Harold had strolled through life, moping around, so quiet that he'd barely existed in her world. Now, he had a purpose.

A clear plan. That plan just so happened to be killing himself over and over in front of a crowd.

"Shit," said Dottie, "someone called the fuzz."

The muffled sound of a police siren grew louder. Soon, the car would pull up into the car park of the ice rink where the tent had been set up and start asking questions.

While Harold stared lovingly at his death trap, Dottie and Pamela started scrubbing.

Three

The wet mop slapped the mat in the centre of the stage. The water in the bucket had long turned red. The figure eights she sloshed calmed her nerves that were still shot from bringing her son back. It always made her feel hollow as an empty bag of crisps. How long until the magic stopped working? How long before she watched her son die for the last time?

She'd been leathered on dark rum when the man with the shifting face rapt on the door. Talking to him felt like she spoke inside a dream, his words were slippy and insubstantial. His druid-like clothes, his face and even his fingers were made of smoke. His offer changed everything.

Since Pete died just before Christmas last year, she'd hid inside the bottle. Harold walked the quiet house like a ghost she did her best to ignore. Truth was, she'd ignored the poor wee guy all his life.

You've got something missing inside, her mum said long ago. *Like God sliced out the caring part. You selfish wee cow.*

The man who she'd come to think of as Old Smokes stood at her front door with his shadowy, ever-changing face, and said he would give her the power to always protect Harold, be there for him like no mother had ever been there for a child. She'd accepted.

"It is done," he'd said. "If the child dies, you can bring him back to life. Just place your hand on his forehead, and that will return his soul to his body."

Harold had stood at the top of the stairs, listening to the deal being made. They argued themselves hoarse for weeks. He wanted to try it out. Be dead. Come back. That's when the cogs started turning for him. That's when the purpose came into his eyes, like he'd found his God.

It had taken Harold three weeks before he killed himself. She found him hanging in his room. The sight broke her heart all over again. She could still hear that swaying, creaking rope. She cut him down, crying into his cold chest. Just when she thought she'd lost the two men of her life, she lay her palm on his forehead. A molten feeling spread through her, bringing him back.

"Think I'm gonna go now, Mrs. Matheson," said Pamela, zipping up a denim jacket over her shiny get up. "Dan, my boyfriend, he, ehm, doesn't like it when I'm late."

"No bother." Dottie reached into her back pocket and handed her three scrunched-up notes. "Will give you a shout for the next one. If there is a next one."

They both glanced at the egg-shaped man who stood in the tunnelled entryway.

"Hope so," said Pamela, twisting the toe of her shoe into the mat. "Really need the dosh. I, ehm, hear you're into horses and that."

Dottie stopped swishing the mop around. "I'll tell Harold you said goodbye."

"Aye, please do. He was marvellous. Never seen anything like it."

"Doubt your boyfriend will like those rosy dots on your cheek, either. Just joshing with you. And if you could keep Harold's secret between us, that'd be very much appreciated. Consider it a term of your employment."

Dottie stared into her shiny reflection in the black mat. An old crone stared back up at her. Even in all the wobbliness of the image, she could make out the dry colour her blond bob had taken on. If Pete could see her now, he'd give her some slagging for getting so old.

Fierce pain ripped through her stomach. She leaned on the mop, letting out a pathetic whimper. When it passed, she punched the mop head into the bucket and pushed down, listening to the reddened water drip.

"You not being paid today," said Zorbo, waddling over like a super-villain. "Destroy show. You and Harold are—"

"I told you he should go on last, didn't I?" she said, muscles aching as she straightened.

"Circus Nightmare is ruin. Refunds." He spat this as if it were a curse. "Refunds! Never refunds."

"You watched him though, right? Put him on last and he'll tear the place down."

"I—"

"After today, the sick fucks will be biting your hand off for a ticket. Trust me. Let him go on last. It's only five minutes. The rest of your show can go on before him."

The man towered over her. He smelled of strange spices and something greasy like sausage fat. There were rumblings and rumours among the stagehands about what else Zorbo was dealing, but she didn't want to know.

His cheek twitched as if he had a twirly moustache that irritated his skin. "Is some act. Been while since I leapt up from seat. Okay, okay.

Others they won't be liking it so much. But next show is Glenrothes. Is shit hole. You go last. Make them scream."

The drive home in her beat-up Land Rover was as silent and awkward as ever. She squinted against the falling evening sun. The death contraption rattled about in a horse box she towed as they made their way along the Standing Stane road and back to Pitlair.

Harold slumped in the back, his nose almost pressed against the window. "Well, that's Pauline never coming back."

"Bell end. Least you can do is get her name right. It's Pamela. And she'll be back. Think she's in a spot of bother. Desperate for money. I know the look. Besides that, I think she's got stones. Nice lassie."

"Whatevs."

A decked Vauxhall Corsa streamed past, overtaking, making her flinch. The grating, rusty noise of the boy racer's exhaust tempted her to slam into the bugger. There were too many people who died on this stretch of road. She watched the tiny car ascend the small rise in front of them and then out of sight.

"Least if you did anything that daft I can pick you out the trees," she said. "Though, if you drove like that, you wouldn't deserve it."

She stared in the rear-view, watching as her son shut her out. He had such a slappable face that looked down on everything and everyone. She couldn't remember if they'd ever shared a joke or a laugh. Her anger fled from her and she concentrated on the road and its overhanging branches that looked like small, eager hands. It was her fault for not trying hard enough when he was younger.

"Tell me what it was like," he said, closing his eyes. "Did the crowd go mental? Did they love it?"

"Looked like you set a starving lion loose among pigeons. Gonna have to do something about this whole stampede business. Don't want anyone dying on us."

"Did they love it?"

"In a frightened-as-fuck kind of way, aye. They really ate it up. Heard a few of them talking in the crowd. Don't think it'll be long before this whole thing goes mental."

Four

The strength of the sun soaked through Dottie's jeans as she sat Jimmy, her beloved black horse. Pete waited ahead of her atop Sundance, his glorious brown steed. A smug smile played up his sun-wrinkled face. The promise in his pale blue eyes melted her through and through. A bumblebee swayed between them before swimming into the perfect, blue sky.

Jimmy snorted an annoyed greeting as if he was saying, *Always gotta show off, eh?* Like her, Jimmy hated playing catch up. His muscular flanks were foamed with sweat, but Sundance was a beast like no other. Same could be said for Pete.

"Harold's somewhere close," he said.

"You actually got that lazy toad to come with us?"

"Got himself a horse. White one. Outran Sundance here."

Her wrists clicked as she tightened her grip on the reins. When she was little, she'd had a recurring nightmare about a rabid, white horse that chased her down the hallway. In the dream, she'd bolt, her bony legs churning. The hall morphed, elongating before her like a camera trick. She'd told her mum that Whitey was gonna get her, eat her up, but all she got was a slap and told to shut her heathen mush. Despite her love of horses, her heart still skipped whenever she saw a white one.

Pete leaned in his saddle and petted Sundance's flank, talking sweetly in her ear. "You'll get that white horse next time, my love. Nothing but a fluke."

Dottie gulped. "Starting to make me feel jealous."

"Let's go get Harold. Show you that pale horse of his." He scratched at the stubble under his chin. "Then maybe we can race up the stairs when we get home. Get all frothy ourselves."

"Have to catch me first."

She tightened her calves and urged Jimmy on and he took off, giving Sundance a cheeky glance that said, *Catch up you slow bastard.* The wind batted her face when she leaned forward, savouring the grassy smells that flowed her way. A sea of green opened before them.

In the distance, a sullen figure with black hair sat a white horse. The sun didn't beam off its coat as it should've, instead the horse seemed to eat the sun's rays. Harold slowly guided Whitey forward, towards a gap in a stone wall where a gate should've been. A few feet from the opening, traffic rushed by on both sides. She could taste the shimmering taint of trucks and diesel on the breeze. An icy hand gripped her bowels. Jimmy snorted under her as if he felt it, too.

"No!" she called.

Her son looked up. His mouth hung slack. His eyes were half-shut. Even from this distance, she could see the silver line of drool on his chin when it caught the sun.

A familiar rumbling sounded behind her and then at her side. Pete nodded. Sundance flicked a sideways glance that said, *That all you got?*

"Pete, don't go," she said, struggling to get the words out. "You're not allowed to go before me!"

"I've got him now," he said, staring seriously at her. "Don't you worry, baby. I'll look out for him until you catch up."

"Don't!"

Pete urged Sundance on, and they steamed ahead. Harold swayed in his saddle, his lolling head nudging the horse toward the road. The roaring sound of cars and trucks whirring past was like jets swooshing by.

"You can't leave me here! I—"

When Pete and Sundance neared Harold, they burst apart like a cloud of black flies.

"No!"

She leaned into Jimmy, willing him on, but he slowed to a trot. Pete, the man she'd spent the last fifteen years with, the man who made her toes curl and her belly rumble with nerves, flew apart like a flock of black starlings.

"Don't you dare leave me again!" she screamed, tears cooling on her cheeks.

Jimmy turned to liquid beneath her. Her hands slipped as they pushed through his skin that turned into a substance like melting wax. She was pitched off, her world turned sideways. As she lay on her side, she watched as Jimmy turned into boiling lumps of black oil. She tasted the tar of it as she pushed herself up.

Cars blared their horns. Harold guided his horse onto the road, his eyes closed, his hands held up to the sky. A lorry hit its brakes, snaking all over the place, smoke churning from its tires coming straight for—

She sucked in a lung filling gasp, falling off her bed. Outside, someone pressed their car horn, yelling abuse at somebody to get off the road. The oily scent of the latex tent and spilled blood still clung to her skin. When she lifted her hand to haul herself up, pain cramped her stomach muscles, making her bunch up on the floor as if she'd been kicked in the side. She closed her eyes, laying her cheek against the musty carpet, waiting for the pain to pass.

The dream had taken Pete from her again. When she'd found him in the bathroom the week before Christmas, it felt as if the house had collapsed on her. It ripped the safety from her life. The dreams gave him back to her in all his sweaty, manly splendour before ripping him away, making the wound fresh again when she woke.

Feeling like a silly wee girl, she'd shared her dreams of living free, riding a horse every day in the countryside. Pete bought her Jimmy. It was his way of showing how serious he was about their relationship at the start. And he'd hoped it would show Harold he wasn't a threat. Harold only rode Jimmy once before refusing to touch any horse again.

Dottie's mouth hung open as she hitched in a breath, trying her best to stay as still as possible, waiting for the pain in her stomach to pass.

She didn't know who Harold's real father was. She didn't have answers to any of his questions over the years. Her mum was right – she'd been a taker all her days, taking whatever thrills life threw her way without a thought for tomorrow. Pete calmed part of that, but their relationship was also a blur of parties and Sunday sessions. It was a wonder Harold hadn't stolen out into the night, never to be seen again. He might've been better for it. A child forgotten about for most of his days.

"I won't forget you now," she said through clenched teeth.

The agony in her core settled from impending implosion to something like a jarring electrical current that she'd learned to live with. It was always there. Dust flitted about in a bar of morning sun that spilled over her bare feet.

She stood on shaky legs, marched into the bathroom, and showered under scalding hot water, trying to scrub the unmistakable scent of blood from her skin. When she was done, she shoved her short legs into a pair of jeans and put on one of her many chequered shirts over a white t-shirt. All that was missing was her cowboy boots and a hat and she'd be ready for an adventure.

"That's right, partner," she said, staring at her bony frame in the mirror, stroking her flat stomach. "Adventure to Sainsbury's for the shopping. Yee haw."

Her bedroom was upstairs in a semi-detached house close to the rough centre of Pitlair. Even at this early hour, she could hear a gaggle of boys hurling plastic bottles around, calling everybody names.

She was about to set her foot on the first step when a shriek like a rat getting strangled crept out of Harold's room. It sounded like he watched a horror film at full tilt. She tapped at the open door and stepped in. Harold always had his curtains drawn like the outside world offended him. He sat on a small plastic desk chair, hunched over a laptop on a desk in the corner of the room. The putrid reek of old socks smacked her as she waited on him noticing she was there.

He watched a short clip over and over. Something like a huge nail ripped into a man's face. The point of view was from the spike, giving a clear view of it entering the flesh. Unseen, a crowd gasped and screamed as one.

"Is that—" she gulped. "Is that you?"

"Awesome, right?" He slammed the space bar to pause the video. "Put a wee camera on one of the spikes. Uploaded it to YouTube and it went mental, but the sensitive pricks took it down. Phone's not stopped buzzing since. Wicked, eh?"

Her eyes widened and she leaned in for a closer look. The website looked like a place where they peddled children and all sorts. The video had 3,239 views and 604 comments.

"Wicked, aye," she said. "This since last night?"

"Nope. Just the last ninety minutes."

"Why?"

"Publicity, Mum. Even you should grasp that. It'll open doors. More people talk about what I was made to do, more people will come see the show. More money will come. Imagine. You could live off me. Live the life of a lush." The look he gave her made her want to lash out with a wicked slap. "Well, you already have the lush part down. You could be a lush with money."

"Did you not think to run something like this by me first? Thought we were a team on this."

"Hey, you were the one cut a deal with that weirdo at the door. What's wrong? Don't you want to see your son have a life of his own? Would that get in the way of you smashing a bottle of rum?"

She stepped back and steadied herself by clutching at the door handle. "We need to take it slow. What if it doesn't work one of these times? I'm not always gonna be here to scoop your guts off the ground, you know."

"Where you gonna go, likes? Think about it, Mother."

The way he said *Mother* made something squirm up her spine.

"If I get this show off the ground," he continued, "show people what I'm made of, then I can get the money so you can muck about with your horses again, get Jimmy back."

"Jimmy..."

The thought of riding her horse again made something physically ache in her chest. She'd had to give him up. Pete was the man with the job, the breadwinner. In fact, he was the only one bringing in any bread at all. She hadn't worked a job for decades, hadn't pitched in to the life they had. All they had to live on right now was the dregs of Pete's life insurance money. She was ignoring the impending doom of finding a job.

He tutted and swivelled in his creaking chair, tapping away at the laptop's keyboard. "Fatso emailed me the string of dates. Says I can go on last. Will be bored as sin watching those useless acts and their—"

"What's it like?"

"Circus Nightmare? Like someone tried to cram a Goosebumps book into a stag weekend."

"Dying, I meant."

The sound of clacking keys stopped. His hands hovered over the soft light of the keyboard then lowered to his sides.

"There's a light somewhere," he said, "but you're underwater. Flashing shapes whir past like grim fish. When you pull me out, it's like I've just hit the bottom of The Big One at Blackpool – like my stomach's being yanked out my arse." He leaned back, staring at the ceiling. "It's like a slap in the face. In a good way, though. Really cracks you awake. The colours are different than before."

Five

"So, he dies?" said Pamela. "Each time. For realsies. And, what, you just watch?"

"Sorry, Judgey McJudgerson," said Dottie. "Suppose that's the gist of it, right enough, though I'd rather not watch the bugger off himself so often. Rather he didn't do it at all."

They sat in the front of her parked Land Rover, watching three track-suited idiots stagger about on their way to the Big Top, vanishing inside its tunnelled entrance, eaten by shadow. Under a blue sky, more of the Glenrothes crowd slalomed around the parked cars that had chewed the field into mud.

The moist grease smell of fast-food packaging was cloying in the small space. Dottie bit into her McDonald's cheeseburger, chewing until it went all globby. In the passenger seat, Pamela dusted her face with a make-up brush.

"Lassie like you shouldn't need to plaster yourself with that much crap."

"Was he always magic?"

"Who, Harold? Magically boring, aye. Technically me that's the magic one, hauling his ungrateful arse out of the depths of... wherever it is you go when you pop your clogs."

"Always believed in magic and faeries and all that. World's far too big and weird for there not to be anything like that, you know? One of my brothers, I've got five of the bastards, he said he was mucking about in the woods in Kirkness one night and saw this wee troop of gremlin looking things that vanished into a portal of light. Mental."

The image of Old Smokes who'd knocked on her door came to Dottie. Where his features should've been was only a grey-black cloud that rolled in on itself. What she did remember was the dead twig smell that followed him. It had lingered in the hallway for days after. None of her nosy neighbours had seen him come or go. It was as if he floated straight to their house, made his offer, disappeared.

Pamela puckered her lips and twisted the rear-view mirror to look at herself. Her hoop earrings swung loose and free. She'd upgraded their stage magician's get up with heels and a tiara. Looked more like a singer in an Abba tribute band than magician's assistant.

Dottie opened her mouth to say as much when her phone vibrated in her pocket. She tutted, took it out. Another text badgering her about—

"Ow," crooned Pamela, "who is DocMan Martin?"

"Never you mind. Just a pal checking in. Again." Dottie stared out the window, resting her hand on her stomach. The pain slumbered for the first time in days.

"You know, what Harold's doing is beautiful."

"Beautiful? Changed your tune awfully quick, hen."

"True, though. Everyone's so frightened of death. To toy with it, beat it, show it what's what by coming back, is nothing short of legendary. By the time you've gone to high school you've seen, like, a million people die on video, right? But to watch it in person – whole new level. People are gonna freak so hard."

Dottie's stomach gave her a rumble of warning. She placed the quarter eaten burger into the white packaging and balled it up. Excepting a packet of pickled onion Monster Munch, it was all she'd had to eat that day.

"Far as everyone else knows," said Dottie, "it's just an act. I'm sure Harold would really appreciate you keeping his secret between us."

Lies. She couldn't remember the last time Harold was grateful for anything. A sullen wee boy grown into a sulky man who thought the world shone out his own arse.

Her mother's cold voice echoed inside her. *You selfish wee cow.*

When Harold was a wee thing, her mum had offered to adopt him, take him off her hands. She'd battled with the decision, eventually claiming she couldn't pass the chance to love her kid, to redeem herself as a mum. It was the benefits, that was the cold truth of it. If she could go back and make that choice over, would she give him up?

Dottie eyed her watch. 9pm and the sun was dropping down the sky. Harold had gone inside, tinkering with his beloved machine. Circus Nightmare would be ramping up to its big finish.

"Let's get our arses in gear," said Dottie, feeling how shaky her smile was. "It's about killing time."

She shook her head, ridding her of the bright spots that sparkled in the edges of her vision. They made their way into the tent, past the candy floss stalls with their white and pink clouds in bags.

On the stage, two men on stilts tried to batter each other. Their faces were painted deep green like forest faeries. Their stilts had been woven with leaves and twigs. The crowd roared as if they watched a wrestling match.

When they entered the staging area, she noticed Harold in the back, still mucking about with his machine. Watching him work welled her up with pride. He coiled a length of rope around his hand and tugged down on it. She'd never seen him so focused, so intent on anything. If only it wasn't death he'd found.

"Make them take notice," she said to herself. "I'll always be here to bring you back, my wee man."

Pamela swanned over to him and placed a petite hand on his shoulder, muttering something in his ear. They both turned and stared at Dottie. She didn't know whether to smile or throw up the middle finger.

"Boy loves his toy," said Zorbo behind her. "Not afraid to work."

"It's his baby," said Dottie, turning to face the planet of a man.

"Make a name for himself quick, ticket peoples tell me."

"Aye, you know how word gets about on the Facebooks and all that."

Zorbo raised a thin eyebrow. "I keep eye on him. Figure out secret. Always figure out secret. My talent."

She squinted up at him, nodded, then slunk past, back out into the action and the cocoon of crowd noise. She took her spot by the side of the stage, draped in shadow. The metal scaffolding she stood beside seemed to vibrate with cold.

She watched the giggling, impatient crowd point at the act on-stage, look at their phones, swig their Buckfast.

A couple of red-faced girls all dolled up for a night on the town, legs out and all, called for Harold, running their thumbs grimly along their necks in unison. Dottie circled figure eights along her stomach as she watched them. No doubt they'd head out straight after this and hit every pub they could find before stottering home, laughing themselves hoarse when they woke up with their minuscule hangovers tomorrow.

A current of pain glazed from her abdomen, curling its cold fingers around her spine. Her wedding ring *clinked* the metal beam she clutched onto. In this state, she couldn't keep up with the young lassies even if she wanted to.

On the stage, one of the stilted fighters toppled over, cracking his head on the floor. The crowd roared in empty appreciation as the winner raised his arms. The loser was hauled behind the curtain and the winner followed after. The lights went out, plunging the tent into darkness.

It was time for Harold.

Six

"Aw, just kill yourself already, you dick," a man screamed, his voice echoing through the dark tent.

Harold stood in the centre of the stage, eyeing the crowd, sizing them up and taking forever about it as usual. The spotlight made his glare all the more intense.

The music started, slow and daunting. Dottie felt its vibrations through the soles of her cowboy boots.

"Get a move on," a girl wailed.

"We want blood," shouted another. "We want blood. We want blood."

Soon, the whole tent had taken up the chant. Harold stood there like the power of his gaze would be enough to stop the rampaging, half-cut Glenrothes crowd from coming onto the stage and killing him first. The crowd stomped their feet as they roared louder. A feeling like cold ants squirmed about the back of Dottie's neck.

"Shit." Dottie glared at the side of Harold's head, willing him to turn and face her. "Do something or get the fuck off the stage."

Harold held his hand up. The beam of light hit his pale palm. To Dottie's surprise, it silenced the crowd.

"Death follows us all," called Harold, puffing up his chest. "Holds us captive. It is a land where no one roams and no one returns. Except I."

She could almost taste the sick ecstasy of the crowd's excitement. Chairs creaked as most of them sat back down, easing in for the show.

"We run from it. Hide." Harold continued like a Shakespearean actor strutting the boards. "It's in every story we tell. Oh, how we love it so."

The violins beat a quicker rhythm and he raised an arm to the side. Pamela wheeled the large, black machine from backstage, walking slowly so as not to fall with those killer heels on. She kept her head down, ignoring the whistles and unsavoury comments. If those comments had been thrown at Dottie, she might not have been able to keep a straight face, but Pamela simply ignored them, exchanging a coy smile with Harold. The smile lingered in her eyes as Dottie watched her trot offstage again.

A few seconds later, Pamela appeared at her side, putting a denim jacket on, covering up the top of the skimpy outfit.

"Sleazy bastards," said Pamela. "Remind me to never come back to Glenrothes."

The sting of rose-like perfume was so heavy that Dottie felt it on her tongue.

"They're like that everywhere, doll," said Dottie, not taking her eyes from the stage.

The crowd murmured as Harold placed a hand on the machine and hauled himself up onto the first step. He basked in the tension, taking it one step at a time until he got to the top step. Then he paused, a look of uncertainty crossing his features like a lost schoolboy.

"What's he doing?" said Dottie.

Pamela laid a hand on her arm. "It's art, Mrs. Matheson. And it's beautiful. He was born for this. Just watch."

Harold shook his head at the top of the steps, regret paining his face. He stepped down to the ground. A *what-the-fuck* groan shifted through the crowd, quickly becoming anger. A bottle smashed on the stage by Harold's feet. Specks of the foamy beer hit Dottie's forearm. The malty scent of it rose to her as she gripped a metal pole, barely keeping herself back from hauling her son away.

The boos tapered off in confusion as Harold lay on the stage, resting the back of his head on the first step. His Adam's apple protruded like an alien when he swallowed. He stared up at the rows of sharp spikes, reaching for a rope that hung from the side of the machine.

"No," whispered Dottie.

He wrapped the rope around his hand, squeezed it tight.

"Harold?" said Dottie, an icy mist settling about her shoulders.

"You want death?" Harold called. "I bring you," he tugged sharply at the cord. The mouth of the machine sent spikes flying down to his face. "Death!"

Its teeth snapped home, ripping through his throat. A gush of blood shot into the air like a trickling fountain. It pattered over his jerking, convulsing form, pooling on the floor by his body.

Dottie felt the air move as the crowd sucked in a breath. The rubbery smell of tent was strong on her hand as she slapped it over her mouth, swallowing a scream.

"Beautiful." Pamela smiled. "He's beautiful."

With a shaking hand, Harold touched a lever somewhere behind his head. The metal teeth shot up to their starting position with a shrieking, silver noise Dottie felt itch her brain. The black spikes rained blood down on the struggling, mangled form.

Like a nightmare thing, Harold pushed himself up to a sitting position. Blood burbled out his mouth. His neck had been obliterated. His head lolled on his shoulders as if about to fall off.

In the cloying silence, a woman screamed a shaky, violent scream. Someone else fainted, thumping onto the ground.

Harold forced a smile on his crimson face before the life drained from his eyes. His head fell forward onto his chest. From this angle, Dottie could see how close his neck had come to being chewed through entirely.

Across the hundreds of people staring down at the stage, she could see hungry eyes eat up the scene with morbid fascination. Most held their phones towards the sight.

By the entrance, a figure caught her attention. Her skin went prickly with heat as he turned to look at her. Old Smokes. The man made of smoke gave a subtle nod to the entrance as if beckoning her to come have a wee blether with him outside.

The lights cut out. An epic, heavy riff oozed from the corners of the tent.

"Ladies and gentleman," a tinny voice boomed from the speakers. "Give it up for the one, the only, Harold the Impossible."

The crowd roared, clapping furiously. As her eyes adjusted, she saw them rise to their feet, shouting between cupped hands, beating the air, whistling.

She looked to the entrance. The figure was gone.

"Now, if you will," continued the voice, "make your way out in an orderly fashion. And do dream of Circus Nightmare tonight. We'll be with you forever. And ever."

Dottie hopped over a small barricade and onto the stage, sinking to her knees beside Harold. The state of him. Blood had soaked into dark puddles on his clothes. The last of the day's light seeped in through the bottom of the tent, giving her some light to see by.

Pamela clopped up to them, dragging a large tarpaulin sheet. As she got on her knees and hauled the cover over herself, Dottie glanced at the entrance again.

Was Old Smokes here to let them know her gift had been taken away? That Harold had abused it?

Pamela shuffled over them, making a sort of windbreaker of herself, shielding anyone from view.

"Please don't be dead dead," said Dottie.

Pamela sucked in a breath. "You can save him though, right? He must be saved."

"Not my fault he's nearly taken his own head clean off. Aw, Harold, you numpty."

Laying there with the softest of light on his features, Dottie saw the little boy he'd once been. The little boy who'd been banished to quiet corners all his days, never saying a word in protest, reading his books. The thought made her sick.

"Please hurry," said Pamela.

Dottie breathed in deep, filling her mouth with the taste of coppery blood and plastic. She laid her hand on his forehead.

Nothing happened.

"No," said Dottie.

"What?" said Pamela, dropping the cover, shuffling next to her. "No!"

"It's gone. It's—"

From nothing, the magic flowered in her stomach, circling through her gut, buzzing up her gullet then down through her arm. Her hand was outlined in gold in the darkness – something she'd never noticed before.

Harold began to knot himself back together with a sound like a team of worms poking their heads from wet soil.

Dottie stood too quickly. She blinked away the dizziness before turning in the direction of the entrance.

"Where are you going?" said Pamela, clutching Harold's hand.

"To catch up with an old friend."

Seven

Dottie followed Old Smokes out into the purpling light of dusk. After the baking heat of the tent, the breeze soothed her skin. She tailed him as he marched across the road, into the grey labyrinth of a blocky housing scheme. Its intersecting paths were speckled with cubes of glass and dog shit. The gloomy buildings seemed to weigh in on her as she called to him.

Old Smokes stopped at the entrance of a piss-dank, graffiti-tagged tunnel. He swivelled round to face her as if he stood on a rotating plinth. She tried to will her body to move, but it would not obey. Soon, her eyes screamed for her to blink. Fillings in teeth at the back of her mouth sang as if she'd bit down on a clump of tinfoil.

The unreal vision of the man-shaped thing made a laugh cough its way out of her. His smoke rolled around the places where his skin should appear. Looking at the hazy way his 'face' shifted was mesmerising.

She forced herself to look away, staring down at her ruined clothes. Blood shined on her t-shirt, almost dry. Harold had given them a show. A shudder trembled her neck bone as she remembered the scraping sound of the machine taking its fangs out of her boy.

How far would his dreams take him and his new found reason for being? Edinburgh Playhouse? MGM Grand in Vegas?

A vibrance of pain in her stomach brought her back to the narrow path and the demon before her.

"Your boy attracts the attentions of many. Brought them out to play. Brought *her* out to play."

Dottie tried to move her hands. They were stuck at her sides, fingers splayed like she was ready to catch herself from a fall. "What the fuck are you?"

"I have done their bidding for many long moons." His voice sounded morose. It made a boulder of emotion sit in Dottie's throat. "Not seen anything quite like your boy. He is a marvel. A wonder. It must make you proud."

"Come to see your handiwork in action, aye? Hope you got your fill. Sick fuck."

"We imbued the gift. How Harold has chosen to use it is rather... creative. Across the veils, they speak of him. His echo grows."

"Can you help me? I should never have said yes that night. I... I was trolleyed. Please? I can't watch him die every day for the rest of my life."

She expected an outburst of anger. Instead, Old Smokes seemed to bow his head, examining the ground. When he shook his head, it was like rain clouds jostled for space where his face should've been.

"I wish I—" Old Smokes straightened. "He has attracted the attention of the old ones. No way back, now."

"Please?"

"She won't let me."

"Who?"

A gaggle of teenagers giggled, swerving around her. A boy with pathetic, teenage whiskers glared at her, something vicious staying locked behind his clenched teeth. She tried to move, but she was held in the gaze of the smoke being.

"Oh, ho," the boy said, his voice laced with the medicinal tang of Buckfast, "check out this total spice bag."

"Leave her," said a lad in a bomber jacket.

The boy marched on, keeping his head down, walking right through Old Smokes. The being burst apart then formed back together.

"You do not like this gift I gave your son?" he said.

She eyed the kids as they swaggered down another close and out of sight. "About as much as a curly hair on a jam sandwich."

"Why did you accept?"

"Let's just say I've a lot of making up to do. Guess you can say I'm not the motherly sort. When you said I can always protect him, I took it as a chance to finally do right by him. So when I fall off my horse for the last time, I can look back on my life and say I done what I could. Sounds pathetic, I know."

"The world is full of regrets. They are my stock and trade, some might say."

Behind them came the rubbery squeal of a pram. A family of four walked by. A pink teddy bear bobbed from the handlebar of the pram as the mother cooed softly to the baby hooded inside. A toddler walked between both mum and dad. They held a hand each as the boy ran and swung in the air between them, a toothy, carefree grin plastered up his elfish face. Dottie caught the scent of talcum powder and milk and new life as they rolled on by, giving her a wide berth, not making eye contact.

Tears tracked hotly down Dottie's unmoving face. It felt like just yesterday she and Pete walked hand in hand with Harold between them, swinging him like that, his hearty chuckle all that she could hear and care for. Every outing should've been like that. Instead, they'd dragged Harold along to sit in the dark, smoky corners of pubs while they got sloshed.

"The look in his eyes when I pull him out," she said. "It's like he's being kicked out of the ultimate high, you know? Like he needs the rush of it. This act is just a way for him to dress it up as 'art'. Why does it feel like you're trying to warn me? Why did you even come here?"

The twitchy way the cloud of his face moved made her think of a child about to burst into sobs.

"This life is tragically unfair at times," said Old Smokes. "I... I can hardly recall the good times. I wonder how long can I hold on. And then I see people like you. People with..."

Dottie felt a hot shiver pulse through her stomach as he seemed to look her up and down. The smell of burning, wet twigs drifted in the space between them.

The smoke of him flitted away into the summer night's sky like a bursting flock of sparrows.

"Her gift is poison," his voice sounded from some great distance. "Do not let her keep him."

Eight

The next day, Dottie soaked into the comfort of her couch and soaked her liver in the sweet spice of dark rum. In two days, Circus Nightmare would move on to St. Andrews, then up to Dundee, finishing its summer tour in and around Aberdeen. She couldn't shake the sound of regret and warning in Old Smokes' voice before he blew away into nothingness.

He has attracted the attention of the old ones. No way back, now.

Her body convulsed like she'd just been zapped with a defibrillator. Agony ballooned in her gut. A line of hot rum fell down her chin as she whimpered and doubled up in pain, drawing her knees to her chest.

"Ride it out, ride it out," she repeated to herself over and over.

After they dropped Pamela off last night, Dottie had tried to corner Harold, speak to him about stopping this whole act, but he sped up the stairs and shut himself in his room, not uttering a word.

The afternoon sun spilled bars of light across the living room. She stared out at the sad, broken street, feeling the alcohol swim its warm way up the back of her neck. What she wouldn't give to be able to fetch her horse, Jimmy and spend the day outside, sitting atop him as they galloped along the beach, giving him his head.

Leaving Jimmy with the old crone at the Drumnagoil Riding School was among the harder days of her life. The crestfallen way he looked at her as she walked him out the horse box on that frigid January day was as if he said, *Leave me here and I'll hate you forever.* She didn't have the money after Pete died to look after him properly.

Martha, the stern-nosed lady that owned the stable, said she'd only take on Jimmy if Dottie promised not to visit. It was the ultimate kick in the shin. She had to tear herself away before she jumped the uppity bitch.

The letterbox clacked three rough times before the sound of paper hit the floor.

"Fuck, what now?" she said, just wanting the world to leave her be.

A shadowy figure shuffled down the small path that led out to the street. She caught the angry stare of Bob, one of her nosy neighbours. His frazzled grey hair stuck out of his head like a clown leeched of colour.

She'd lived in some dumps before moving to this street in Pitlair, but she'd never been in a place where she felt eyes on her constantly. It was as if her neighbours all pointed telescopes at her. It was impossible to shake the feeling of being watched no matter what time it was.

There was a stack of unread mail from the NHS and some red bills. She kicked them to the side. They joined the others that lay against the skirting board like giant, scattered playing cards.

She lifted the card Bob had posted with its scratchy, desperate writing. The pen had been pushed down so hard she felt bumps on the underside of it.

To whom the devil concerns,

The Lord beggeth you to stopeth this evil abominination. You have a stain on you. Its not too late. I can help smite the evil that has your family in its evil clutchs. I know its face.

Your saviour,

Bob.

PS – Actioneth will be taken if you dont acept

When she scrunched the card up, a papercut sliced her index finger.

"You can crameth thy fist up thy arse," she said.

From the bottom of the stairs, she could hear Harold *clack, clack, clacking* away at his laptop. She went up and found him hunched over the screen, his tongue hanging out his mouth as he scribbled on a notepad. The laptop showed scenes of death after death, a reel of blood-letting that had her turning her face away like it stank of rotten fish.

"That even legal?" she said.

"Just gathering ideas," he said, not turning around. "Keep my act fresh and all that. Need some serious pops next time."

"Got plenty enough last night."

"Pamela took a video of the crowd so she could show me. Nice, eh?"

Dottie clutched at her wrist, pressing down, twisting, needing something to steady her. "Aye. Nice."

"Wish I could've pulled off that whole beheading thing. Maybe next time."

"If you need someone to rip your head off, I can do it right now. Near gave me a heart attack. Maybe not be so extreme next time. Enough of the Mary Queen of Scots shite."

"Och, stop worrying. If everybody sees what's coming I'll get pretty stale."

"Smell that way already. There's a washing basket, you know?"

Harold beat the pencil off the notepad. "Needs to be fresh. Got a wee list here, if you're alright with sorting me with money?"

"Not got a lot left. Besides, that was Pete's dosh. He wouldn't want anything to do with—"

"Fuck that prick! Bastard quit on you in the worst way. Deserves that hole in the ground. He made it himself. Let him shout his fake cowboy shit up at me from his spot in hell."

"I... I didn't know you felt like that."

He spun in his chair. His neck muscles stuck out in thin wires as he spoke. "How did you think I felt, Mother? Jesse James wannabe pretending to be my dad when actually he's just here to tank you up and make me watch SpongeBob SquarePants while he rides you like a banshee."

"Harold!"

Her hand stung before she realised she'd lashed out, slapping him across the face. The sound of it seemed to reverberate around the dark room as he stared up at her with childish hurt.

His hand came up to the side of his face, rubbing where she'd smacked him one. The hand looked as thin as a skeleton's – no skin or muscle at all.

"I was so sick of you and your fantasy world," said Harold. "This isn't Lonesome Dove. You don't get to ride into the sunset on your noble steed. Here you have a golden chance for us to do something together, for once. To make the world bow down to us. To rake in the cash. But no, you don't want to." His sour breath drifted over her when he sighed. "I'm glad he died."

"You can't—"

"Is that what you're dreaming about when you're passed out on the couch, whimpering like a bairn?"

"Stop."

"How he left? How your sweet chestnut—"

"Don't!"

"—went into the bath and opened himself up like a can of tuna? Fucker didn't even leave a note. Just left his bloated face for you to stumble across."

The image of it pressed into her. The way Pete had been submerged in crimson-stained water that almost spilled over the tub. He'd been curled into an S-shape, his head resting on the porcelain, staring up into dead white nothing. As well as the gaping wounds up his wrists, he'd cut little grooves into his hairy chest. To Dottie, it looked as if he'd tried to spell something out as he faded away.

The peppery smell of diluted blood and the papaya body wash that lingered on the air when she'd found him seemed to circle around her as she stared down at the vindictive man her son had become.

"Don't forget what he did to you." Harold turned his back on her, picked up his pen, whacking it off the paper in a machine-gun rhythm.

"He done more for me, for us, than you'll ever know. He'd hate seeing you top yourself again and again. And for what? The love of a bunch of half drunk wankers. He'd hate that I let you do it."

"Let me? Let me? You made me into this, Mother. And you know what? It's fucking amazing. You should feel it. The rush. It's like being dropped out of the sky."

"Would you—" a pain like hot tweezers gripping and twisting in her stomach made her lean against the cool wall. "Give it up. I've a bad feeling about it all."

The pencil stopped its *tap, tap, tapping*. "I thought we were a good wee team. You and me, finally doing something together. You know, when I was at primary school, I used to dream that you would read me books. Used to fantasise about showing you how good I was getting on with my reading. I'd learned way ahead of my class. Memorised The Giving Tree, by Shel Silverstein – not that you'll know who that is."

"Harold... I..."

He hit a button on the keyboard. Violent images played on the screen. A hunger filled his eyes.

"I didn't know," she said, one hand pressing down on her stomach. "I didn't know."

"Just get out. Got a lot of shows to plan. They won't know what hit them."

She started towards the open door, looking back over her shoulder, a world of unsaid words dying behind her lips. How to go back and change it? Pay attention to him. Ask the questions. To care.

You've got something missing inside.

"Looks like you were right, Mum," she said to herself, going back down the stairs.

In the kitchen, dishes and pots lay stacked and uncleaned, nearly toppling over like the world's worst game of Jenga. The room was caked with the stench of old food and grease.

Her last remaining friend lay in the freezer. She scooped him out, unscrewing the lid. The delightful dark of the bottle of J. Gow Revenge rum flitted around her nostrils. After this, she would have to stock the cheap stuff.

"Some mum you turned out to be, Dottie," she said to herself.

She raised a toast to the silent kitchen and downed the drink. Fire swooned in her bones. It reached her stomach, a familiar numbness oozing outward.

When she lay on her couch, her phone buzzed. She hauled it out of her tight pocket, frustrated that she had to yank at the thing to get it out. Another message from *DocMan Martin*.

"Fuck sake, leave me alone!"

She launched the phone across the room. It hit a photo frame on the windowsill that crashed to the floor, face down. The *crack* it made promised broken glass.

She picked up the remote and turned on the telly, laying back on the couch, her rum resting on her stomach. The news anchor's dulcet tones made her want to sleep. She ignored what the moustached prick was saying, only wanting the noise so she wouldn't feel as lonely.

On the path outside her house, she saw three girls pointing at her through the window, before they giggled and ran off. How long before they chapped the door, demanding a first-hand demonstration of Harold's abilities?

She felt more than her forty-two years in her aching bones. Not so long ago, she'd been a spritely filly. Oh, to have a horse steaming under her again. She placed the glass on her lips, whipped her head back, the remainder of her drink galloping down her throat.

The sound of the bathtub upstairs filling with water startled her. She wiped at her chin with the back of her hand. Dizziness flooded her like a warm blanket. It felt as if an alien thing was inside her stomach, rummaging around, ready to burst out in an expulsion of black blood.

She scrunched herself into a pathetic ball on the couch, closing her eyes, trying to ride it out. The glass tumbled out her hand, fell to the carpet, and rolled in a curve until it hit the couch, empty.

"And finally, a magician from Pitlair in Fife has gone viral," said monotone news man. "Harold the Impossible was filmed during an appearance with Circus Nightmare in Glenrothes yesterday, appearing to have died onstage, only to be spotted leaving the event unscarred. His act is said to be so realistic that people in the audience have fainted. An ambulance was even called to the scene just to be turned away. We cannot show you the act as it's too gruesome for TV, but we caught up with Zorbo, the owner of the circus, to—"

She pushed the off button on the remote so hard the plastic casing creaked.

Just what they needed. Harold on the BBC. She could already hear her phone *durring* in the corner with messages. Since watching the fevered way the punters at the old miner's club in Methil had looked at him when he performed for them, she knew the act would take off.

On the mantelpiece in a silver frame, Pete's smile beamed down at her. It had been one of the only pictures she had of him smiling. He was more of a stare-down-the-camera-like-you-hate-it kind of guy.

They'd always talked about setting up shop in the States once Harold was settled with a life of his own. She stared at the blue sky outside. It had not a cloud to disrupt it. She could do it. Pack her stuff. Bugger off to America with the money she had left. Find a crappy little job to pay the bills. Work with horses somewhere. Start over.

Above her, the rushing water ceased its hammering. She heard Harold's muttering as he mucked about before stepping into the bath.

She braced herself as she sat up, expecting a fresh electrocution of pain. Instead, she felt the warmth of the rum flood her extremities. She could put some Springsteen on right now and dance around the room like she was twenty – put some shake in that shimmy.

The haunted look on Harold's face when he said he was happy Pete had died crashed down on her.

It was her fault. If she could have it back, she would do it all different. She could've had it both ways, spoiling her little man, while riding into perfect laughter with the man who made jellybeans flip in her tummy when their eyes met. She could've had it all. She did have it all.

She started her slow way up the stairs, going over what she could say to sew up their relationship. With her hand on the wooden banister, she resolved to always be there for him. They were a team from here on out. She would guide him, be the mother he always needed. If she could persuade him away from a life of killing himself, then all the better. There was room for happiness still. There was a new beginning, somewhere.

The *plink* of the dripping tap in the bathroom cascaded down the hall, making her wince each time it hit the water. The door was ajar. She stood outside of it, suddenly unsure of herself. Barge in on her adult son?

"Seen it all before," she said, though she didn't like the shaky leaf note of her voice.

The door creaked when she pushed it open. The heat of the bath misted over her, sticking to her skin.

"H-Harold?" she said, stepping slowly forward, the tangy scent of orange shower gel mixing with the ozone-like smell of rank water. "No…"

His head lay against the taps. His skin had started to yellow already. His unblinking eyes held a coy, knowing look in them.

The water was red.

She turned her head and threw up on the linoleum floor. Her knees buckled. When she tried to catch herself from hitting the floor, her hand slid in the chunky sickness. The burning sensation of rum shot out her gullet as she spewed a second time, the pressure behind her eyes building, causing tears.

She gagged a few times before she sat up and knelt beside the bath, staring at her dead boy.

"I hope it hurt," she hissed. "You absolute bastard. How could you? How could you?"

Nine

The next morning, she lay on her bed, staring out the window at the unkempt back gardens that belonged to the street parallel to their house. The hypnotic swaying of the cluster of bluebells at the top of her own garden held her. Her mum planted them as a gift, always using them to give Dottie a row for not keeping them in order. She hadn't cared about the flowers with their large hanging cups of pale blue and violet, but an urge to stand in the middle of them, run her hands over their long stems, breathe of their summer perfume, suddenly grabbed her.

A stomach protesting burp eeked out her mouth, burning her gullet. She really should lay off the sauce for a while.

She'd left it too long to bring Harold back from the dead. Just thinking about it made anger throb in her temples. How dare he off himself in a parody of Pete's suicide? It would've been too easy to leave him there. Call the cops. Call it a day on being a mother. No one would know the real story. All except Pamela, but Dottie could've dusted her off with an easy lie about the magic running out.

Downstairs, the bottle of rum lay open on the kitchen, misting the air with its heavenly spice. She wrestled with herself before screwing the lid back on and sliding it into the freezer.

Overnight, Harold had been crowned Fife's *Angel of Death*. She scrolled through her phone. All the Scottish news sites carried the story along with blurred out images of his demise. The comments sections ranged from people proud that they'd seen him in person, to shouty all-caps proclaiming he was the devil.

You have a stain on you, Bob's note had said.

The fact her own flesh and blood had riled up so many people brought the first smile of the day to her lips.

Her phone buzzed in her hand. DocMan Martin again.

Holy magpies, where's that boy been hiding? Take it that's why you been ignoring your letters. Get phoning me or drop by the surgery to see me. I'm serious. We need to talk. x

Her thumbs tapped out a snarly response to leave her the fuck alone. A cramp laddered its way up her abdomen. A ghostly moan escaped her as she gripped the counter. She deleted the message and typed, *Gotcha big 'un. I'll drop in soon. Promise.*

Harold marched into the room, opened the fridge, took out a can of Pepsi, then smacked a kiss on her cheek. He left without a word, leaving nothing but the cough-inducing reek of woody aftershave behind. She felt the house rock in the soles of her feet when he slammed the front door closed.

"Where you off to with that much spray on?" she said, trying to cluck away the taste of it.

She saw what lay ahead. More shows. More action. People wanting a piece of Harold. Cameras. Headlines. Questions.

The urge to see Jimmy overwhelmed her. The old cow who ran the riding school had said she wouldn't be allowed to visit, but the thought of him not seeing her, wondering why he'd been ditched to slowly carry bairns on their first rides made her ache inside.

MOTHER DEATH

The Land Rover bounced her around as she drove up a small country road on the way to the Drumnagoil Riding School. Drumnagoil was a rural town not far from Pitlair. She'd heard about the things they brought into the warehouses attached to the farms at all hours. The bottom basement of the criminal underworld thrived here. The sprawling green land wasn't nearly as idyllic as it looked.

Her tires sloshed through bumpy puddles when she brought the vehicle to a stop. The riding school was a series of barns and stables filled with God's most beautiful creatures. She hoped the kids who got to ride Jimmy realised just how special a character he was. Did he reveal himself to them?

Jimmy was all alone. Sundance, Pete's horse, had died of a strange wasting disease three years ago. Pete hadn't been the same since. In a way, Sundance's slow death had marked the start of their downfall.

What now? The place seemed quiet enough. Sneak in? Find Jimmy's stall in the stables?

A tap on glass made her jump in her seat. Familiar, disapproving eyes glared at her as she rolled down the window. The scent of mud and horse shit leapt at her.

"If you think you can just show up here like a stray cat, think not," said Martha, the owner of the school. "One does not simply make such intrusions. I was most clear about my instructions for not paying Jimmy a visit."

Martha said the name Jimmy as if it tasted of sour lemons. Dottie wanted to reach down and grab the wide woman by the scruff of her riding shirt and slap the poshness out of her.

"I-I'm going away for a wee bit," said Dottie. "Please. I need to see him. Just this once. I swear."

Dottie unclipped her seatbelt and threw the door open. The woman had to step out the way to avoid the door slamming into her.

"Do excuse me, but I believe it was you who abandoned him. We've been through this countless times, Dorothy Matheson. One who gives up a horse does not deserve to see that horse again."

"Aw, quit it with the accent. You were born in Pitlair just like me. Owning a horse doesn't make one a queen."

Martha lifted a leg that looked like it should be holding up a grand piano. She pivoted and turned her broad back on Dottie like a soldier doing an about turn. "Goodbye."

"Martha, please." Her voice broke. "Just this once. I promise. Haven't you ever loved a horse so much you felt it hold part of your soul?"

Martha's shoulders sunk like her resolve had puffed out of her. When she spoke, her voice had none of the hoity royal speech. "Aye, alright then. Five minutes. That's it. And don't let me see you crawling around here again. People who abandon their horses are worse than murderers in my humble opinion."

The sharp tang of horse pee and straw assailed her as she entered the stable. The fly-inducing smell took her back to simpler days. She followed Martha into the cool darkness until she stopped by a stall. A lonely black horse whinnied. All the other stalls seemed to be empty.

"Five minutes. That's it." Martha stomped off.

Dottie walked up to the stall. She leaned against the metal bar, feeling its cold spread through her chest. "Come here, my big guy. Come see momma."

Jimmy lifted his head and blew a sharp breath out of his nose as if to say, *Who the hell are you, likes?*

"I'm a terrible person for giving you up. Trust me, I know. I miss you, you huffy bastard." She set her boot on a metal bar and hoisted herself up, leaning over it to get closer. "How about I piss the old bitch off and saddle you up? Ride out. Me and you. What you say?"

He turned his muscular body away from her, grunting and sliding into a shadowy corner.

"Och, don't be like that, Jimmy. My big guy. Come here."

Slowly, he swayed forward. Dim light caught his bright, all-too-intelligent eyes. He kept looking past her and around her as if she were the black sheep at a family dinner party.

"Let me sniff you just one last time."

Her stomach protested as she stretched out, testing the limits of her balance. She could feel the heat radiating from him as she reached, almost touching the side of his nose in the way that he always crooned over.

Jimmy reared up on his hind legs. His front legs cycled in anger, his head scraped the low ceiling. When he brought his hoofs down, the loud noise trembled in her lower intestine.

"Jimmy? Calm down, my son. Ssshh."

He was getting himself into a froth, pacing back and forth in the small space, baring his teeth. A line of white spit hit her cheek as he shook with the promise of violence.

"What's gotten into you? Can't you—"

Jimmy turned and head-butted the back of the stable, making a high-pitched shriek that she'd never heard a horse make before. He struck the wood again and again, pawing at it, trying to stomp his way out. She felt each thud in the chambers of her heart as she looked around, panicked. She longed to jump into the stall, pet his sides, to sing and soothe him. But it was her. She was the thing making him panic.

You have a stain on you.

"Stop. Jimmy? Please!"

"What on blue Earth have you done?" Martha roared behind her, pushing her to the side.

"I don't know, I—"

She felt the air change. Jimmy had knocked through the wall. Fresh wind brought the smell of salt and blood. A jagged tooth of a plank of wood stood stark against the sky on the other side. Blood streamed down that wood and Jimmy's neck. The wound was a blackened smile. He shook his head in a vicious snarl, staring into Dottie's eyes.

"Jimmy!" she screamed as Martha fumbled with the lock to the stall.

The life drained from Jimmy's eyes.

The ground shook when he slumped to the floor, legs snapping under his weight.

A long, final breath sighed out of him, and he was gone.

Ten

She couldn't remember getting home. Or opening the bottle of rum. Or finishing it.

Sat on the singular step outside her back door, she watched the bees hover around the bluebells. They were the only thing she had left of her mother's. She'd died in a nursing home with nought to her name but a selfish, ungrateful daughter named Dorothy and two dead sons.

The flowers stirred in the breeze, sun dazzling off blue-purple petals. They were so bright, so eye-achy.

Each house on their street had a long, thin garden which ended where the next street's gardens started. If you looked out an upstairs window, you could see rows of what looked like unkempt tennis courts, seeing what everybody was up to. Dottie felt the creeping sensation of eyes on her, but was unable to locate who or what was staring down at her.

"It's all fucked," she said, knocking back a bottle of beer. She gulped until the burn of it threatened to come out her nose.

"Back stoop drinking, aye?" said Harold from the kitchen behind her. "Proper redneck, you. Look, Mum, I... I'm sorry I done myself like that last night. Shouldn't have—"

"Jimmy's dead."

She heard a moist noise like a mouth clicking open. "Shit."

He mucked about in the fridge, opened a bottle of beer, and joined her on the small step. Their thighs touched. He clinked her bottle with hers before taking a snappy drink.

"What happened?" he said.

She gulped down some courage, then told him about how she'd begged a visit, and how Jimmy had gone mental. When she finished, she buried her tearful face into his shoulder. After a moment, she felt his arm go around her, drawing her close.

The reek of perfume on his clothes was familiar. "You been winching? Wee casanova. Can smell her on you."

He took his arm away and drank his beer, staring out at the top of the garden. "Maybe I was, maybe I wasn't. You gonna be alright? Know that horse meant a lot to you."

"Wasn't mine anymore."

"He'll always be yours."

She used the sleeves of her chequered shirt to wipe away the tears from both cheeks. "Must think I'm a pathetic old bag, seeing me like this."

"Would you stop that already? Cutting about complaining like you're ninety and headed for a retirement castle."

"I feel old. Feel it in my bones."

Harold stared down at the uneven slabs that led up the middle of the garden. He let out a dry chuckle. "Mind ages ago, that Ronnie appeared at the door a few times, wanting me to come play? Only reason he wanted to be my mate was because he had a torch for you. Not gonna repeat the filth he spewed, but it was a pretty big crush."

"Where is that slimy wee fucker?"

"You might've been the reason we had a... falling out, let's just say."

The sharp, yellow taste of pollen floated around her. This was nice. Her belly didn't scream pain at her for once, and she couldn't remember the last time they'd had a drink together.

"I know you don't have much reason to believe it," she said, "but I love you, alright? Know I don't say it enough."

"Can't remember you *ever* saying it."

He sat straighter, ran a hand through his hair. Somehow, her gawky teenager had bloomed into a man. His hair looked like a ruffled raven perched on his head. He'd lost his puppy fat and now his jaw was square and muscular. His pronounced nose gave him a distinguished air.

"I love you too, though," he said. "And this isn't just all for me, this killing business. We could have a life if we play it right. You won't have to get a crummy job at the shop or wherever. I can *be* something."

"I think you're already something, the way my phone's been buzzing."

"Just getting started." He scratched at the brown label on the glass bottle, pulling it back piece by slow piece. "I don't think you're a bad mum. Do I wish you were there more when I was growing up? Aye. But I know you'd scrap for me, do anything to protect me."

The bottle clacked against her front teeth when she forced a long swig. She eyed the large plastic buckets that were stacked in the corner of the garden. The bluebells swayed towards those bins as if reaching for them. The sloshing, glugging sound Harold's blood made as she emptied a pale of it into the soil beneath the flowers rushed through her. Had he deliberately held his hand over the bath so blood would cover the floor?

"Promise me we'll do it together," she said.

"There's no other way."

He finished his beer, then stood, swotting away a buzzing bluebottle that zipped around his head. "Suppose I should tell you about what's happening later."

She felt dread knead her stomach. "What did you do?"

"Been getting calls all day to speak to the papers and all that. Figured a wee demo might be in order. Get this one right and we can shoot to the top of the world. We can branch out on our own and ditch Zorbo and his collection of weirdos."

"A demo?"

"Get your best shirt on, the beeb will be here in about an hour."

"You invited the BBC to our house? It's a tip. I-I'm half plastered. I haven't cleaned in—"

"Told them we'd do it out in the street. Figure a wee crowd couldn't hurt."

Eleven

A grey van screeched to a halt outside their house. The rusty van looked more like a paedo had come to steal Harold away than a news reporter for the BBC. A bank of dull clouds covered up the evening sun. Harold fiddled with his jacket before swooping it around his shoulders. She followed, pulling her shirt tight around her, guarding against the cooling air like it was mid-autumn.

The van's doors drew open, and a petite woman spilled out, clutching at her large microphone with the BBC logo writ across it. She quickly combed her hair and checked herself in the van's mirror, then clopped across the road.

"Harold, I presume?" she said, offering her hand.

Harold took his hand from his pocket and shook it. "Aye. That's me. This is Dottie, my mum."

"How do you do?"

Dottie shook her hand, impressed by the firm handshake. The woman had shoulder-pads straight from the eighties. She bit down on the urge to joke about it. The world seemed to weave around her like she was on a boat.

All around them, she saw curtains being pulled back, windows opening, oily children standing on windowsills. Some opened their front doors and gawked.

"Once my cameraman is done arsing around," she aimed this over her shoulder with a roll of her piercing blue eyes, "I'll ask you a few questions, alright? The simple bish, bash, bosh kind of stuff. Just keep looking at me, forget the camera's there, and we'll be fine. We'll be live, so no swearing. This'll be my first stint on the six o'clock news, so don't bugger me off, okay?"

Dottie's belly felt like a snake coiling into itself. The pressure of it had her noticeably swelling up. Her stomach pushed at her jeans like she was in the first stages of pregnancy.

"You mind?" the burly cameraman spat at her. "In the shot."

The tree-sized man looked at her through the camera balanced on his shoulder. She moved round, opting to stand next to the hulking figure to get a good view of Harold. The cameraman smelled like three days of hard partying.

"Right, Harold. I'm Monica, by the way." Monica leaned forward, forcing out three barking coughs into a balled-up fist. "Just waiting on the signal from the powers that be, then we'll roll, okay? Sorry, no time for run through."

The cameraman grunted, a red light shining out the side of the big box on his shoulder.

Monica held her hand against a small device in her ear, then turned to face the camera. She glanced out at the crowd that shuffled around them like slow zombies, turning her nose up like they'd throw monkey shit at her live on camera.

"Thanks, Daryl," said Monica in a practised, newsreader voice. "That's right. I'm standing here with Harold the Impossible, who's agreed to give us an exclusive chat about his show." She turned, her perm bouncing to a stop. "So, Harold. Tell us, what's your act all about?"

The silence became a thing Dottie could almost taste. She bit into her balled fist, tempted to march in and rescue him.

A radiant smile blossomed up his face. "I'm the angel of death."

"You've caused quite the stir, with people saying your act is so realistic they swear they saw you die on stage." She held the mic out to him. Her hand trembled in the silence between them. "W-What do you have to say about that?"

"Death holds us captive all our life. It is the cage that makes us stop living. We pray it doesn't visit upon us, yet who hasn't wished it upon others?" The cameraman shuffled nervously when Harold turned his attention on the camera, speaking directly into the living rooms of thousands. "I've roamed the fields of beyond. It teaches me things. I'm the symbol of mankind's long fascination with death. I court her. Come watch me. I'll give you a show you'll never forget." He turned his attention back to Monica. "We all wonder what it's like to watch someone die. Isn't that right, Monica?"

Around them, a semi-circle of milling neighbours in nightdresses and half-dressed kids watched them with hungry, whispering eyes.

"R-Right," said Monica.

"I'm touring with Circus Nightmare. We'll be in St. Andrews tomorrow night, then Dundee, and up the coast. Don't bring the children."

"So, you fake it? Celebrate death, is that it?"

"I see it's no use trying to explain." Harold took something from the inside of his jacket. It glinted in the afternoon light. "Let me show you."

Monica yelped at the sight of the knife, taking a step back. "This interview is—"

He punched the knife into his stomach. It made a wet, dull sound when he took it out and stabbed himself over and over, his hand a blur. Blood splattered over his hand and at his feet.

"Y-You're a baddie," said Monica, tripping over herself as she ran back to the van.

Half the gathered crowd gasped and left. The other half turned their phones at Harold who continued to hurt himself. Veins pulsed at his temples. He stooped over his stomach. Dottie burped up sick and covered her mouth. She could see the purple and black knots of his intestines poking through slashed skin.

"Stop," said Dottie.

"Barry, come on," pleaded Monica, opening the van's door. "Shift your hairy arse."

The cameraman stepped closer to Harold. "No chance."

Harold waved the blood-dripping knife at the eye of the camera. "This hit the spot, Scotland? This real enough for you? Come see me."

When he tried to step back, his leg folded under him. The blood dripped from countless wounds in his gut. Dottie felt the electric pain of it like it had transferred to her.

Monica hauled the cameraman away. "Both get the sack after this."

Dottie knelt beside her son. "Could've picked a less painful way, you dafty." She lifted her head and raised her voice, trying to make herself sound as calm as possible. "You've all had your fill. All seen the show. Now, beat it."

The news team slammed their van closed and whored it along the street, almost knocking over some of the milling crowd.

The moving bank of clouds reflected in Harold's dead eyes. It should get easier, watching him die over and over, knowing she could pull him back, but it stung fresh and powerful each time.

She grabbed him under the arms and lifted, feeling something stretch too far in her back. Grit and small stones on the path scraped under her boots as she shuffled and pulled his weight, slowly dragging him back to the house.

The crowd of mobile phones zoned in on them, lighting the zombied gazes of their owners.

A figure stepped out from them, his tufts of grey hair flowing in the wind like clumps of dust about to blow away. Bob stared down at her with one eye half open. "Devil woman, be gone!"

"He dead enough for you, aye?" she screamed, her voice breaking with effort as her legs strained with the weight of him. "Get a good look."

No one came to help as she dragged Harold inside, leaving a long line of red blood on the concrete.

Twelve

Each time the Land Rover crested one of the many hills on the twisty road to St. Andrews, Dottie's stomach lurched. Yesterday's hangover still clawed at the back of her throat.

"You feeling alright?" she said, looking in the rear view at Harold who was sprawled over the back seats.

She'd fainted after she eventually managed to haul his heavy arse into the house last night. When she woke up, she was face to face with him on the floor. The yellow of his skin snapped her awake and she threw up all over his face. She hadn't shared that particular detail.

"You seen any of the stuff from last night?" she continued, trying to coax a conversation. "They cut the feed right after you stabbed yourself the first time, so there's a lot of questions. Neighbours got a good few videos going though, where you can see your intestines worming out."

"How long?" croaked Harold.

"What? Your intestines?"

"How long was I gone for?"

"I dunno. However long it took me to haul you into the house while our beloved neighbours snapped pictures." She rolled her shoulders. "Feels like I went rowing all last night. You're about as light as a Transit full of goats."

She'd taken paracetamol and ibuprofen and a quick swig of rum before she climbed into the Land Rover. When she had to time to drop in on Martin the doctor, she'd beg for stronger stuff, whether legal or illegal. The pain was all-controlling and the stuff they sold in the shop barely approached it.

Harold shifted in the back, staring out at the rain that pelted the jeep.

"Are you alright? Seem a little off since I dragged you out."

"Packs a kick sometimes."

"Is it worth going on then, if it hurts? Not gonna lie, I've seen better looking smackheads."

"Doesn't hurt, exactly. It's... It's like getting pulled through a tunnel at warp speed. Once I've been back a while I get all wobbly, like I can barely fend for myself. It's a buzz, though. I can still feel it now, like it's still crawling in my veins."

"Hope it's not frying your brains, cutting the air off like that all the time. If you end up a vegetable, I might just have to kill you myself, ha."

"You can't—" Harold huffed a sigh down his nose. "I'll be fine. I'll make sure it's a walloper of a show tonight."

"A walloper? You mean, you've been playing it slow and easy all this time? Jesus. I think I'm one more ambulance call away from getting fined or some shite. That's two fine-looking paramedics I've had to apologise to, lying out my arse about you being alive."

"I give the crowd what they want."

She turned a bend. The Land Rover's tires went blasting through a huge puddle. The sound of it hitting the chassis under them had her heart thumping in her ears. The death trap contained in Jimmy's old horse box behind them rattled around before righting itself. She gave the engine some juice. The bonnet tipped up as the power of it thrust them forward.

"Martha keeps texting me," she said. "Says she's gonna wipe me out."

"Who's Martha?"

"That old crone at the stables where Jimmy's kept." The leather of the steering wheel creaked in her grip. "*Was* kept."

"Your point?"

"You wee—" She was tempted to slam the brakes on, make him jerk forward and scone his head off something. "Point is, I'm not made of money and she might be about to take what I do have."

"I don't think that'll be a problem for long."

"Might as well call us the Elephants, cause Zorbo's giving us peanuts."

"Big picture, Mother. Big picture."

She drove through the centre of St. Andrews and the sun appeared from behind the grey clouds. The place looked a million miles from Pitlair, with its clean cars and happy families smiling their ice cream smiles. The big top came into view and she drove towards it, the Land Rover skidding to a stop in the gravel car park outside.

She killed the engine, eyeing the huge queue that snaked from the tent's entrance, through the car park and along the neighbouring field. She placed her hand on the door handle when Harold sat up straight, leaning between the two front seats.

"Wait," he said. "I kinda have something to give you."

"What? You shouldn't have."

He fumbled about at a bag by his feet and brought out the object. He set it on his lap, tracing a finger over it before handing it to her.

It was a mask. An ugly, vulgar, pointy looking thing. Staring at it made butterflies panic in her stomach.

"You really, really shouldn't have," she said.

"It's a Venetian Bauta mask. Pretty sharp and wicked, eh?" He looked down at his hands, spidering his fingers like he was a big ball of anxiety. "Figure things are getting a bit too crazy to have people recognising you out and about. Would rather you remain hidden. Besides, you can't deny the mask looks awesome. Will add a wee bit of mystery to the strong woman running things from the shadows."

Dottie thumbed the masks intricate details. It looked wicked, indeed, like something an opera villain would wear. It was big enough to swallow her whole face, but had a protruding, pointed chin that stuck out from the mouth so it didn't need mouth or nose holes. It was bone white, with diamond shapes that covered each eye. One eye was painted black, the other was livid red. Gold rusted over the forehead and down the pointed bump of its nose.

It smelled of plastic and leather with the ghost of glue when she placed it over her face, fixing the elastic strap behind her head so it'd stay in place.

"Fits perfect," she said. "Like I'm not wearing a mask at all. Can breathe and everything."

Her heart sang when a happy, childish smile beamed up Harold's face. "Let's go shock the world."

Thirteen

With the mask on, she strode into the circus, a buzzy thrill running through her each time one of the muscled stagehands gawped at her. The constant pain in her stomach circled like slow, drowsy sharks. She slunk to her shadows at the side of the stage, watching Harold help hoist a large, heavy object up into the rigging above the stage.

She felt the gravity of Zorbo's presence next to her. He ran his hand down the sides of his mouth like he smoothed a moustache, eyeing the stage. "Biggest crowd tonight. Find hundreds of extra seats. Not easy." He pointed at Harold who was directing traffic on the stage, telling them when to haul the large black box on its pulley. "I know how your boy dies. Well, how he fake."

"You do, aye?"

"All plastic parts, not metal, intricately prepared. Skin make-up already applied so he just rip off top layer. Have pump for fresh looking blood on his person. Look nice and freshly dead."

"If it's that easy, you not think everybody else would have done that by now?"

He let out a little rumble of a laugh and slapped his belly. When he turned to face her, the laugh wheezed itself out. He clutched his chest. His yellowed breath hit her when he stuttered and pointed at her mask.

"*Masca rea*," he said in Romanian, stepping back. "What do you bring here?"

"What, this?" Dottie tugged at the pointed chin. "Fetching, eh? Suits me down to the ground."

The air between them grew thick. For a second, she thought he was going to burst forward and rip the thing from her face and stomp it into flat nothing. Someone called on him, snapping him out of the tranceful gaze. He turned and stomped off, throwing a worried glance over his shoulder.

A couple of hours later, a different class of drunk filled the stands and the spare plastic seats around the edge of the circular stage. There wasn't a bottle of Merrydown or Buckfast in sight. Instead, the ground was already littered with clanking green bottles of lager.

Pamela had arrived, and asked Dottie to come backstage to prepare with Harold, but she stayed out in the crowd, secretly pleased whenever anyone noticed her mask and let out a little gasp.

She wrapped an arm through the thick metal bars by the side of the stage, delighting in its radiant cold. The packed-in crowd had turned the heat up. With the rain from earlier, the tent was a damp and mud-swollen oven.

She wondered if Sundance and Jimmy were rollicking around under a perfect sky somewhere. Pete would be watching them, his shirt rolled up to his elbows, the sun sprinkling off his unshaven jaw.

Sundance would snort at Jimmy as if to say, *What took you so long, slowcoach?*

Jimmy would glare back, *I'm here now, ain't I? Let's race.*

Would they be missing her? Waiting on her? Watching her?

The sharks in her stomach bit down. She seethed in a breath and doubled over, drawing the attention of a lady where the row of seats ended. The woman looked more like she waited on the bingo numbers being called rather than watching a bronzed, topless man jump about on his squeaky pogo stick. Dottie saw the look of concern flit across her face, then she turned her attention back to the bouncing act.

Dottie pulled herself up, forcing herself to straighten her back, tasting the thin, metallic taste of the bar she held onto. As she watched the first act, zoning in on the man's six-pack, the pain finally ebbed away.

She watched all the acts, in and out of a state of blinding pain. The crowd seemed up for it, cheering and clapping away, unlike the brazen folks of Kirkcaldy and Glenrothes.

"And now," a booming voice announced, "it's time to end the show."

Dottie's heart lurched when the crowd leapt up and roared like the man had just announced the Beatles were here. Fog machines pumped out smoke. The chalky taste of it clung to the roof of her mouth as she took in the crowd's adoration. Her Harold had done all of this. He was becoming a real somebody.

A jarring heavy metal riff started. The spotlights criss-crossed each other, making ghosts in the smoke.

"This is not for the faint of heart," the voice continued. "Please do not call the police or an ambulance. At Circus Nightmare, everything is under control."

The music cut off after drums *dom-dommed.* A taut silence stretched.

"And now, St. Andrews. Please welcome. Harold the Impossible!"

Harold stepped into the centre of the stage, smoke eating up his legs. He breathed in the crowd's wild adoration. To Dottie, it seemed as if he were a balloon filling up, nearly light enough to start floating. The look in his sharp eyes was of fevered hunger.

"Set them alight, wee guy," said Dottie, tightening her grip on the pole.

"Good evening," bellowed Harold, his voice carrying despite the noise. He waited until the cheer died. "Death. We fear death. Death stalks us. Death awaits us all. Yet, we cannot avert our eyes. Scottish legend is steeped in its tales. The BBC have even started showing it on the news."

The crowd roared in a laughter so hard Dottie felt it shake the small bones in her ears.

"How very brave of them, though the real show I gave them went on longer." Harold stepped to the side of the stage, shooting Dottie a wink before settling his attention back on the crowd. "Who wants to see death unchained?"

The crowd clapped themselves hoarse as Pamela wheeled the gnarly death machine to the stage. Her walk was much more of a strut this time round, although there were markedly less whistles. She stood next to the machine, giving her best impression of a magician's curtsy. She gave Harold a coy smile, holding his gaze for a long, pregnant moment.

"Oh, doll," Dottie said to herself, feeling the breath mist under her mask. She knew what that look meant. She recalled the cloying perfume that had stuck to Harold's clothes when he'd come home the day before.

Harold nodded at Pamela, suddenly looking scared. Then Pamela sashayed off the stage and back through the curtain.

"You want blood?" yelled Harold.

The crowd screamed back as one, leaning forward in their seats.

The music began. He'd changed the song. He'd done away with the eerie, gothic music and gone with something that sounded like a grating cross between Metallica and Dubstep. It annoyed the fillings in Dottie's teeth.

Harold whipped his cloak off and threw it into the crowd. It flapped open, soaring through the air like an oily bat-thing, before two girls caught it. They wrestled with it in their grip until one girl clawed at the other girl's face, making her let go.

Harold quickly stepped up the centre of his death machine. He eyed the spikes that overhung him, promising another gushing death.

This should get easier. Instead, it felt like she'd have to bolt to the toilet. She hated seeing his dead eyes stare back at her. They seemed so accusatory. But, she couldn't deny the prickly excitement that pimpled her arms.

The music popped and screeched in a jarring cacophony. The crowd pointed their phones. Harold held his arms out, slowly reaching up, up.

He clenched his fists. The signal for Pamela to push the button.

The spikes squealed, rushing for him.

The air in the tent changed.

The crowd gasped.

Harold leapt from the machine, landing on his chest, his arms splayed out.

The metal teeth bit into nothing.

He stood, shaking his head.

"What you up to?" said Dottie.

A beer can hurtled through the air. In the silence, she could hear the lager foam in a puddle around Harold's feet.

The boos thundered. Harold held his palms up in apology, looking every bit like the kid who'd been caught giving the teacher the middle finger. He stared up at the tent's criss-crossing scaffolding.

Dottie clutched at her t-shirt, stopping herself from dragging him off the stage. Some of the crowd rushed forward, angry fingers pointing.

A grating noise came from above. Harold shouted something, holding his hands up, pleading at the crowd to stop leaping over the small barricade.

The heavy box Harold had tinkered about with earlier dropped from the rafters.

It landed on him, turning his body into mulch.

The people who'd jumped onto the stage leapt back, falling over each other. Some got so close that they were dotted in Harold's blood.

Something fell close to Dottie's shadowy corner. She peered over the barricade.

One of Harold's arms. Its fingers moved slowly open and closed like a dying, upturned spider.

"Don't panic!" came a voice from the speakers. "Exit in an orderly fashion. A-And come back to Circus Nightmare." The voice took on a whispered, hissing quality. "Hit the music you fanny. Quick."

From under the black cube, Harold's blood seeped out in rivulets.

The music started up again. The lights dimmed.

Her grip on the metal bar turned to jelly. Her legs crumpled beneath her. She fell in a pile on the cement ground.

White specs fizzled in the corners of her vision as she stared at the top of the tent through the mask's eyeholes. The crowd started clapping. Then they whooped and cheered.

With a smile rising up her face, darkness claimed her.

Fourteen

Dottie gagged on the mothball smell of the house she'd grown up in, stepped through a doorway with no door on its hinges, and tiptoed over the shit-coloured carpet to stand beside her mum. Dottie was small, nimble, light. The ball of iron in her stomach had vanished for the first time in forever.

The dead light of an autumn day spread over her mother's lap and the purple-maroon chequered blanket that was constantly over her legs. The rocking chair eeked its dry, cracking rhythm as it swayed back and forth. Her mum had been a small, compact-built woman, but when you looked Nora Inglis in the eye, she was a giant.

"Your brothers pay me visits," said her mum, not taking her eyes from the curtain-less window. "Awfully nice of them, eh?"

Trevor and Barry hadn't crossed her mind in years. They'd both died young. Trevor had been steaming down a country road on his beloved motorbike when a tractor pulled out in front of him. Barry had joined the forces in Afghanistan and never came home. Neither made it past twenty.

The cloying certainty of a dream washed over Dottie. "I'm not dead yet. Am I? Am I dead?"

"You're gonna wish you were," said Nora. "Just like you to court death rather than lay down and die for it like the rest of us. Whore."

Dottie stepped in front of her, hoping to catch her eye, but she only shifted her gaze, refusing to accept her. That had always been her way. Her mum had been proud as a prancing show horse when it came to her two boys. Dottie had been a stain on the family.

"Mum, I—" she stopped at the sing-song sound of her own voice, filled with youth and vigour. "I should never have been a mum. Not cut out for it. Tell me what to do so I can make it right."

"Here to beg for help after what you did? What a selfish trollop you turned out to be. Bet you haven't been keeping my bluebells going in that scummy garden of yours, either. They protect, you know. They wash away the dark. Not that you'd care about tending garden. Takes skill. Discipline. I guess those spades hit other people."

"I-I didn't mean for it to be this way." She reached over and grabbed her mother by the chin and glared down into her grey eyes. "I know I've been a shite mum. A shite daughter. But it's not too late, is it? I can give my boy all the love he needs. Make up for it. And—"

"Just so you can feel better about yourself?" Her mother's sour spittle rained on her cheek. "You don't know what love is. Don't pretend you wanna do this for Harold. This is for you, so you can square away your wasted, pathetic life."

Dottie let go of her mother's chin. Cyclones of green flamed in her mother's irises. The dead weight in Dottie's core returned. She crossed her arms over her flat stomach and stumbled backward, hitting the dusty windowsill. The skin over her abdomen seemed to inflate, puff out with painful life.

"You don't know what it takes to love something unconditionally," said Nora, her voice seeming to echo inside Dottie's mind. "You never had a motherly bone in your body. What were you thinking? Or is that it? You weren't thinking at all. Far as I'm concerned, you deserve every last death you get. You'll leave my bluebells to rot as well, won't you? Left me to rot in that awful care home. You know what it feels like to do nothing for hours on end? And did you visit? No. Not even after my fall when they said I didn't have long left."

"I was gonna. I-I swear."

"No use lying now, is there? You were a rubbish daughter, and now a rubbish mother."

"I... I can fix it. Still got time. I'll make up for it."

Her mother shot up from the chair like a sprung cat. The blanket tumbled off her lap. The back of Dottie's head knocked against the window as her mum pointed a gnarled finger in her face. Emerald smoke swirled out of Nora's mouth as she spoke.

"You've got something missing inside." Her mother's voice doubled, tripled inside her head. "Take, take, take. You selfish wee cow."

Her mum held up a cupped hand, a hungry smile on her face as she stared at the black-tipped claws at the end of her fingers.

"Mum—"

Nora stabbed her hand through Dottie's stomach. Black blood oozed out, flowing onto the carpet. Dottie blinked as the pain assailed her, looking down at the unreal sight of her mum's hand deep inside. The hand grabbed something, stabbing with sharp nails, twisting. Blood coughed out Dottie's mouth and down her chin.

A grey tongue wormed out her mother's mouth, licking the tip of Dottie's nose. When it slithered its way over her cheek, it left a thick coating of slime.

"You selfish wee cow," said her mother, pushing her hand deeper inside until Dottie felt pressure at the bottom of her spine. "You selfish wee cow!"

A flash of pain stung her cheek. The sound of the blow clapped its echo around the small erected space behind the stage curtain. The familiar smells of sawdust and blood came to her. The tent. The act. The block that had crushed Harold into paste.

Pamela's blond curls swam above Dottie as she leaned closer. Tears made silver streaks down her face. "H-Harold. You have to. Have to put him together. Quick."

Dottie sat up. The memory of her mother sending taloned fingers through her gut awoke the pain within her. She groaned and placed her hands on her stomach like a pregnant mother about to give birth.

The dark space was empty apart from the two of them and Harold's death trap. Sticking out the top of a large plastic bin was a leg with a familiar black shoe.

Dottie turned and puked up a gush of burning vomit. It splattered on the floor, flowing hotly around her hands as she gagged on all fours. A silly laugh escaped her at the thought of looking like a cat heaving up a clot of fur. Within the creamy soup of chunky sickness, a glob of thick blood spread its tendrils out.

"Put him back again," begged Pamela. "I don't know how long I can hold off the others from coming in. They helped me move that cube thing that crushed him so I could bundle his parts into that bucket. I didn't know... I didn't know..."

"That he was planning on squishing himself like a tube of red toothpaste? Neither did I, hen. We'll have a wee word with him, shall we?" She eyed the bucket and the limbs sticking out the top. "If I can put him back together again."

"This world needs him." Pamela gasped in a shaky breath. "I need him."

Dottie got up, righted herself, then aimed a kick at the bin. It slopped over, spilling her sons remains onto the floor. The shattered parts looked like something from a crappy horror film. A thing that looked like a burst football with hair stared up at her with one eye. The brine-like stench of it all made her turn her head and gag.

When the sickly feeling passed, she knelt by the thing that might once have been a head. How would this work? Did they need to assemble him like a Lego man? What if a leg was pulverised and impossible to find? With Pamela's help, they did their best, though some of the parts were hardly recognisable.

Dottie knelt by Harold's head. Something white caught her eye. By the knocked over bucket, her mask lay in a puddle of thickened blood.

"Here goes nothing," said Dottie.

Nerves coalesced in her stomach, smacking her with a pain she felt all the way up in her teeth. She clenched her jaw, and set her palm on Harold's mangled forehead.

Nothing happened.

She tried again, aiming all her energy at him.

Nothing.

"No..." said Dottie.

"It's not his time to go," said Pamela. "Don't you see? His art. He was just getting started. Bring him back!"

"I... I can't."

This was it. He'd taken it too far, broken some rule of physics, made it impossible for any God to stitch him back together. She'd watched him perish. And she'd been so pleased with the way the crowd roared for him, basking in it before she'd passed out.

She covered her face with her hands. The sound of Pamela's hitching sobs made her want to lash out. A real parent would've known how to handle this whole mess, stopping it before it got this far. But she'd seen the opportunity, hadn't she? Seen the oncoming stardom.

She eyed the mask. It seemed to catch some passing light, although it was dim as a fox's arsehole in the small space. She leaned over and grabbed the mask, placing it across her face, securing the band at the back.

"M-Mrs. Matheson?" said Pamela.

This couldn't be it. She refused. She'd do whatever it took. Old Smokes said she could bring him back no matter what.

You selfish wee cow.

"No," said Dottie, placing her hand on his forehead again.

"Sorry? No, what?" Pamela batted away the running snot from her upper lip.

Dottie closed her eyes and breathed in, digging deep within herself, willing her son to come back to life. She'd give everything, anything, for him to be okay.

It worked. She kept her eyes closed, ignoring the crackling, moistening sounds working their magic under her touch. She pictured Harold as he was onstage – vibrant and full of energy.

He stirred beneath her. His head reattached to his torso. His dented skull puffed out like a dented car being fixed by a giant magnet. Where they hadn't been able to find a body part, web-like material formed, morphing itself into whatever part he needed, filling the gaps. An awful, wet sound gargled out his mouth.

Dottie placed a hand on his cheek. "Hang on, big guy. Let it sew you back together. Ssshh, relax. Mummy's got you."

"Y-You're really here," he croaked up at her. "You came back for me."

"Babe!" Pamela collapsed to her knees on the opposite side of him, planting a kiss on his cheek, burying her head into his shoulder. "I thought we'd lost you."

More limbs knotted together, making him whole again.

"That mask. Made for you," croaked Harold. "D-Did it work? The box?"

"Worked like fuck," said Dottie. "Crowd went ballistic. You, ehm, really did a number on yourself. Was touch and go for a bit, there."

"Zorbs is gonna go mental," said Pamela. "A few seconds later and you'd have taken some of the crowd with you." She ran her hand through his hair, tracing it behind his ear. "You had them, H. It was wonderful."

"H? Real cutes. Does your boyfriend know you call him that?"

As soon as it left her mouth, she wished she could have it back. Pamela stared at her, mouth agape. Her chin bobbed up and down like she tried to find a retort or an excuse.

Harold tried to sit himself up on his elbows. He shook like a fragile leaf and flopped back down again. Sweat shown at his temples. She still didn't like the fever dream cast to his eyes. It was like he wasn't all the way here. He did a lot of sighing, like he was in the middle of a sordid fantasy or a hit of ecstasy.

"I'm sorry," said Pamela, staring down at Harold. "Dan ain't what I'd call a noticer."

"Wee girl. Watches me from the trees," breathed Harold. "She smiles so green."

"Right, mister," said Dottie, patting his hand. "Take it easy."

"More."

"More what?"

Two iron cables of muscle stood out on both sides of his neck. His dilated pupils looked like the bottoms of empty glass bottles. She wanted to push his head back down, tell him to shut up, force him to sleep. A maniacal look creased its way across his face, making him look like a man of sixty.

"She sings such a sweet song, Mother. She wants *here*. And she sings just for me."

Fifteen

The night sky was an iridescent band of rippling toffee. Dottie walked, neck aching from craning up so much. She fancied she could poke a finger through the sky's gloopy centre and swirl the stars around her head like a lasso.

Everything that surrounded her, the trees, the swishing water, the dangling moths, the smell of dirt singed by summer sun, felt so alive, pulsing with energy. She wanted to somehow wrap it all up and smother it inside of her. Such wondrous colours.

She walked alongside the river as it trundled by like a machine scooping up shopping trolleys and crisp packets. Its burbling was hypnotic. She wondered how deep the river was, how cold.

Ahead of her, beyond rows of sparse trees, two green orbs floated.

Dottie giggled. "Wee faerie lass from beyond. Come watching for me, are you? Bring me sweet rhymes and playful sparks. We're alone now."

She took one skip forward before she froze. The colours faded. Her connection to the vibrance around her washed away, leaving her shivering.

"Where the fuck?" she said coming back to herself, buttoning up her shirt over her dirt-smeared white t-shirt.

MOTHER DEATH

The moon cast its cold colours down on her. She stood beside the river, feeling its muddy water spec her face. This must be the River Dourie that ran through the dusty heart of Pitlair. She'd warned Harold away from this place many a time when he was little.

"Never go down to the Dourie," she'd told him. "It's where humanity curls up into a ball and injects itself with sad sauce. Swear, there's more needles down there than blades of grass."

She stepped away from the river and under the shade of trees, stepping as lightly as she could.

Her stomach kicked like someone played ping-pong in there with a spiky ball. She held her hand over it, applying a slight pressure. Her life seemed like it was a never-ending quest to find new ways to find comfort, or position herself as to not ignite the fire.

"Why the blue fuck are we here, Dots?" she said to herself, batting a moth away from dancing around her face.

She tapped her pockets. No phone. No keys.

Last thing she remembered was getting good and loaded on the couch. Harold took himself to bed early. She didn't like the sweaty sheen on his face when he mumbled a quiet goodnight.

Both their phones had gone *ding-dong* non-stop since videos of Harold mashing himself into red goo done the rounds online. Requests for interviews. Sickos wanting to pay for a demonstration. Righteous folks who rang just to call them a bunch of scrupulous cunts. She stopped answering after a while and got herself steaming on rum.

Shame spiralled, blossoming into heat in her face. She closed her eyes and rubbed at the centre of her forehead.

Martin, doctor, chum from school, and one-time lover had text her again, demanding that she pop in to his clinic. Her skin crawled as she remembered texting back something about her sitting on his lap and talking about the first thing that pops up.

"Why you have to be this way?" she muttered. "You embarrassing mug."

The effects of the rum still throbbed in her ears, but the feeling of being alone in such a foreboding, silent place sobered her up quick.

She found a concrete path that twinkled with glass. The cubes of it stuck to the underside of her boots. She hoped the scraping noise it made wouldn't invite anyone to jump from the wild bushes and plants that seemed to be in the process of eating the path away.

After a while, the path ended, covered by a makeshift fence held in place by two large bollards of concrete. She didn't trust it to hold her weight if she tried to climb. The only option seemed to be to try go round it, risking either falling into the water, or wading into the wiry plants, hoping nothing nefarious lay beneath the tangle.

She shook the fence. It jangled, but held firm.

"Mayhaps you're trapped for good reason," said Bob, standing on the quiet road on the other side. "Punishment comes to all sinners."

"What are you—" A snuffly dog ambled its way around Bob's slender ankles, sniffing at the air. "Aw, look at the wee guy. Looks like someone put a nose on a mop."

"You leave Biscuit out of this."

"I got your nice note, by the way. How neighbourly of you. You have a grand time watching Harold's insides crawl out the other night? Your eyes seemed to eat it up. You get off on that sort of thing, Bob?"

Bob placed his hands in the pockets of his duffel coat. The thin bars of metal cast criss-crossing shadows over his face and his moist, bulbous nose. He seemed to chew his tongue inside his mouth. "He plays with forces beyond his ken."

"Beyond his what?"

"You have no idea of the forces you invite in. They fester. They will not leave. They will thin your life to brittle nothing. And I can see plain that you are not up to the task. She will rip you senseless. Take everything."

With his face so close to the bars, Dottie considered clawing at him, trying to take an eye out. "You hobo-looking bastard, if you know something, then—"

"You're a harlot. A jezebel." The dog leapt up onto its back paws and leaned against Bob's leg, a pleading look in its black eyes. "Not now, Biscuit. I'm having words with the lady."

"*Lady* is it now? Thought I was—argh!"

Agony tightened its claws in her gut. The fence jangled when she rested a hand on it to stop from falling. Biscuit let out a squeak like a concerned mouse.

"If I am right, you've got a tough road ahead." Bob sighed. "Here, let me help you out of there."

Sixteen

Dottie breathed in the entombing silence of the Land Rover, happy for the chance to try and straighten everything out in her head. Bob's insistence that she was courting the devil. Martin's demands that he see her after all the tests he'd ordered. Harold's freakish deaths and the gone look in his eyes. Harold having an actual girlfriend. It was all too much.

Her darling son lay sprawled across the backseat, his head in Pamela's lap. Dottie watched her make twists and twirls in his hair as she stared out the window, looking like a girl being sent to the airport for a flight she didn't want.

"Seems rather taken with you," said Dottie as she tried to peer round a bouncing tractor that had them going fifteen miles an hour.

Pamela stared down at Harold, a slight smile tugging at her full lips. "I'm not usually like this. Got sucked in by his aura, I guess you could say. He's just a magnificent creature. You're so lucky to have him."

"Pft, you can keep him if you want. No charge. Boy's got an aura like a stale sock."

"You don't see him like everyone else does."

The road straightened ahead of them and she gave the engine its head, roaring around the big red tractor and its bales of straw. She felt her heart quicken. Putting her foot down always gave her a thrill.

"Just don't go breaking his heart," said Dottie.

"Not me."

"That boyfriend of yours better not break his jaw, then."

A knot of concern crossed her features as she moved a lock of hair from Harold's eyes. "Does he seem alright to you after yesterday?"

"How do you mean?"

"I guess things are going a bit mental. I saw my brothers all joking about inviting him over and killing him to see if it was real. Can't be murder if he can't die, right? Scared the hair off my scalp, the pricks. What other nutters are out there thinking the same thing?"

"Too late to pull the plug, now. It's the way he wants it."

"Will you always be there to put him back together again?"

They crested a small hill and she had to put the anchors on. The brakes moaned beneath them as she came close enough to the back of another tractor to see the dried mud caked on its arse.

"Fucking Dundee," said Dottie. "Every second thing's a farmer."

"Will you?" persisted Pamela.

They will thin your life to brittle nothing, Bob had said before yanking out a section of the fence, allowing her to crawl through a gap in the bars. She'd quizzed him about what he'd meant. The old witch melancholy seemed to swallow his fire, and he only said he'd rather not revisit those wounds, only that she needed to stop Harold before there was nothing left.

The temperature in the Land Rover dipped. She checked the knobs on the centre console to make sure the air con wasn't on full blast. Harold had mentioned something about a wee girl in the place he visited when he died and how she watched him from the trees.

A shudder wracked its way through her, making her lose her grip on the steering wheel. The vehicle banked to the left. She grabbed control again, pointing it in the right direction.

"Woops." Dottie slapped the plastic dashboard. "Old lassie got away from me there. Mind of her own, this one."

Harold stirred and shook himself awake. He sighed and stretched, then grabbed Pamela by the back of the neck and dragged her down to him, kissing her long.

Dottie coughed. "Make me wanna bleach my eyes out."

They arrived at Camperdown Park. Dottie caught the glares of worried parents as she put a towel on the vehicle's hood, climbing up, watching the little kids enjoy the summer sun. They seemed that freaked out that she touched her face to make sure she wasn't wearing her mask.

In the green field across from the car park, a small crane helped erect the big top. She sighed as Zorbo turned, then started to waddle over to them.

"Here comes old walrus face," said Harold who stood beside the Land Rover. "Watch out, Mum, he looks serious. Might ask you on a date."

"Think I gave him the shits with that mask," said Dottie. "Acted like his balls shot up into his belly."

"You've got that effect, sometimes. Me and Pamela gonna head on down with the machine. Catch you down there."

"Aye, cheers son. You go leave me with the big, angry Romanian. Nice."

The trilling laughter of tiny humans filled the air. It was a strange place to pick for an over-eighteens circus. The bright-coloured place was made for children and their wee smiles. A persistent bluebottle buzzed its way around her head in jagged, square-like patterns.

"In all my years," said Zorbo, out of breath from his walk, "I never see thing like your boy. *Mare afacere.* A big deal. Phone go all day. TV crews want in, see show."

She swatted at the fly. "Give him his due, he doesn't do anything small."

"The scare he made with big cube crush wasn't small, either. Acting like kill self on stage one thing, would ruin my family if he killed crowd."

"We've had a wee word about that."

Well, she'd spoken and Harold had nodded like a zombie over his uneaten Weetabix that morning.

"He is special, your boy. But he not make ruin of himself for fame."

"Is that—" she leaned forward, peering at the crowd of workers who mulled around setting up the circus. Three men pulled a cage across the grass, struggling with the effort. "A lion? You go on about Harold being a danger and you've added a fucking lion?"

"Bessie is old girl. No harm. We give her happy pill before show. Not able to hurt unless close."

Bands of children pointed at the animal that lay on its side like a dead fish. Its tail hung limp from a gap in the thick iron bars. Even from here, Dottie could tell it was a mangy old beast.

"Poor wee thing," she said.

Zorbo left her. The sun lost its sting, hiding behind a thick cloud. The sticky smell of ice cream wafted from a nearby bin.

Her phone chirped in her pocket. She sighed and took it out, thinking it would be some journalist or whatever after Harold.

Ehm, just gonna ignore what you said last night, doll, read the text from Martin. *Still, though. When you coming to see me? Don't make me hunt you down. Seriously, though, you NEED to speak to me. Phone if it's easier. We need to talk. M x*

She twirled the phone around in her hand before deciding to put it back in her pocket.

On the field, Pamela guided the traffic of small containers that made their way over the grass like a baggage train. The tent was now erected and swallowed half the field it sat in. Pamela stood by the entranceway and pointed two men around the back, looking like she was having an argument with one of them. The girl had stones and more smarts than her skimpy magician's assistant get-up would have you think.

"Don't break my boy's heart."

Seventeen

Wearing her mask meant Dottie didn't need to hide the grimaces of pain. The feeling bloomed from her gut all the way up to the space between her shoulder blades. The vibrations of the thunderous crowd rose through the soles of her boots, up the backs of her legs, irritating her to her core.

She fought the tears, but it was no use. Soon, her face felt moulded to the mask. A nightmare vision sprung in her mind of not being able to get the thing off, tugging and ripping at it until it took half her face off.

The crowd were awed by the lion and its jittery tamer, but soon grew restless. Bessie was so scrawny it looked like it would keel over and die.

There was a moment when the lion seemed to focus on Dottie, its glazed eyes turning predatory, its head stooping low. She barely contained the primal instinct to bolt before the tamer tugged at its thin rope and paraded the limping thing around the stage.

As the crowd clapped listlessly, Pamela swanned her way over in her jeans and denim jacket. She gave Dottie a long, squinty look as she ran the back of her thumbs under the mask, wiping the tears.

"You okay?" Pamela stood so close Dottie could feel the anxiety baking off of her.

"Aye, fine." Dottie struggled to keep the wheezy note from her voice. "Is that all the act is? Walk a lion around a stage?"

"Poor beast used to cut about Africa, hunting with her fellow lionesses."

"Dundee's hardly the place for exotic wildlife."

"She's been reduced to this. That's what happens when someone tries to confine you to a place you don't want, don't belong. They need to thrive, to be let loose, to fly. Such beasts are rare."

The wide-eyed tamer tried to get Bessie to stand on a box, but it slumped down, flopping onto its side. Each slow attempt at a trick was met by a slight round of token applause whether it succeeded or not.

"Someone die, already," yelled a man near the front of the stage. "Paid twenty quid for this shite."

Bottles crashed onto the stage, followed by half-eaten hotdogs. A beer foamed the lion's front paws like a wave hitting a shore, but it sat on its bony arse like its brain had been switched off long ago.

Pamela tugged at Dottie's arm. "Shit."

She pointed at the stage. Three bald men clambered over a small barricade. Quicker than Dottie thought possible, Zorbo waddled from backstage, standing between them and the lion, holding his palms up. The three men halted, staring at each other. They nodded and raised their fists.

"Gentleman," said Zorbo, "no need to—oofmph!"

One of the men decked him. Everyone in the tent seemed to stand up at once. The tamer crept slowly backward, tugging on the rope of old Bessie, but the lion refused to budge.

"We should go," said Pamela, holding her hand, trying to lead her away.

Dottie shook her off, gripping tight to the metal railing. "Not going anywhere, yet. Look."

Harold waltzed onto the stage, whispered something in the lion tamer's ear, then rushed to place himself between the three men and Zorbo. The high and mighty look he gave them made Dottie wonder why the men didn't clobber him. Instead, they stopped, confused. More drunks lumbered over the partition, mischievous glee in their eyes.

"Good citizens of Dundee," Harold roared. The rush of people froze. It fell silent enough that Dottie could hear the wind sighing under the flaps of the tent. "If you would kindly return to your seats, I'll be happy to give you what you came for."

"Shit, shit, shit," muttered Pamela.

The spotlight beamed over Harold. "I have a special treat for you, this evening. Death as you've never seen it."

The crowd who'd hopped the barricade hopped back into their seats. All except the three men that started it. Harold glared at the one that struck Zorbo, holding his eyes with such a fiery gaze that the man stepped back. The other two cowed and followed after, and they slunk away like injured dogs.

Harold nodded to Zorbo who also left the stage, then raised his hand, motioning for the lion tamer to come closer.

"Aw, shite," said Dottie.

"Some say a lion can rip you to shreds in the blink of an eye," said Harold. "I bet old Bessie here used to have a wicked bite on her. What do you think?"

A nervous titter of laughter circled around the tent.

Harold leaned over and whispered something in the lion tamer's ear, gesturing at the beast who still sat on its arse, staring out at the crowd, a drugged look in its amber eyes.

Dottie leaned closer, catching a whiff of the dry, vital smell of the beast. She watched the enraptured audience. They all hunched forward, sitting like kids waiting to be told they could go downstairs to rip open their Christmas presents.

The lion tamer leaned close, tickled the beast's throat and it opened its huge jaws. A strand of saliva hung like a thick spiderweb between sinister, bone-white canines.

Beside her, Pamela was unable to stand still, pawing at Dottie's arm, placing a hand on her face, sighing, shifting from foot to foot. "He can't get killed by a lion. Not *that* lion, anyways."

"I'm pretty sure you can get killed by anything if you try hard enough. Turns out my son's a trier. I'm more concerned about how pathetic the old thing looks. Can't heal him if he's still alive. If it rips half his face off, he'll have to live with it. Well, until he dies the next time. I think."

"Now," said Harold, stepping around the stage, drawing the eyes of the audience, "is time to say my farewells? Death calls its sweet call."

He turned on his heel with a dancer's flourish. On his way back to the waiting lion and its open maw, Harold tipped Pamela a jaunty wink. Dottie adjusted the bottom of her pointy mask, steeling herself for what was about to come.

"Are you hungry, my love?" said Harold, standing inches from the lion. "How about a wee snack?"

He leaned forward until his head was inside the lion's mouth. Someone in the crowd let out a pale shriek. The crowd shifted, craning their necks, trying to get a better view. Long seconds passed as everyone held their breath.

Dottie could hear Harold mutter to himself in the silence. "No need to be scared, now. It's all green. All green. She's there for me. Waiting. Like she said she always will."

He shoved himself forward, forcing his head into the back of the lion's throat. It spluttered and gagged, tossing its head to the side, lifting Harold into the air. The sorrowful tamer jabbed Bessie in the side like a grandad telling a toddler to stop his tantrum.

The lion bit down.

Red spilled over the sandy fur around its jaws.

Bessie jerked herself forward, pulling Harold to the ground, wrapping her paws around his body like a cat caught a mouse. The taste of blood turned the mottled old thing into a frothing beast. The tamer kept tugging at the lion's rope as it sunk its teeth into blood and sinew and bone.

Dottie turned and took Pamela into her arms, murmuring that it was all going to be fine, watching the beast rip her son apart.

Eighteen

"Got to hand it to you, son," said Dottie the next morning at their small kitchen table, shards of burnt bacon on a plate between them, "death by lion is a new one. Didn't that hurt like fuck?"

Harold chewed his sandwich, working his jaw like he ate a piece of leather. There was a faraway look in his eyes she didn't like. He'd been that way since she dragged him back to life.

"Saved the show," he said, "didn't I?"

"Your show's nearly done. Had to beg the lion tamer not to spill his guts because now he knows the truth, doesn't he? It's not a show. He just willingly murdered someone with his mangy pet lion. Not sure if I got through to the poor guy or not. Couldn't even tell you what language he spoke."

"You done?"

"Done? Done? You wee—"

The smell of grease and blackened bacon crisped the air as she closed her eyes and took in a breath to keep back the mounting rage. She opened her mouth to let it out when something thudded against the front door.

It had been like this all morning, people throwing stuff at the house or chapping the door and running away. She heard the unmistakable noise of spray paint exhaling all over her door earlier, not wanting to know what it said on the other side.

She turned her back on her son, staring out the window at the blue summer that begged her to come play. The echo of Pete's loss hit her like something physical to the chest, then. The force of the ache almost pulled her down to the linoleum floor.

They both hung out in the kitchen due to the news vans and randoms peeking in through the living room window. No chance she was leaving the house before they had to. They had a good few hours until they had to leave for Dundee for the second night's performance and whatever fresh hell Harold cooked up for them.

"Got to hand it to you," said Dottie, "life sure as hell isn't boring. Thought that lion would just suck on your head like a baby with its dummy. Rag-dolled you like a pitbull with rabies."

"It hurt." He rubbed at his shoulder as if he could still feel the lion's teeth. "Was good, though."

"Good? You sicko."

"You know what I mean. Like that feeling you get when you can't stop scratching an itch. It just gets redder, your teeth clench up, but you can't stop cause it's like it's lighting up part of your soul. Like that, only a thousand times deeper."

She picked up her coffee and took a sip. She'd made it so black it was almost soup. The whisky she'd slipped into it when Harold wasn't looking tickled the back of her throat. On the counter, both their phones trilled and buzzed and danced about. Journalists. Friends. Former friends coming out the woodwork. All wanting a piece.

She set down the mug on the table and took a seat opposite her boy. "Do this next show, then that's it. I'm out."

Harold stared into the depths of his stacked bacon sandwich like it was a mountain to climb. He placed it on the plate with a singular bite taken out of it, dusting his hands of crumbs. "Why?"

"Because it's sucking you in. It... It's taking you longer and longer to get back to yourself after I pull you back out. I don't like it. Not one bit."

"You wouldn't understand. It's too beautiful. And her... She watches me. I feel her closer each time."

"And that would be a reason to stop, wouldn't it? Creepy wee fuck."

"The sun's brighter over there." He scratched at his weedy bicep, the clawing of skin loud in the small space. "You're being really selfish."

"What the hell is happening? Feel like the last week or so's been lost down a K-hole."

Harold sniggered and she opened her mouth to ask how he knew what a K-hole was and if he'd taken any ketamine before and—

The cold of his hand as he covered hers shocked her racing thoughts away. He leaned in and gave it a gentle squeeze, trying to get her to look him in the eye.

"We're a team, Mother. You and me. We're in this together."

Her phone buzzed again. She picked it up.

"Zorbo, my man," she said. "You got as many news bastards outside your house as us? Where do you live any—"

The harsh sound of his voice made her blink her eyes like someone had just slapped her one.

"We're done. Finish."

"Aw, Zorbo, don't break up with me like this. What's wrong? Not enough paper to print all those tickets Harold's helping you sell?"

"You not watch news today?"

Cold misted over her as if someone held a block of blue ice close to her face. She fiddled with a button at the bottom of her black and yellow checked shirt.

"What you talking about there, Zorbo?"

"I hope you can live with what you created."

"Zorbo? Don't." Dottie held her phone in front of her face, checking that he'd hung up.

"That me out the circus?" said Harold.

"Maybe it's what you needed. Can stop it with all this—"

"Stop?" Harold chuffed out a laugh dripping with spite. "Just getting started and you're talking about stopping. The circus was just a vehicle, Mother."

"The news."

Dottie stomped through the living room and pulled the curtains closed, but not before seeing she'd been spotted. She ignored the kids' taunts, turned on the telly, flicking through the channels.

She caught a warbled reflection of herself in the blank screens between stations. A worn-out witch who hadn't seen a lick of sun in decades stared back at her.

Where had the years gone? Once, she had a tight body that men fought over. All she was now was a used up, selfish old bat.

"...details following the death of Tonya Lafferty from Paisley," a stoic lady said in a power-blue suit, one arm leaning on a desk like she spoke to someone at the pub. In the top corner of the screen was an image of a gawky looking girl with braces. She looked like the type of girl found in libraries, nose-deep in a book.

"Earlier today," the newsreader went on, "it was reported that the ten-year-old's body had been found by her parents who were taken into custody as key suspects. Fresh information now suggests it was a suicide. Tonya left a note, citing that she was copying Harold the

Impossible. Harold Matheson, from Pitlair, Fife has made headlines recently for his shows that portray his death in realistic, gruesome fashion. More on this story—"

Dottie killed the telly, noticing how ghostly her reflection had become in just a few seconds.

"No," whispered Harold behind her, staring at his hands like they were painted in blood.

"This wasn't you," she said. "They can't blame you for this."

"They did already."

Dottie almost leapt out of her socks as a sharp knock from the front door bellowed through the house.

The walls seemed to close in on her, like things alive, pressing down, suffocating. No more shows. A crowd waiting to hurl abuse at them or worse. A sweet little girl dead.

Harold collapsed onto the couch. He leaned forward, holding his head in his hands, tugging at his messy hair. It looked as if someone ran him through with a sword. She hadn't seen such a look of pain on him despite seeing him mutilate himself over and over.

She walked over to the window, peering out a gap in the centre of the curtains. Crews chirped and laughed on the street, speaking to passers-by, getting the full scoop on Harold no doubt. And what would they say? That he was always a quiet weirdo. Always knew something was up with him. Bound to be messed up when his mum does nothing but hit the sauce all day.

"You can't be held responsible for this," said Dottie. "She did it on her own. Young as she was."

"Her name was Tonya. Can at least say her name."

"Right. Tonya."

Her heart tripped over the name. She tried to imagine what it must've been like, stepping into a wee girl's bedroom, finding a scrawled note beside a body, spatters of blood on the floor.

"You got what you wanted, eh, Mother?"

"What?"

"Didn't you want me to stop? Prayed for it, even. Well, you got your wish. Again."

"Don't you dare lay this on me."

"This wouldn't be happening right now if it wasn't for you. Old Smokes gave you a choice and you took it. Same old selfish cow."

She stepped forward and slapped him across the cheek, really leaning into it.

"Shit," she said, rubbing her hand.

A snarl rippled across his features. He stood, stared down at her a long moment. The creases on his forehead made her think he was going to strike her. And why not? Wasn't he right? She had granted Harold his gift.

"Harold?"

"I... I need to think this through."

He turned his back on her and strode into the hall. The whole house seemed to groan as he loped up the stairs to his room.

"I'm sorry, Harold. I really am."

A sound like a rotten tomato *splatted* the window, making her flinch.

"I guess we are in this together."

Nineteen

"Mrs. Matheson? Is Harold inside?"

"What do you think about people calling him a demon?"

"Does Harold take full responsibility for the death of Tonya Lafferty?"

That one stung Dottie like a mad wasp. She stopped mid-step, turning, glaring at the bank of reporters who shoved their microphones and recording devices at her. The small crowd shuffled forward as one, a pincushion made of sharp-dressed journalists. They'd erected small spotlights around the path outside their home, the cones of light aimed at her, burning in her vision.

"Listen to me," said Dottie, putting her hands in the pockets of her jacket. She flicked her gaze at her dark house and the red *Sicko* painted across the door. "Harold didn't kill anyone. Got that? We'd like to give our condol—"

"Tonya slit her wrists because of Harold. How does that make you feel?"

Watching from across the street, neighbours pointed their phones. Some had bags of drink at their feet, sitting in their deckchairs, making a night of it, hoping to get an appearance from Harold.

"We'd like to send our condolences to Tonya's family," said Dottie. "Harold never meant for anyone to copy what he does, what he did, and—"

"So, you admit it's his fault?"

"I didn't say that."

"Will you let him on stage again, given what's happened?"

"Let him?" She hid the chuckle that escaped her with a cough, covering her mouth. "Harold will not be performing for the foreseeable future."

"How do you respond to those who call him a murderer? That he's the devil reborn? Have the police pressed charges?"

"Listen to me right now, you bunch of seagull looking fucks. Harold did not do anything wrong, he—"

"He killed a lion," yelled a boy from across the street.

"Been pumping that Pamela behind her boyfriend's back," yelled another.

"He needs a haircut," said another.

The three tittering boys ran when the reporters turned their spotlights on them, but not before lobbing a glass bottle that smashed in the middle of the road, sprinkling its harsh cinnamon smell into the muggy summer night.

Before the lights turned back on her, she took her chance and marched in the opposite direction, away from her house. They turned, calling for her to come back, but not giving chase. She guessed they didn't want to miss the chance that Harold would waltz out and give them a show.

The air pawed at her face. She felt bare without her mask. Maybe if she'd worn it she'd have scared the crowd away.

The wind picked up like it tried to push her back in the direction of her house. She walked on, reaching the end of Kirkland View and onto Kirkhaven Place. A long, tired stretch of council houses appeared before her and she put her head down, leaning into the driving wind.

It was a wind that Jimmy would have relished. That horse would steam along the beach like an unstoppable train, leaving blasts of sand in its wake. Jimmy would churn up the sand while Dottie held on, all thoughts of the world forgotten, leaning into the moment. That horse had gotten her through the worst of Pete's death. She'd even left Harold on his own while she rode Jimmy along the beach all Christmas Day. But, the money had dried up quickly and she had to give Jimmy up. That had been the worst January.

"There's no one left to run with," she said to herself, zipping up her jacket.

Someone walked behind her. She glanced over her shoulder. The figure seemed to haze into existence making Dottie's nerves turn to liquid.

"The devil take that witch and your boy to the swamps of hell," said Bob, limping after her.

He stepped under the light of a lamppost. His eyes were frazzled with religious fervour. With his pock marks and anger reddened skin, Dottie thought that in olden days Bob would've been classed as a leper. He smelled like he'd had a bath in cider without taking his clothes off.

"Where's Biscuit?" said Dottie, stopping, waiting for him to reach her.

Bob looked around him like he expected the dog to be there. "I... I must've left her inside. Don't want her near the likes of you."

"What happened? You were so close to being nice the last time we—"

MOTHER DEATH

"You murdered a child, is what happened. You and that corrupter. How could you, Dorothy? I thought I warned you of this. She'll breach the surface. Scum like you must be perished, along with all the other uncaring mothers who—"

Dottie stepped up and shoved Bob in the chest as hard as she could. He stumbled back, leaning on a small fence to stop from falling over.

"Shut it, Bob," she said, pointing a finger in his face. "You've no fucking idea what's happening. Don't make me lodge my boot up your urethra."

He leaned forward, lowering his voice, speaking into her ear. The flesh hung loose on his neck. He was so close she thought about pinging the loose skin and seeing if it rocked back and forth like a pendulum.

"God will bleed you slowly in his own way. Do the right thing, Dottie. When he dies next time, don't bring him back. Wouldn't that be so much easier?"

"How do you know—oofh!"

He sent his fist crashing into her stomach. Pulsing strobes of light exploded in her vision. She wheezed in breath, doubling over, falling to her knees. The pain was nuclear. She spat on the ground. In the dark, she could see the eye of red in the saliva.

"Until then," he said, "may your days be short and agonising."

"Help. Bob. Please."

Tears blurred her vision as she flopped over onto her side, stared up at him.

He glared down, shaking his head. "You can't let her in." He stomped off, muttering a strangled, "Sorry," before she lost sight of him.

She coughed up line after line of blood spattered mucus. The thick puddle of it on the concrete shone in the streetlight. The dots she saw at the edges of everything turned into encroaching circles of purple and brown. They swarmed her entire field of vision. Her body turned spongey. The world spun, then her shoulder thudded against concrete.

She fought her heavy eyelids, forcing them to stay open as she stared up at the diamond streaked blur of the streetlight above her. Her tongue was made of acid and iron. The sour stench of blood and spit from her sickness made her gag and sit up. The pain ignited, begging her to stay still, to quit, to die right here. Give in.

If she pushed down on her belly, the pain wasn't quite so blinding. At least she could stumble back to her house, figure out what to do. She watched curtains wiggle about as she stumbled onward along the cracked concrete path.

"Thanks for the help, you bunch of bastards," she said, watching people cower from her glare.

The crowd still gathered outside her house. She turned onto a neighbour's path, up to a house with no lights on, sneaking around to its back garden. From here, she could see the rows of low fences that separated each garden. The creamy scent of dandelions accosted her as she made her way over to the first fence.

"Here we go, old gal," she said, eyeing the windows to make sure no one was watching. "Been a while since we hit the hurdles."

Seven fences later, she flopped over the last and into the bed of bluebells at the top of her own garden. The night sky seemed so very far away, like she was being sucked down, down, into the earth by the inch. Sweat ran off her temples and into the soil. The crowded flowers pawed at her, soothing her with their papery noise when the wind shifted through them.

She was one big heartbeat. Each thump sent agony rippling through her gut and up her spine. She could feel her heart through the stems of the bluebells it seemed.

"What's happening to me?"

Her voice was a sigh. She lay exactly where she'd landed. Her breaths were thin and insubstantial. A cloud of dizziness swept her up.

She watched as her own soul floated out from her chest, rising above her, looking down like an apparition in an old film. Ghost Dottie was translucent, laying flat on its back, staring down at her as if it lay on some unseen ceiling. A ball of charged fury let out branches of tiny lightning from the ghost's stomach.

It offered Dottie its hand. The look of sorrow on her ghost's face made fresh tears fall down Dottie's cheeks. It was making her the final offer. Come soar with me. Be free. We don't deserve this pain.

"No," she said. "I won't leave my boy. I can't."

The ghost nodded, returning its hand to its side. Then it melted out of existence.

"He needs me."

Twenty

Dottie opened her eyes. The morning sun blazed low in the sky, heating up her insides. The bluebells crackled and swayed above her, like they, too were woken by the sun. A fuzzy bumblebee hovered from one flower to the next, its weight making the plant droop closer.

She smiled. Hot puke foamed out her mouth, over her chin and down her neck. It clogged in her throat. She turned and coughed up the rest into the flowerbed where she'd emptied Harold's blood before.

A panicking clipshear wriggled around in her pale sickness, flipping itself over and over before swimming to the safety of the chocolaty soil. The lumpy liquid was covered in pinpricks of red.

"How did I make such a mess of things?" she said.

Bob had blamed her for the death of Tonya, and had he been far off the mark? Everything she touched turned to rank shit. She should've thought about what the world would do if it saw Harold playing with death. And why wouldn't he find fame for that? It always seemed like the responsible, adult thing to do was just beyond her ability.

She walked into the house through the back door. The caked puke and rum seeping out her skin took her back to days where she'd get trolleyed in the park until someone had to help her home. The look on her mum's face had been worst on those days. Good times.

It was like she stepped onto a struggling ship at sea. The floor swelled under her as she made her way to the sink, chucking her guts onto the unwashed dishes.

A *thump* from upstairs rocked the whole house.

"Aw, you wee bastard, not now," she said. "I... I can't be this anymore."

It took her an age to muster the confidence to check on Harold. A sense of unreality washed over her as she scaled the creaky stairs. How would he have done it this time? A carousel of dead Harolds turned over in her mind as she hauled herself up.

Did Tonya's parents have any idea what their daughter was up to? Or did finding her wee body smack them in the chops like a hammer blow? Dottie was a river of nerves, despite how many times she'd seen Harold take his own life. It never got any easier.

Her legs felt as flimsy as liquorice whips by the time she made it to the top of the stairs. She traced a thumb around the jagged edge of a photo hung on the wall.

She looked so pleased at life sitting atop Jimmy. Pete leaned back against Sundance, folding his burly arms. Harold must've been the one to take the photo. She looked down the row of photos that lined the wall. Only one in twenty had Harold in it. She should've encouraged him, made a horse-lover of her son, found him the perfect horse. That's what was missing.

A cloth of mist settled over her skin. She couldn't shake the feeling that someone, something, was watching. The dream she'd had of Harold riding Whitey, the horse that had scared her into wetting the bed when she was younger, came to her then. The memory made her press her thighs together as if holding her bladder. She suddenly felt as small as an ant in a jar. Looking over her shoulder, she expected to see the pale, red-eyed creature at the bottom of the stairs.

"Calm yourself, hen, we're fine," she said to herself, laying a hand over her pounding chest. "We're fine."

Harold's door was closed. She moved over, set her hand on the door handle, demanding herself to breathe slow. She closed her eyes and pushed the door open.

A fetid warmth pawed over her face like she'd just stepped into a different atmosphere. She opened one eye, expecting a crimson mess on the bed. Nothing.

Harold let out a choppy snore from the corner of the room that nearly had her leaping back into the hall. He lay with his head on top of the closed laptop. A thick notepad lay beside him. The pencil he still held pointed up at the ceiling like an exclamation mark.

Everything was fine.

She watched the rhythmic rise and fall of his back, thinking that if she were strong enough, she'd lift him up and lay him in his bed, tucking him in. A pang of sadness swelled in her throat.

He was all she had.

She didn't have anything else. No job. No husband. No lover. No passion, save the art of losing herself in a bottle of dark rum.

Maybe she needed Harold's act as much as he needed it himself.

She felt the sweat cool on her temples as she tiptoed closer. Her big toe cracked when she hit something heavy. A pile of books looked like they'd tumbled off the desk. That must've been what made the noise earlier.

"I might be a shite mum," she whispered, "but I'm here now, alright? I'm not going anywhere."

She straightened, flinching when her stomach seemed to expand with white heat. She was about to leave when the list Harold had been writing on the notepad caught her eye.

IDEAS-

Stuntman?

Science Experiments? do they pay you for that sorta thing?

Die for good?

Spiritual?

Find the green girl? Why is she watching me from the trees? I want to follow her, but she won't let me. It's a cruel game she plays. I'm getting closer each time.

Am I losing it? Am I even really here?

Sometimes I think I was never really born at all.

Twenty-one

When the police arrived, the gathering of some twenty-odd folk outside their house roared in applause, saying that Harold was being carted off to jail, where such devils belong.

They'd spent the day watching the crowd morph from rows of girls with love-heart signs, to a gaggle of drunken idiots braying for blood, to the sewing circle of collected old hens who chirped bible verse at them. Bob's lot, no doubt. Dottie's lips tightened at the thought of the bastard. He'd get what was coming to him for smacking her.

A detective introduced himself as Detective Larvor, Paisley Burgh Police, like it was the most important job on earth, before taking a seat on the couch opposite Harold. Larvor looked like he wanted to cross his legs and smoke a pipe, and his legs twitched beneath him like the couch offended his very being. His partner, simply referred to as Anya, stood in the doorway, her massive arms almost touching each side of the frame.

"Mr. Matheson," said Larvor, flicking through the world's smallest notepad, "just you relax. I understand that the spotlight has been on you for several days now, but it'll pass, no doubt. A tragedy. That wee lassie. You know the details, yes?"

"Aye," Harold coughed into a balled up fist, leaning forward in his chair. "It was painful to find out about it. That she copied me."

"I'm sure it was painful for the family to be the ones to discover her."

Dottie sat on the arm of Harold's chair, tempted to take his hand, to show that she was there for him. Larvor raised his eyebrows at her expectantly. She knew it was good manners to offer a cuppa and biscuit in these situations but she was wiped. She leaned back, holding her arm across her stomach.

Larvor turned his attention back to Harold. "The girl. Most fascinating. She left a note, you see. For the parents to find. And it is our duty to ascertain what such things really mean. Isn't that right, Anya?"

Anya grunted and folded her arms, glaring at Harold like she wanted to send a fist through his face.

"Indeed," said Larvor. "Mr. Matheson, do—"

"Harold, please."

"Very well. Do you have any inclination as to the phrase *circle of green eyes*."

Harold glanced at the ceiling and quickly back down again, fumbling with his hands. "I... No, I don't think so."

"Why so pale, all of a sudden?"

"It's—"

"Been a long few days, officer," said Dottie.

"Detective."

"Right, detective. Been a right bastard of a week and he's knackered. So am I."

"Did the note say anything else?" said Harold, his voice almost pleading.

Larvor sat up straighter, the couch complaining beneath him. "I'm afraid I'm not at liberty to share such—"

Anya let out a booming cough, then glared at Larvor, nodding in Harold's direction.

"Oh, okay," said Larvor, turning his attention to Dottie. "That woman always makes such eloquent arguments." He dug into his pocket and handed Harold a crumpled piece of paper. Harold tried to grab it off him, but he kept hold. "It's a copy. Read it, but you can't tell anyone, you understand? I'm sure the fellows at Broadshade would love to play a game of who can kill you the hardest."

"His act isn't real," said Dottie, feeling as if she watched the conversation from a dark corner on the ceiling.

"Oh, I know. I don't think the inmates have the same deduction skills as I, however."

Harold's face looked as if it'd gone yellow. Dottie leaned over, reading the note.

Their is a gren girl in the trees, she stink of pickle and ham. But sweet so sweet. Tell me of place Grammy went after hospital go beep beep beep. Says she waitin on me. We wil play jigsaws again in her caravan. Says Harold has answer. Harold vsits place in his act. She says its real, and I see her circle of green eyes. If Harold can I can. I will. I WILL. Grammys waitin on me. Ill bring her back.

Dottie felt her chin screw up as Harold handed it back in a rush like the words stung. Tonya had signed it with a zigzag drawing of a bear next to her name.

"Harold…" said Dottie.

"I have no clue, detectives." Harold stood and marched towards the door. "I don't know why you think I would."

"You understand," said Larvor, "we have to cover all bases. Some cases are not what they seem. And just a word of advice. Maybe not perform an act faking your death where kids can easily watch you do it. They are mimic machines. They confuse reality with what they see through a screen."

"None of those videos were his," said Dottie.

"Doesn't matter anyway," said Harold. "They've cancelled me. There is no show." He turned and glared at Anya. "Excuse me."

A tense moment followed where she thought her son would lunge at the hulking detective, but Anya stepped aside and let him through as gracefully as a bulldozer reversing out the way.

Dottie showed them out, glad to close the door behind them. She leaned against the cool of the door, listening to the gathered crowd boo the cops for not dragging Harold away in shackles.

"I dunno about you," she called at the bottom of the stairs, "but I could use a drink. You coming down? Keep your old lady company for a wee bit."

Nothing but silence came for her.

She shuffled her way to the kitchen, being careful to place her socked feet gently on the floor to not jar her stomach unnecessarily. Chasing four paracetamols by opening a fresh bottle of OVD probably wasn't all that sensible, but she was past caring. All she wanted was for the pain to leave her the fuck alone. She had enough shit to deal with.

Ice sparkled and tinkled about in her glass as she carried it to the back step. The sunlight that spilled over her legs felt heavy as a blanket. She leaned her head against the concrete wall, her eyes drawn to the lazy sky and the flocks of seagulls blaring their squalls as they dipped and swooshed.

The first glorious sip of the spicy, amber rum held notes of metallic blood. The sip turned into a gulp and then an upended glass.

"That's the stuff," she said, feeling the warmth of the drink grab the back of her neck.

"You come here often?" said Harold behind her.

She flinched and turned, clutching her empty drink.

"Woah, don't glass me." He stuck his head in the fridge and opened a beer, then joined her on the step. "It was an attempt at humour, Mother. You know? Ha ha."

"Funny cunt. Scared me half to death."

"Look like you're more than half way there." His eyebrows dipped as he seemed to examine her. "You sure you're alright?"

"Aye. Fine. Just... Been a lot going on. Still getting over what Pete did to himself. Now this," she stared at her hands, "gift. Being the reason you can die and come back. Jimmy. Tonya. Those pricks waiting outside our house like they've got nothing better to do."

He sighed and pinged his finger off the glass bottle. He opened his mouth, then closed it again, eyeing her glass. "I'll top you up."

"Woah, it's not a pint, son. Nearly overflowing."

"You'll drink it though, right?"

"Wheest it and sit down."

She took a large drink, just to make sure it didn't flow over the glass. Across the gardens, on the shaded back doors of the street opposite, she noticed people clocking them, pointing their phones. How long before someone hopped the gardens and tried their back door?

"Bluebells creep me out," said Harold, gulping his beer. "Look like some alien, undersea thingy with a thousand eyes."

"Always thought it looked like an anemone from hell."

"Not sticking that up my arse."

"That's... That's not—" she chuckled and took another delicious sip. "What did you mean when you wrote that list, saying, *She won't let you in*?"

"What?"

"On your notepad. Saw it in your room while you slept."

"Creepy old crone."

"That's me. What did it mean, though? That girl you said you saw, is that who Tonya saw, too? How's that possible?"

"Some magical dude showed up and granted you powers that shouldn't exist. Who's to say what else is out there? What old Gods are kicking about here that we've forgotten to write about? We're not the ones who know how this works. As much as we like to think we are."

"She won't let you in where?"

He took a long drink, cream coloured foam sliding down his mouth that he wiped away with his thumb. "Hard to explain what it's like. I... When I die, I slip away. I feel all the pain, and it resonates as I get pulled through to the other side."

"Other side?"

"We're taught all this shite at school about going up or down, but it's more like being pulled through a veil sideways. I... I don't think there's just one place, either. God, it's so fucked." He put his head in his hands, the bottle resting against the side of his face.

"Guess you're the only one in the entire world who can say they've experienced it."

"There's this field I go to, surrounded by these massive trees, all swaying as if they're one living being. When I pass through, I go to this field. And I'm—" He straightened and closed his eyes, looking as if he was reliving it, "I'm trying to find something. I can see her through the gaps in the trees on her white horse. I can never quite bring her into focus. The longer I'm gone, the closer I get. And her eyes are as green as green gets. Fiery. I can see whole worlds in those eyes. I dunno, maybe I need to try harder. She won't let me through."

"White horse?" Dottie shook all over, clutched her drink. "Harold, you can't stay dead for too long, it'll fry the circuits in your head."

"You'll never understand."

"What do you—" she stopped the rising anger that wanted to burst forth. He looked so worn out, so gutted. He'd been through a lot, too. "Hey, I tell you what, once this dies down a bit, bet you'd get a heck of a book deal. A tell all thingy sharing what death is really like. Probably crumble civilisation and religion as we know it, eh. That'll be cool."

"Whatever."

A silent, heavy minute passed as they both sipped their drinks, staring at the nothingness of the gardens that joined each other.

"Hey you! Magic gadge!" someone yelled. Dottie followed the sound of it. A bald man with mirrored sunglasses hung over the railings of his upstairs flat. With his thin vest, he belonged more to Ibiza than Pitlair. "Gonna gimme a private show, aye?"

"Only if you go first, you sunburnt prick," Dottie called back.

The man stuck the middle bar at them before going back inside.

"Can you believe some people?" said Dottie.

"Private shows." Harold stood. "Maybe that's the way."

"Woah, slow down, Flash. Private shows?"

He marched back into the house and through the kitchen, calling over his shoulder. "Gonna work on it. Could be just what we need."

"Wait, I—" It was too late. She could hear the creaking of the stairs as he loped up them. "Cheers for the drink."

Twenty-two

Dottie didn't let the lack of company stop her from getting rat-arsed. She also didn't keep track of what pills she took and when. All she needed was the pain to leave her be for long enough that she could have a good, drunken think about things. Sort everything out.

Visions swam around her like yelling ghosts as she gripped the couch, staring up at the ceiling. Larvor's judgemental features. Tonya's bookish smile. The look in Pamela's eyes when she gazed at Harold, calling him *H*. The red and purple anger on Bob's face as he'd punched her. Jimmy going mad trying to get away from her. Pete in the bathtub.

The world spun itself out of control, and she was powerless to do anything about it. She drove her sharp thumbnail into the side of her temple, slowly rotating, breaking skin.

Upstairs, Harold humphed and stomped about in a fever, getting angry with himself. She hated the numpty for giving him the idea – private shows. The thought of it weighed on her. Lord knows what he was cooking up, but she knew it would be coated in red.

Darkness had come, and Dottie decided to forego the glass and drink directly from the bottle of rum. The crowd outside changed to drunken neds hollering, calling for Harold to show them the goods in their reedy, pathetic voices.

She went to tip the bottle back to take another drink when her stomach sent tentacles of fire coiling around her innards. The bottle fell from her grip, tumbled to the floor, the dark amber liquid glugging into the carpet. She felt as if her eyes would pop out of their sockets as she watched the brown stain expanding.

"Shit," she said, knowing she should do something about the spilling drink, but not giving a crap.

It was as if the pain was sentient, waiting on her to move so it could pounce. She held one arm across her bloated gut, summoning the will to stand, to get herself another drink.

She slapped the armrest and pushed herself up. Her vision cut out, her knees gave in, and she crashed to the floor, her face mushed into the dusty carpet. All she could do was suck in short, even breaths, praying for this wave of agony to subside.

It was getting worse.

Her stomach had become a ball of taut muscle, expanding, ready to pop. She had the image of a blackened alien ripping through her skin, leaving her for dead while it slithered off into the shadows.

"Harold," she tried to shout but it came out a croak.

She could feel something slipping away like she was being dragged under. Lifting her head was a struggle. Each time she tried, the world seesawed before her and she'd hawk up a line of yellow bile.

"Harold."

She coughed. The pain was magma pooled in her gut. Blood trickled down her chin, hitting the ruined mess of the carpet.

Somehow, she hauled herself into a sitting position. Getting her phone from her pocket was a pathetic experience. She shook like a broken twig.

I'll b with you tomorrow, big guy, she typed to DocMan Martin. *I need help here. I'm sorry. I really am. Should listen to you in future eh? Dots xx*

She sent a text to Harold asking him to come down, with little hope that he actually would.

She willed herself to sit perfectly still, to ride the wave, let it pass as it always did. The pain had never seared into her this hard before. Every time she closed her eyes, the drink and the pills crashing through her system would shoot her down a steep rollercoaster, bringing up fresh, insubstantial puke with it.

This was it.

Something was seriously wrong.

She'd been denying the doctors since she got all those tests done, refusing to acknowledge what they might say. Ignore it, chuck it in the quiet corner. With any luck, it'll go away on its own. That was her answer to everything.

She eyed the open doorway, hearing Harold pace around upstairs like an idea-maddened scientist. He'd do fine without her. He'd done fine until now.

Slip away. Into the dreamy dark. Let it come. Let it win.

Her eyes shot open. "You fucking selfish cow, you—" A torrent of twisting agony sparked in the pit of her stomach, but she pulled herself up to her feet. "Fuck, fuck, fuuuccckk."

Somehow, she dragged herself out to the hall and to the bottom of the stairs. Her weak voice refused to make it to Harold's room. She sent a photo frame toppling to the floor, but still Harold didn't come to see what was up.

She set a hand on the banister, looking at the stairs as if they were Mount Everest. An icy mist descended on her bare shoulders like a baby's shawl. The frothy, straw-like scent of horse was on the air, mingling with something dusty, dry and ancient.

Whitey watched her from the top of the stairs.

The horse stepped closer to the first step, baring its ragged teeth. Its skin was pulled taut around its head. Dottie could see the creature's skull through its almost translucent skin. A froth of spit hit the floor, sizzling into the carpet. The scent of burned fibres stung Dottie's nostrils.

"No, no, no," she said, fever sweat breaking out on her brow. "You're not real. You can't be here. I-I've been good."

The horse stepped down, stomping its hoof on the first stair. Dottie felt the vibration shake the bottom of her heart, a fresh wave of pain taking her, making her clutch the banister, doubling over.

She forced herself to stand straight and the world sizzled away. Her skull made a muffled *thud* as she fell backwards, striking the floor with the back of her head.

Through the haze of her vision, she saw the shape of the beast descend the steps slowly.

Whitey was here. Here to finally take her.

"Go away," she said, her tongue thick and useless. "You were never here. Never here."

Its pale, pink eyes glared into her as it stepped down, its muscles rippling in the light.

The corners of its white, foamed mouth rose in something like a clown's smile. Its rubbery lips, wobbled, dripping more acid onto the carpet.

The horse vanished.

After a moment of swimming vertigo, she sat up on her elbows. Wisps of smoke curled from the spots where the beast's acid had burned the floor.

"Harold!"

Twenty-three

The yellow walls and paintings of blurry daffodils in the doctor's office tried too hard to instil a sense of comfort. Instead, they made Dottie's fillings cringe in her molars as she waited to see Martin. She'd arrived at the reception desk like a cat who'd fallen into a bath and wasn't pleased about it. The muggy rain that had streamed from the sky all morning had seeped into her clothes. What a day to decide to leave the Land Rover at home and go for a walk. The rainwater weighed her down as she sat on the tiny plastic seat, avoiding eye contact with the coughers and scratchers around her. When she got called into the doctor's office, it earned her a few spiky glares.

The cedar desk that took up half the small office reeked like the inside of a church. She took a tacky looking seat and examined Martin who sat with his fingers steepled. A sly grin showed a hint of his yellow teeth.

Despite them going to school together, he still looked as young and spritely as he had when he'd been a teenager. His eyes were a bit too bright. His movements a bit too jerky.

"Dorothy, I—"

"Don't *Dorothy* me. Dorothy. Pft. Never called me that all my days, don't start now."

He pressed his lips together and folded his hands over his non-existent belly. "You really haven't opened any of the letters the team at the Vic sent, eh? They've been going nuts in my ear, telling me to do something. If it wasn't for all that shite your boy has got you involved in, I'd have kicked your door down. Trust me, I was a couple of days away from doing it."

"Nobody's got time for letters, Martin." When she ran a hand through her hair, some warm rainwater dripped onto the floor. "Not got time for this damn rain, either."

His eyebrows shot up. "Gonna come in here and talk about the weather? Really?" He leaned forward, sticking his neck out, trying to get under her gaze so he could look her in the eye. "I'm worried about you."

"Can we skip to the part where you tell me what you've been badgering me about?"

"Badgering? This woman, jeez. Never mind the fact it was you begged to come see me, remember." He sniffed like he had a cold. "I've been *badgering* you because you need to know what those tests came back with. You know, the ones where you made me come hold your hand while they stuck a camera down your gullet."

It felt as if her eyes had been glued half-shut. She forced herself to stare at the dirt-streaked floor. "Did they…"

"Aye. Aye they did. And it's the big one. And I'm so fucking sorry."

"I always did like big ones."

"Dottie, for fuck's sake." Martin slapped the desk, sending a pen hurtling across the room. "Would you be serious for once?"

She closed her eyes. A tear cascaded down her cheek.

The white horse. Had it been a messenger? Or was it a being sent to collect her?

"H-How bad?"

"Bad bad. When you skirted their letters, they called me about it. Told me their prognosis. Cancer's a bitch." He let out a shaky sigh, covering his mouth with his hand. "I wish I didn't have to be the one to say this to you. Been my bud since we were wee. We're not old by any stretch. Are we?"

"I feel old."

She set the tips of three cold fingers onto her forehead, leaning into them until it began to hurt. It was just supposed to be a hitch in her giddy-up. Some growing pains. After a life on the sauce, she knew she'd pay for it later. But this?

When the stomach cramps and aches got so bad it felt like it did when she'd been pregnant with Harold, she asked Martin to help her out. Something was growing in there, she joked. He'd referred her for some tests, and then some more. Then the little black snake forced down her throat snip, snip, snipping at tissue inside. Samples to be tested. Nurses with apology-laden smiles.

"I... I appreciate you helping me through this, Martin. You always were a good mate. W-What happens now?" She looked him in the eye and instantly regretted it. The sorrow made her own eyes well up. "What now? They carve it out, or what?"

"It's not like that, Dots. I... I'm sorry. Aggressive. The cancer's progressed, they said. Stage four."

"What are you saying?"

He opened the drawer by the side of his desk, picked up a straw and sniffed hard. He kept his eyes closed as he shook with the hit of the coke he'd just inhaled. It had always been his vice. She had her drink. He had his coke.

"They want you in for some more tests to monitor the situation, but they said it's the worst. Malcolm, the mad chap I know on that team, said he'd seen less cancer on a dead body. Sorry, sorry, that's too crude. I shouldn't have shared that." He sniffed and wiped his nose. "Dottie? You alright there, pal? Need anything? Wee bump do you any good?"

"He needs me and now I'm gonna be gone. He finally needs me. Don't you get it? And I'm about to take that last ride into the sunset."

"Maybe it's time to get your affairs in order."

"Affairs in order? Ha. What an awfully cold, adult way to put it. I'm done. I... I think I knew that. Why I was skipping finding out, I guess."

He stretched over his desk and set a hand on her shoulder. The cold of it jerked through her.

"I'm here for you, pal," he said. "I'll send you away with a prescription for some extra heavy stuff. And a baggie of my own personal flavour to sort you out. Make you as comfortable as possible."

"Is that it? Nothing else can be done?"

He settled back in his chair, scratching at the space between his eyebrows like a bug wriggled under his skin. "They said it's all about comfort at this stage. It's spread like a motherfucker. Showed me the X-ray. They wouldn't even offer chemo or any form of surgery, no matter how I begged or bribed. Hopeless."

"Hopeless."

"Go spend some time with that boy of yours."

"That's the worst bit, I have been. For the first time, I feel like I'm actually there for him, and now..."

"Just you gimme a shout if you need anything. On or off the books, okay?"

Rainwater splashed over her brown cowboy boots as she stumbled through the backstreets of Pitlair, walking with no aim. The rain had long since soaked through the thin, useless material of her jacket. One of Martin's pills in the bottle he'd sneaked her was already doing the trick, making the world marshmallow soft.

It wasn't fair. She wondered if Old Smokes knew something about her condition when they spoke in Glenrothes right before Harold's fame smashed them all in the gob. Old Smokes seemed rather sorrowful when he'd given his warning about the old ones taking notice.

This life is tragically unfair at times, Old Smokes had said when she was frozen to the spot. *I... I can hardly recall the good times. I wonder how long can I hold on. And then I see people like you. People with...*

He'd broke off then, but the more she thought it over, the more it seemed Old Smokes had been looking at her stomach. Did he know? Did he sense the cancer growing there?

And now, Harold would have to stop his act. She'd get what she wanted one final time. She could only hope he wouldn't hold it against her, cursing her as she died.

Was there a field waiting just for her? A horse? Jimmy and Pete and Sundance? What if Jimmy wanted nothing to do with her in the afterlife?

She stumbled over her own feet, tripping onto the road and into a huge, oily puddle. She'd landed on one knee. Cold soaked its way through her jeans.

A cackle erupted from her. The acidic smell of rain was on her hands as she stood and wiped off the dirt. The laughs spiralled into something mad and out of control. It doubled her over. Her stomach protested, but the pain was like a switchboard light going off somewhere in the dark distance. Martin's magic pill saved her from the worst of it.

No one stopped to ask if she was alright. She was just another loon on the street between the doctor's and chemist's where druggies queued, itching to get their methadone.

MOTHER DEATH

The rain drowned the sound around her as she set out to join them. The list of drugs on her prescription was lengthy.

Her time on this blue marble was nearly done. She'd felt it in her bones for a while now, denying it, putting it off, scared to find out the results. What was left now? The lump that lodged in her throat at the thought of telling Harold was like something real, something sharp.

She remembered sitting on the balcony of a cheap hotel in Greece, Pete sitting on a deckchair beside her, looking like a star from Miami Vice with his curly body hair. With her son playing in the small bedroom, she'd clinked glasses with Pete, saying that she was here for a good time, not a long time.

You've got something missing inside.

She collided into the shoulder of a woman who wrestled a pram up a steep kerb, almost sending both of them flying.

"Shit, sorry, sorry." Dottie held her palms up.

"Jakey bitch," the mother growled in a deep voice.

"I'm not, I—" she looked into the pram. A bundled up baby girl cooed and made spit bubbles. "Here." Dottie lifted the bottom of the pram and set it on the path. A brown, spit-riddled teddy bear hit her on the back of the head as she straightened.

"Aw, did you drop your teddy-winkles?" said Dottie, holding the teddy out to the baby in its comfy cocoon, protected from the rain.

"Na, na, na, naaa!" yelled the girl, swaddled in purple, bright eyes lit up the way that only a baby's eyes could be. Before the world leeched their light away.

"Cheers, doll," said the lady with a gruff voice.

Dottie nodded and watched her go, her vision blurring. The baby continued to coo and squeal excitedly. She felt her chin wobble and before she knew it, tears streaked down her face joining the raindrops. She let them fall.

In the sheltered doorway of a boarded up supermarket, she sat on a step, ignoring the smell of piss and rotten food. Hugging herself tight, she watched the pram bounce down the street.

Twenty-four

She made it home safely, despite the people who loitered outside the pharmacy clocking her paper bag full of painkillers. She'd glared at the guys, daring them to try it, but they left her alone. Just an old hag, clutching her pills.

Four girls swayed under a large, purple umbrella, watching as Dottie leaned into the howling rain, stepping past her Land Rover in her gravelled driveway. The lassies were dressed in what could only be described as *gothic funeral*. Their sad eyes pleaded with Dottie for their saviour to be set free.

She went inside, managed to haul her boots off before having to rush to the toilet and throw up what looked like lumpy custard into the downstairs toilet. Her gut retched, protested, retched again. It felt like her brain was trying to press its way out her nostrils.

When she cleaned herself up, she ran her tongue over her teeth, feeling one of her canine's wobble.

"Belle of the ball, you are."

The hag in the mirror had been what she'd spent her whole life avoiding. She never wanted to grow old. And here she was, oldened before her time. Cancer on her doorstep.

"Dust is dust, and rust is rust," she said, no idea where it came from.

She set her pill haul on the kitchen counter. The sharp smell of lemon dishwater permeated the air. Harold must've gotten sick of the mess. One of them had to.

White boxes toppled out the brown paper bag, tumbling onto the counter with their calm blue labels and plus signs. Tramadol. Codeine. Oxycodone. Oral Morphine. The lot. The bulky pharmacist behind the counter had raised an eyebrow and spent some time going over the prescription to the point of phoning Martin to check it was legit. He'd come back, handed her the bag, telling her that it was to be taken in a certain order. Tramadol first, then going through the others if that didn't touch the pain, ending on Morphine, but only for a little while. That M-word had pricked the ears of the people in the queue behind her.

She opened a bottle of red wine that had perched in the back of the cupboard for years, and filled herself a glass. She didn't have any proper wine glasses, so into a pint glass it went.

She sipped at the bitter drink while she picked up all the letters she'd ignored from the NHS, reading about her diagnosis and the next steps written in their calm, condescending words.

"Down the hatch," she said, sticking two of the green and yellow Tramadol pills into her mouth, chasing them with the wine.

The little cellophane baggie Martin had given her had more Oxy in it and Fentanyl patches. She wondered what the street value of it all would be and laughed.

The letters were grim reading, telling her about how advanced her cancer was, and where it had spread to, and how they'd already ruled out chemo-therapy before referring to the sad leaflets about planning for the end of your life. *Don't be sad*, one pamphlet read, *death can be beautiful.*

"About as beautiful as a screwdriver through the eye."

Harold. What was she going to do about Harold? She owned the house, but apart from that, she had nothing to leave him. No insurance, no money, nothing.

At Christmas, when Harold had been four, her mum had bought him a copy of the Gruffalo. He'd tugged on her hand, begging her to sit in the corner with him and read it. She'd been so mad at her mum, then. Looking back, she had no idea why. Was it really such an inconvenience to read to your boy? If she could have that moment back, she would read fuck out that book, over and over, doing the stupid voices and whatever else it demanded. She'd never read to him. That was the horrid truth of it.

She took a long gulp of wine. The Tramadol seemed to have taken effect, but they only danced around the pain instead of taking it by the hand and dealing with it.

Standing at the bottom of the stairs, the memory of the pale horse flooded over her. Shaking off the feeling of a hundred cold eyes roaming all over her body, she pulled herself up the stairs. When she reached the top, the hallway seemed to lengthen like a hotel corridor in a horror film.

"Calm it, missy," she said. "Breathe."

She rested her hand on the door handle to Harold's room. Maybe the fact she'd been a shit mum all her days would make this easier. Maybe the lack of an attachment was a good thing.

"Thanks for doing the—" she said, pushing the door open, her heart thumping in her chest at the sight of him sprawled on the bed, his skin yellow and pallid, "dishes."

The stench of puke hit her nostrils so hard she backed out of the room, covering her mouth. The frothy, green sickness clung to his cheek, down his side, down the bed, and to the floor like bubbled frog spawn. It was enough to make her own gullet contract.

He'd found his own pills. Three boxes of paracetamol lay discarded on the floor, next to the empty, shimmering pill cases.

She couldn't think of a worse way to go. She'd heard horror stories of lost teenagers overdosing on paracetamol and how the stomach ate itself for hours afterward – a slow, agonising death if there ever was one.

The sight confirmed something she knew, but hadn't wanted to admit. He enjoyed the dying. Not just the show, not just the adulation of a crowd, but the pain and the crossing over.

Her hand hovered over his forehead. A note lay on his chest, its edges caked in hardened puke.

Leave me here a while. I'm gonna go get some answers.
I need to listen to the green girl.

Twenty-five

Dottie's legs dangled high above the rollicking, foaming river below. The sun blazed its heat, sizzling the crown of her head. Harold sat beside her, his long legs dangling, too. They hung over the edge of a rickety bridge, leaned against the interlocking bars of rusty metal as they stared down at the River Dourie.

"Why so wistful, Mother?" said Harold. "Act like I died or something."

The sun's rays seemed more intense than usual. It prickled through the green trees and wild plants that ran alongside the river. The thin taste of rain was still on the air. About an hour ago, the sun had come out, turning the concrete into a wispy, ghostly landscape as they'd walked together, ignoring the shouts from open windows.

"It's hard for me, you know," said Dottie, "seeing you like that. All dead and shit. When I bring you back, it's like I'm pulling you from a fire, but you wanna keep on burning."

"Aye, but you're always there to save me. You know it'll work."

"Doesn't make it any easier."

"Doesn't make it any easier, pft." Harold itched the side of his face. The noise grated inside Dottie's brain. "Pretty sure Tonya's folks would disagree with that sentiment."

"Och, I didn't... Whatever."

She felt her own fire slip away. The tramadol went well with a rum chaser. It felt as if she'd floated down here, unable to remember much of their walk. Just a half-dead mum, with her half-dead son, stumbling to the Dourie where the kids are told not to roam.

Harold leaned back on his palms, knocking his battered Reeboks together. They made a rubber *thud* that made Dottie's eyes twitch each time.

"You should've seen her," he said, bathing in the sunlight.

"Who?"

"The girl. The girl with the green eyes. Went to visit her special. Did you not read my note?"

"I'd rather you went to see Pamela more than visit a... demon."

Harold chuffed out a sharp breath. "She has a horse."

"A white horse. I know. You told me. I... I've seen it."

"How?"

"Listen, does none of this freak you out? You're playing along like this is the natural order of things. Things like Old Smokes don't come to your door to make magical offers. Creepy wee lassies don't stalk your dreams riding pale horses. People don't die and come back to life."

"I do. She says I'm the most impressive thing she's ever seen. That I'm making all the worlds stand up and take notice. It pleases her. Makes her stronger."

"And that sound like a good thing to you, does it? Most impressive thing she's ever seen. Pah. That a reason to smile like a cat with a mouthful of tuna?"

"Some team we turned out to be."

She stared at him, catching his eye. Now would be the time to spill. Drop the C-word and tell him she wouldn't be around for Christmas. That she'd love to finally read that book to him, or have him read to her. Anything to go over to the other side feeling that they'd at least spent some quality time together at the end. Too late to fix everything she'd done wrong, but it would make all the difference, instead of using the last of her time to pluck him from death every day.

She opened her mouth to speak when he turned his head away.

"Harold, I—"

"Shared my ideas with her. Gonna show this world something they've never seen. Feels like I've finally arrived at myself, you know. Found that thing that makes me sing inside."

Dottie felt the ghost of pain trying to awaken itself inside her. Its fire slowly spread around her gut, promising agony when the pills' effect clouded away.

"She needs them to know," he said. "Need to see the glory of it."

"The glory of what? Death? It can stay the fuck away from me. The bastard."

"You'll never understand."

"Make me understand, Harold. Look—" she sucked in a breath through her nose, willing calm. "You know I'll do it. Be there to bring you out again. But what happens when I'm not around anymore?"

"Talking like you're turning eighty. What's into you? As morbid as a visit to the graveyard. I've almost ironed out my plan. She said they can feel me through there. We're building something powerful. And if it works, we'll be sorted for money. Loaded, even."

Dottie felt her palm warm her stomach as she ran her hand back and forth. The trees *shooshed* in the distance.

"You can be my Mother Death again," said Harold.

"Mother Death?"

"Aye, with the mask and that. Some folks already been calling you that online. You not seen it? Figured we could make a wee persona out of it. Mystique sells."

"Blood sells, more like."

"Get this. I set up a page on the dark web, invite people to watch me die. If they pay enough, they can even choose how. Give them a show. We can do it from our house. Get real inventive about it. Then you come along, Mother Death, and revive me. Then I do it all over again. I'd set some terms. No mega-deaths, like explosions or that. Just the standard kind."

Dottie snorted. A sharp knot of pain unfurled in her stomach. "Aye, just plain, standard, excruciating death. Sounds rather... messy."

A figure shuffled out from the cover of the trees, walking the path that ran along the side of the river. When the sun lit the woman's skin, it looked as if she'd been hiding in the trees for months. Her skin was almost grey. Dottie leaned closer, squinting down at her. She could taste the orange of rust on her tongue.

"Can you imagine it?" continued Harold, heedless of the figure making its slow way to them. "What do you think people will pay to watch me off myself? Could fix that wee problem with Martha. Even get you back into horses."

Dottie concentrated on the woman ambling towards them. An exasperated *tsk* escaped her. The shop doorways and parks of Pitlair were littered with heroin junkies. She'd dabbled with a few drugs in her time, coke, weed, ket, ecstasy, but she feared heroin. It seemed like such a cop out. A giving up of life, to hand yourself over to its clutches.

The lady stumbled, staring up the incline at them. The pale, blond hair seemed to wash to grey. The sun bleached it, turning it shock white, hurting Dottie's eyes. The hair started to fall away in clumps, flowing into the slight breeze.

The thing coming to them wore the same cowboy boots as Dottie wore now. She looked at her own hands, almost able to see the bones poke through skin.

The thing was her, she realised. Some ghastly, nightmare vision.

It jerked forward as if its feet were stuck in sludge. Its skin boiled off. Red sinew and muscle tore apart from bone. Its eyes melted out their sockets in a spume of white custard. Teeth crumbled out its mouth, each making a dry *clink* like dice as they pinged off the concrete, bouncing away.

"No..." she whispered.

The thing had become nothing but a skeleton. It reached a hand out, begging Dottie to come help, to save her. Then it crumpled in on itself, creating a dust cloud, then there was nothing left.

The bridge swayed under her, turning into something liquid. The noise of the water seemed to explode in her ears, getting ready to swallow her up. Her palms slapped the metal bar in front of her. Her whole body went rigid as she clung on. "Jesus!"

Harold stared at her like she wore a fuzzy clown hat. "What the heck was that?"

"I—" She stared down at the spot where she watched herself crumble to death. "Thought the bridge was collapsing for a sec. Fine now. Sorry."

He went on staring at her like she'd grown a third eye.

Tell him now. Let it out in one long torrent about the tests and the drugs and the cancer and the short time they had left and how she couldn't promise to be there to save him for much longer.

Her heart *thud, thudded* in her chest. She took a deep inhalation.

"So," she said, "when were you thinking of starting these shows?"

Twenty-six

The breath wheezed out of her as they walked up the brae on their way home. It felt as though her bones were hollow, her tank empty. Harold purposefully slowed his pace to a crawl. Sunlight sprinkled of cubes of glass that littered the path and the road as the heavy river roared on in the distance behind them.

"You're gonna charge how much?" she said, hating the breathy quality of her voice.

"That's my low figure," said Harold. "The, ehm, lassies that do this sort of private show thing charge ridiculous amounts. Or so I've heard."

"Heard? Aye, right. Think I was born yesterday, pal?"

"You're an ancient, dusty old thing. Probably best you don't go looking. It'll offend your turn of the century beliefs."

"Hey." She slapped his arm. "I know the internet."

"Yeah, no one calls it that. God, you're such a mum."

A broad smile hooked its way up her face. Being a normal, run-of-the-mill mum. It was a plain thought that normally would've spiked her with a craving to go get pished. "Aye, that's me, alright. Mum as fuck."

He shook his head, laughing as they continued their slow walk up the steep road. Her throat burned for a drink. The pain in her stomach started to blaze like a spinning firework. She'd carry her pills with her from now on, she decided, as she did her best to remain upright, not show Harold the pain she was in.

"Can we," she said once the blurred edges of her vision encroached everything. "Can we sit? For a minute?" She plonked herself down on a small wall that ringed a grassy area littered with dog shite.

"Nearly there, slow coach. Let's—" said Harold, leaning in, studying her. "You sure you're alright?"

"Aye. Beat. Just beat is all."

"Look like I just showed you the inside of a seagull."

"Argh, thanks for that image." A shiver galloped through her. "Can't we just rest a sec? Actually, no, I'm not alright. Got something I really need to tell you."

This was it. Just like the brochures said, with their pastel-coloured blobs that were supposed to be soothing. Let it out. Let your family know the truth. Make it straightforward. Be prepared for tears. Would he cry? The thought of him not caring in that moment made her play with her tongue inside her mouth, stretching out the silence.

Above them, the trees continued to watch, making a loud noise like surf splashing on a beach. The scent of baked pavement rose to her, mingling with the road dust. She wished she'd brought a camera. Just her and her boy on a wall in the sun like a holiday snap.

"Here we go," she said. "I've—"

"Found you, you slippy cunt!"

A young man around Harold's age marched towards them, his bald head reflecting sunlight. He looked like a cross between a rottweiler and a wolverine. The stranger walked up to Harold, sticking his neck out, getting right in Harold's face.

"You been rimming your mum or something," said Harold pushing the man in the chest. "Breath's honking. Get out my face."

"I know about you and Pamela."

"Aw, shite," said Dottie, standing, the world pitching around her. She stood between her son and the raging guy. "Is it Dan, I take it? If you get anymore riled up, your neck's gonna eat the lower half of your face."

Dan's fetid breath wafted over her, clinging to the hairs in her nose. "Out my way, you old boot."

"Hoy!" Harold stepped up, pulling her back. "Get the fuck away."

Dan stomped his foot on the road, then shoved Harold in the chest, sending him reeling back three steps. Red seethed its way up Dan's neck. "Good to see you're not a total pussy. Come on, then. You a big guy now? Think you're hard?"

"You know." A creepy smile shadowed its way up Harold's face. "I think I mind Pamela saying something like that the last time we—"

Dan's fist cracked Harold's jaw. A burst of spittle clouded the air as Harold tumbled backwards, placing a hand on the ground. Dan stepped up, swinging his leg back as if Harold's head was a football.

Dottie slunk in front of him, palms up. "Woah, there. Calm it, big guy. You've burst his lip. Probably deserved that. But that's it. Just go. I'll have words with him. No more fighting here."

"Fighting's the least of his problems." Dan took something from the pocket of his ripped jeans, clutching it in a tight fist. A flash of sunlight swam across the blade. "Always was curious to see how he does his wee magic tricks. Guess I get the chance to find out if it's real or not."

"Dirty bastard," Harold muttered, getting to his feet.

His eyes swam with fright as he saw Dan's blade. A line of blood dribbled down his chin from a fattening lip. He shoved Dottie aside, pointing in the direction of the path, away from danger, but she stood her ground.

"I'll get the cops down here," said Dottie, wrestling to stay in front of Harold, to protect her boy.

"It's Pitlair. Wouldn't show up even if you were the fucking Queen."

"Least make it a fair fight. No need for the steel to come out, alright?"

Dan stared at the knife clutched in his fist. He looked like he was considering putting it away. Harold sprinted and speared him right in the gut, sending them both tumbling to the concrete. The breath whooshed out of Dan. He held his arms by the sides of his head like he expected a barrage of punches, but Harold grabbed the hand holding the knife and slammed it into the ground, sending the knife skittering away.

Dottie stood on the path, fumbling at her pocket to call the cops. Harold rained blows down on the bigger fellow, fighting with a fire she hadn't seen before. Dust from the road kicked up as they scuffled, Harold getting the upper hand. She was overcome by the urge to race forward and stomp on Dan's skull.

She dropped her phone, swore and picked it up again.

Dan delivered a punch to the underside of Harold's jaw, making his teeth click together. The sound shuddered its way up Dottie's spine. Harold fell backward, rolling away from Dan.

They both got to their feet, growling at each other. She saw bloody murder in both their eyes. Harold pounced, catching Dan off guard. Dan was lifted into the air as Harold churned his legs, carrying him, then slamming Dan onto the concrete like a wrestler.

She'd typed 999 into her phone, but her thumb hovered over the green call button. Harold was quite the wee scrapper. Pride was the wrong feeling to have in this moment she knew, but that didn't stop the smile spreading up her face. Maybe he could see Dan away, win the fight, send a message that he wasn't to be messed with.

The blows came slower, more laboured. They tugged at each other's t-shirts, rolling around on the road.

Dan punched Harold in the stomach. A sharp blast of pain burst from Harold's mouth. They both stood, Dan's hand still against Harold's stomach. Then Dan withdrew, a coy smile rising up his rubbery lips.

Harold clutched his side. Blood pattered beneath him.

"You dirty bastard." Dottie grabbed a loose brick on the wall and raced forward.

Dan saw her coming. He stared at his red-coated hand, realisation shadowing its way across his features.

"Pamela likes it deep, too," Harold said, his voice strained.

"She's all I have," said Dan.

His hand blurred, stabbing Harold three times before putting the knife in his pocket and turning to flee. Dottie lobbed the brick at him. It thudded off his lower back, making him stumble before he righted himself. He turned to face her. The grizzly anger had faded to childish petulance.

"You got him," roared Dottie. "Had your revenge. Pamela doesn't love you. I've seen the way she looks at my boy. All love-sick. No one will love you that way. Now, go. Unless you want to mess with Mother Death."

"Mother Death?"

"Aye, that's me. Don't you forget it."

Harold shuffled about on the road, turning in agony, wheezing in wet, gargled breaths.

Dottie watched Dan race up the brae before kneeling beside Harold, planting a kiss on his forehead. The salt of his sweat stung her dry lips.

"He can't touch you, alright?" she said. "No one can hurt you. Not really. You're a god amongst these people. You hear me? You'll show them all."

A tear slid down the side of her nose. She felt him going. Had seen it enough times to recognise the slippy attention in his eyes, the change in the flow of his blood. She held onto him, using him as an anchor while white pain lanced around her own stomach, up her gullet, catching her throat with its molten fingers. She swallowed it down, held on.

What was Dan going back to? Should she phone Pamela to warn her?

"One problem at a time, Dots," she said, kneeling beside her dead son. She stroked his hair. "If you're talking to that lassie with the green eyes, tell her I said to fuck off, alright? She can't have you."

She took a deep breath, tasting the coppery blood mingle with the summer air, and set her hand on his forehead.

Twenty-seven

"Fancy a drink?" said Dottie.

In the kitchen beside her, Pamela dried a plate, pressing the towel against the dish so hard her knuckles turned white. "Fuck aye. Sorry, didn't mean to swear. But, yes, I could really use one."

The room still tasted of garlic and spaghetti bolognese as Dottie reached into the warm dishwater, pieces of translucent onion bumping against her skin. She watched the bubbly water swirl as it got pulled down the drain.

"What'll it be then?" said Dottie, drying her hands on a tea towel with a black Scottie dog on it. "You a wine chick or what?"

"I'll have what you're having."

They settled in the living room in a comfortable silence, listening, waiting to see if Harold would come down to join them. After she'd made him call Pamela, made him bring her here away from the murderous Dan, he'd gone straight to his room like an artist with an itch between his ears. She could hear him now, pacing and mumbling.

Dottie sipped at her drink. She hoped Pamela or Harold hadn't noticed just how little she'd eaten. The pain made it hard to think. She turned her head, eyeing the kitchen cabinet where she'd hidden her stash of pills. The tramadol wasn't cutting it. On to the next tier, she mused.

"Thank you for this," said Pamela, sitting cross-legged, staring out at the quiet night outside the window.

"Think nothing of it, dearie. Can crash here as long as you need to. Look after my Harold for me. Maybe teach him that a lassie's job isn't to cook and clean for him, though, eh?"

"You must've spoiled him too good."

Spoiled? He'd been nothing but. She wished she had spoiled him, at least a little.

"Think Dan will calm down?" said Dottie.

"Honestly? No. No, I don't think he will. He's not the calm type. Dunno how I got myself mixed up in that relationship. Know how... Never mind."

"No, out with it. Know how, what?"

"Well, when you first took me on, I was saying how I needed the money?"

Dottie thought back to that day of their first show with Circus Nightmare in Kirkcaldy. It seemed like years ago now, when Pamela had swanned in and took Harold's attention.

"That damn circus," said Dottie. "Wish I never begged that Romanian brute for a spot. Maybe things would've turned out differently."

"I wouldn't have met H, that's what you mean. You don't think I'm good for him."

"No, no, no. Just that things got crazy after that." Dottie gulped at her drink, enjoying its fire. "You were saying about that fucker, Dan?"

"He was starting to joke about selling me to pay up his debts. Has a bit of a drug problem. Not the small stuff, either. The sniffy, sniffy stuff, if you catch me." Pamela stared into the depths of the glass, tracing a delicate finger over its rim. "I got the feeling in my gut he wasn't really joking. He was in deep, and I knew one day he'd force me into it. Just had a feeling, you know."

"Why didn't you leave him, then? Seem like you can give as well as you can take."

"I did. It's hard, though. Then I met H. Sweet boy you've got there. Wrote me little notes. Actual handwritten, who does that anymore? Was gonna break it off with Dan, but it was never the right time. I just feared I'd hit a nerve one day and make a murderer of him."

"Harold beat you to it."

"Aye, he did."

"Sorry about the job, hen. Circus act is no more."

"H says I can help with his new plans. Sounds exciting."

"You actually love him, don't you?"

"Love him? Ehm, maybe. I mean, kind of. I guess I do."

"Don't break him."

"Break him? I would never do that. H is... different." A smile lanced up her face, shining in her eyes. "He's the sweetest boy."

"Sweetest? Didn't learn that from me, anyways."

Thoughts of how Dan's knife had pierced through Harold came to her, and the sound those practised, lightning-fast strikes made.

"Well," said Dottie, tanking the last of her rum, "I'm gonna head out for a wee spin. Clear my head. You two lovebirds don't do anything stupid while I'm away. And suit up if you do."

Pamela's face turned scarlet. Dottie stood, strode through to the kitchen, quickly grabbing a box of pills.

"I'm away, Harold," she shouted at the foot of the stairs.

She paused, but there was no response.

MOTHER DEATH

She grabbed her car keys and stepped outside.

Twenty-eight

The Land Rover bucked like a horse when she put her foot down. It was like she could only think straight at full speed. She'd swallowed two pills, chasing them with one of the bottles of Irn Bru she'd bought at the shop. The pain tingled in her abdomen before finally going to sleep.

Pitlair was a shite-hole and Leckerstone Walk was the very worst of it. Barred windows. Spray-painted *PYT* over every available surface. Everyone she locked eyes with as she roared past had an offended, angry look about them. Everyone was a powder keg, ready to go off at the slightest perceived insult.

She found the place. The Land Rover bounced her around as she mounted the kerb, coming to a stop. She reached into her pocket and took out a batch of pills in their silver packaging and considered popping an extra one into her palm and swallowing it, but she set it back in her pocket. She needed to be semi-straight for this.

The warmth of the night air flowed over her face. She walked up a narrow path to a door that looked like someone had tried to kick it down. If she studied it closely enough, she was sure she'd be able to make out the size of the boot that had been used.

Before she got the chance to raise her fist and knock, the front door flew open.

"Aw, shit," said Dan, leaning against the door, breathing heavy like he was having a heart attack. "This is it, isn't it? You're here to get me. Haul me back to Broadshade. I can't, man. Said they'll chib me in next time." He stared at the street behind her. "Wait. Where's the cops?"

Indian sitar music played from somewhere inside the house. A smell like black tar walloped her nostrils, making her turn her head.

She tried to keep her voice steady. "Not here to dob you in to the police. I need a word. I've been speaking to Pamela. She has a message that she wanted me to give you. In person." She turned on her heel and walked down the path, past the long grass that pawed at her calves. "You coming, or...?"

Her insides quivered when she slammed her driver door closed and started the engine. Hot bile tickled the back of her throat, and she rested her head on the plastic steering wheel. The vehicle shuggled when Dan climbed in. His freshly applied aftershave made her open her window a crack.

"Seatbelt on, Old Spice," she said, crunching into first gear.

"Fair enough, doll." Dan clipped in his belt with such concentration that she wondered if he'd ever worn one. "What did Pammie say? You taking me to see her?"

"Let's go someplace quiet where we can really get into it." She fished a flask out of the centre console and handed him it. "Might help."

"What is it?"

"I call it a frothy ginger. Dark rum and Irn Bru. Go on, take a drink. Ease up a bit."

Dan looked as if he'd been crying all day. His eyes were raw and puffy. She wondered how he explained away the blood he'd stumbled home in. He'd been such a brute when he'd fought Harold, but now he sunk into the seat, watching Pitlair roll by like he was only half taking it in. He met her gaze, holding the black flask before his mouth, unsure, and then something seemed to sag in him.

"Why not, eh?" he said. "Not every day a nice lady comes to pick you up."

"That your attempt to butter me up after butchering my boy?"

"Look, ehm, Mrs... Harold's mum. I didn't mean it. Is he alright? I didn't hurt him too much, did I?"

"Hurt him too much? Aye, you killed him. But it's all good. He's fine now. Mother Death brought him back."

"So, it's true, then? It's real? He really dies?"

"Drink up, dude. I'll explain all."

Dan tilted his head back and took a long swig before coughing half of it back up. The orange liquid foamed down his chin. He sucked in a breath through gritted teeth as if he'd just had a plaster ripped off a gnarly wound. "Jesus, that's a heavy drink. Can feel it going to town on me already. Man." He scrunched his face up and pressed his hand over one eye like he had brain freeze. "How does it work?"

"Just kinda gets in your blood stream, and before you know it, you're in blotto town looking up at some stranger, wondering where the fuck you are."

Dan shook his head, blinking his eyes. "Not that. Know how the drink works, trust me. Harold, I mean. Him dying and that."

"I'm Mother Death. I bring him back. That's the truth of it. That's the big secret. And he's about to show the world what he's made of. Literally and figuratively speaking."

"I don't know what that means."

"Just you enjoy that drink. I'll stop soon and we can have ourselves a nice heart to heart."

They drove in silence. The streetlights lit the inside of the Land Rover a dull amber until they got outside of Pitlair. The country road was dark and twisty. Her phone buzzed in her pocket, but she ignored it.

Soon, the landscape turned into nothing but trees and fields and cows on the road to Drumnagoil. Her thoughts turned to Jimmy and that awful day he'd ended himself at the riding school. That bitch Martha and her high and mighty attitude.

You have a stain on you.

"Might as well add to it, then," she said.

"Wha?" mumbled Dan, half-asleep.

"Just about there, cowboy."

"Why you being so nice, likes?"

The brakes squealed as she slowed, then turned onto a pot-hole filled road with trees lining both sides. Ahead of them, rabbits bounced out of the way, and black shapes burst from treetops. Weeds and tall grass itched at her doors. This was a road hardly driven.

When her stomach could take no more bouncing, she pulled over to the side, killing the engine. With the headlights extinguished, the world spread its darkness around them.

She turned to face him, and he flinched. She opened her mouth to speak, glancing out the back window. Something white on the back seat drew her eye. Her mask. It seemed to stare up at her, inviting her to put it on. She couldn't remember leaving it there.

"What's wrong?" he said, looking out the window on his side. "Weird place to come for a chat. Just tell me what Pammie said and we can go back to how it was. Was gonna propose. Nothing's too late for fixing, likes. You know that. Lady of your age."

"Careful."

He sighed and ran a chubby finger around the lip of the open flask. The gingery scent of Irn Bru reached her. He took another sharp drink, tipping the flask right back, finishing it.

"Fuck me. Woah." He rubbed at the bridge of his nose. "That's the stuff, likes. I... I guess I knew something was up with Pammie. I know I don't treat her right. Things right now are super-stressful. Brothers always riding me at the garage. All money, money, money. Me and Pammie can fix things, patch things up." He fixed her with a desperate, dilated stare. "What did she say? Is there any chance?"

"No. And if Harold didn't have Mother Death looking over him, you'd be back in Broadshade behind those horrid red walls."

"You wanna drink?" Dan's voice was thick, like his tongue was too large for his mouth. He stared at her with one eyelid almost closed. "Think some's left. Nearly polished it off. Good stuff that, likes." He shook his head like a fly buzzed around him.

"Plenty more where that came from."

She took the flask and set it in the centre console, then leaned down to her door, pulling out two plastic bottles of Irn Bru. She held them up to the light before handing one to Dan.

"Always bring a spare," she said.

"Woman after my own heart."

All was quiet around them save the trees dancing above them in the gentle breeze. She opened her bottle and drank the juice, while Dan opened his one eagerly, tucking in.

"Pammie ain't coming back, is she?" he said. "That wee bastard stole her away."

"Hey, you watch your mouth. But you're right. You don't deserve someone like Pamela. Heart of gold that one. And you broke it."

His face scrunched up. He covered his mouth with his hand, trying to hide his sobs. "I know. I'm a fuck up. I ruin everything. Like

I'm marked somehow. Like I've got some fucking stain on me or something. What do I do now, eh? My life was all about her. Had our daughters' names picked out and everything. I just... I just... I... Woah."

The bottle dropped from his grip, and he pawed at his door, trying to find out how to lower the window. Sick erupted out his mouth, splattering the glass, dripping down the door. It slimed its way down to the carpet where the upturned bottle of drink glugged its fizz and white foam.

"Great," she said.

He heaved again, this time covering his lap in a sea of milky, creamy puke. She leaned over and pulled the door-handle and shoved it open. Dan flopped out. His hands clawed uselessly at the air. The back of his head thumped off the dirt-packed road. He let out a pathetic groan, trying to turn himself over, not able to move.

Dottie picked up the flask from the centre console. She screwed the lid off, wincing as the strong spice of rum hit her. When she licked her finger and ran it along the inside of the flask, her finger came away with white, chalky marks. Her tongue tingled when she licked it off. How long would the pills take to have their full effect? Did he spew out all her hard work?

Pain jarred up the back of her legs at the impact of getting out the vehicle. The pain awoke the black monster in her stomach.

"Fuck," she whispered as she walked around the Land Rover.

Dan flopped about like a slow, upturned turtle. When he tried to raise his arms, they became limp and dangly. He reeked of acidic puke. The sickness had darkened to something that looked black.

She put her mask on. Despite the thing's pointed edges, it fit her to the point where she could see and breathe perfectly – like there wasn't a mask at all. The moonlight shone in Dan's wide eyes as he whimpered and redoubled his efforts to roll over and escape.

"Love is a fickle thing," said Dottie. "Get to my age and you'll realise how much things can change between two people. How even if you think you know someone inside out, they're never really yours. You can never really know anybody. One day, you'll wake up and everything you love will be taken away. Like a magic trick. Poof. Bath time. Cheerio."

An owl hooted somewhere in the distance. She eyed the dark road. All was silent.

"I'm sorry," said Dottie, stepping closer. "I am. It's just that I can't have people knowing the magic is real. All sorts will queue up to kill him. They'll make sport of it. Butcher him every day like he's some trophy. I can't watch him go through that. Not when I won't be here to save him."

Dan managed to turn himself over and army crawl his way to the grass at the side of the road. She watched as he made it to the base of an oak tree, hauling himself into a sitting position. He turned to face her. His breath was uneven and shallow. His front was covered in puke and dust and dirt.

"Bitch," he spoke, although he struggled to form the words. "Spiked. Bitch. Cunt."

"Charming." She leaned in close, whispering in his ear. "No one messes with Mother Death."

He gazed up at her. His features slid to one side like they started to melt off his face. He rested his chin on his chest, continuing to spew until something got caught in his throat. His eyes begged her, pleaded. He didn't have the strength to turn his head, to take in a breath.

The wind moaned through the gaps in her mask as she watched him slip away.

Twenty-nine

Sweat made the mask cling to Dottie's face as she stood in the corner of the shadowy room, watching Harold about to knife himself through the throat. They'd set up three cameras in the spare room beside Harold's. What little light that did exist, bounced off the plastic sheets that covered everything to make it easier to clean up the mess. As she worked, the scent of churned earth seemed to cling to her hands no matter how hard she scrubbed them.

Pamela had rigged up the tech, telling her what each camera would do and how it would work, but since she upped her dosage, moving beyond the tramadol and onto the codeine, the words flopped around in her mind like her brain was a bean bag chair. She'd slipped herself some of Martin's oxy as well, a wee extra to chase away the look in Dan's eyes as she'd watched him go.

Harold held the knife against his Adam's apple. Red blood dribbled down his neck and onto his white t-shirt. He spoke into a camera on a tripod that pointed at the bed in the middle of the room.

"You all have the privilege of being the first to watch my show. Your support has been humbling. And thanks to user ilovecats_1984, I will let you all watch the blood seep out of my neck before I die. As you can see," he held his free hand up, gesturing at the bare room behind him, "there's no magic here. It's just me and Mother Death.

If you switch to camera three, you'll see a shot of the whole room, so you can see there's no trickery. There is only death here. Beautiful, numbing, insatiable death."

She couldn't help but tut in impatience. He whipped her a warning look, knife still held close to his neck. The orders were clear. Stay in the corner with your mask on, confirm the death, then look into the camera, nod, then turn it off.

What a sick world they lived in. In her day, everybody shouted disgrace if a character died on Eastenders. Now they needed the real thing.

Harold made the cut. He grimaced, letting out a high-note of agony, trying his best to look cool and mysterious for the camera. For a while, the blood streamed out of the cut, but it stemmed off, quickly healing itself. He looked at her, then back at the knife, perplexed.

She resisted the urge to shake her head. The films made it look so easy, but she knew you had to cut deep to actually do any real damage. When she mimed stabbing her own throat, trying to emphasise the fact he had to go deeper, an image of Jimmy's last breaths came to her, making her feel sick.

He nodded, closed his eyes, and punched the blade deep, and made jerky, sawing motions with the blade before the pain got too much.

Blood spurted out of him. Soon, the small room was filled with the metal smell of it.

He picked up a small camera, holding it close to his face, smiling a jack-in-the-box smile that sent a shudder rippling through her. His blood looked almost black as it spilled out of him. She stifled a cough as he worked his vocal cords, a moist, drowning sound sputtering out of him. The cords moved around inside his throat like he'd taken the casing off some kind of machine.

Harold tried to speak again, but the words wouldn't come. Life flooded out of him in one long breath, then he flopped onto the bed.

How were the anonymous onlookers reacting? Did they feel like throwing up? How many of them were in the room with her and her freshly dead son?

She leaned against the wall and made her way over to the camera, standing directly in front of it. The mask shifted about when she gave her instructed nod, then she turned the thing off.

This had been Harold's playroom long ago. It was where they chucked Harold when she wanted to play her own games in peace. She felt a spike of guilt at the thought of trying to add up how much of his life he must've spent in here, the loneliest wee boy in the world with his train sets and mountains of library books. Now, he played with different toys.

Pain twitched in her stomach. She held a hand over the bloated thing. She'd tell him, but not yet. Let him build up a wee pot of money in the bank before she whipped it all away.

By the time they did four shows, she was cream crackered. Each time she pulled him back took something from her, sapping her of all strength. She had to slap him out of his mumbling stupor the final time around.

These shows tested his limits in new ways. It wasn't about the big impact, the instant gore. People wanted slow, torturous deaths. By the time the sun had retreated, Harold had sliced his throat open, drowned himself, drank anti-freeze, and suffocated himself.

"You'll break your head doing all this, you know," said Dottie.

They were in Harold's room after a lengthy cleaning process. Getting rid of blood was a motherfucker. They split the buckets of blood between the sinks, the bathroom, and took some in pales out to the garden, pouring it into the soil of the bluebells. After last night's antics, her very bones screamed for rest.

Pamela sat on Harold's lap in his room, one arm around his shoulders as they scrolled through the comments section.

"Och, I'll be fine, Mother. They love your get-up. If it wasn't for me, you know, murdering myself, you'd be the star of the show. Three grand for a few hours work. Not bad, eh? Let me see if there's enough requests for us to do another—"

"I'm done."

"But, what—"

"I said I'm done. Takes something out of me, too, watching you splatter yourself to the wind."

How could the body create such rivers of blood? The smells of leather and dusty carpet hit her as she stepped down the stairs. When she got to the third step from the bottom, her foot seemed to wobble, refusing to go where she intended. She thumped down the final steps, clutching onto the banister. Her knees sang in pain as she got back up to her feet, laughing at herself for being so clumsy.

The memory of a white horse at the top of those stairs cut her laughter off.

When she fixed herself a large rum, she gulped down an extra two pills. The way her stomach tensed itself up, she knew that the medication was the only thing keeping her going. She'd hardly ate a thing since she'd somehow dug a shallow hole for Dan's body and shoved him into it. Did she bury him properly? Would a random fox see a boot hanging out the dirt and run off with it?

Some fuzzy time later, Harold and Pamela burst into the living room, faces red and fresh from showers, giggling and slapping at each other. The sight filled Dottie with a happy glow. How nice it would be to have someone as capable as Pamela looking out for her boy when she wasn't here. Have someone to finally be there for him like he deserved.

Dottie tried to haul herself up to a sitting position on the couch and failed. She trembled all over with the effort of it. When she set her head back on the cushion, staring up at the ceiling, it felt as if her whole being was made of marshmallows.

"You two had a cheeky wee boink in the shower, aye?" said Dottie, giggling. "Scrub-a-dub-dub."

Harold stopped mid-step on the way to the kitchen, an uneasy croak escaping him, making him sound like an annoyed crow. "Made a killing with that show."

"Aye, you made a killing alright," said Pamela. "You're one messy bastard when you're dead."

Dottie looked out at the window. Under the streetlight, opposite the house, she could see three shadowy figures swaying. They swayed in unison like they were made of jelly, being rocked by the wind.

"Jelly, jelly, jelly people here," said Dottie, raising the glass of rum to her chin. "Splat the carpet, they will. Enough ruined carpets around here, thank you very kindly. Pesky jelly bastards. All of you. Get yourselves to fuck."

Harold came into view, taking a seat on the chair opposite the couch. He leaned his elbows on his thighs, his face in his hands. "You alright there, Mother dear?"

"No." She swallowed a mouthful of alcohol. "Been growing in me an awful long time. Got me. Enough of this Mother Death, shite. The mask fits too good. Skin... Skin..."

"Mum!"

He darted forward just as she tried to get off the couch. Her hand turned to mush under her and she rolled into her son's waiting arms.

"Did I really never read to you?" she slurred. "Was I that much of a cunty mum?"

Harold kneeled on the floor, resting her head on his lap. She looked up at them both, her breaths coming in short and desperate gasps. Both Harold's and Pamela's faces refused to focus in her vision.

Dottie turned her head and spewed onto the floor. It tasted of sharp metal. Above her, Pamela and Harold gasped, their faces turning white.

Dottie tried to raise her hand to hold Harold's face close, to feel him. Each inch seemed to awaken the pain in her core, but she fought through it.

"I'm gonna shower you with trains. And books. Lots of books. Read them to you. I'm sorry. I'm so sorry. The world's went awfully spinny. Stop it, you bastards, slow down!"

"What the fuck are you talking about?" said Harold.

Everything looked like she stared up through a dirty kaleidoscope. She threw up again, not able to turn her head. The hot liquid soaked into her t-shirt and down her jeans, making it feel like she wet herself.

"Bluebells," said Dottie, coughing out the stuck chunks of puke from her gullet. "Look after the bluebells. I slept there once. They watched out for me. Stop looking at me like that!"

She swung a pathetic slap at Pamela, but Harold caught it and held her hand in his. He looked at his new girlfriend with panic in his big, bug eyes. "Phone an ambulance. Please? Quick. Mum? Mum? You're okay. I'm here."

"Hey, Pammie," said Dottie. "Any messages from Danny boy on that sleek phone of yours? Didn't think so, ha!"

The laughter seemed to roar out of her. Harold held her close and she spewed again. When she rested her chin on her chest, she spied a half digested pill. She picked it up and swallowed it.

Her spine straightened. She went rigid. Pain rooted deep in her temples. Her facial muscles seized up.

"Holy shit," said Harold, his two black eyes wobbling about. His voice sounded like someone blared a foghorn at her. "Help's coming."

She tried her best to stop her violent shaking. Harold set her on the carpet as she continued to convulse from the inside out.

From the hall, something clomped its way into the room. Dottie pushed her head back, looking at the doorway upside-down. "No..."

Harold followed her gaze, darting his head around to see what she stared at.

The pale horse stood there, watching her.

It stood in the doorway like a patient guest waiting to be invited in.

"Come get me, you white bastard," whispered Dottie, her mouth barely moving like she was freezing cold. "Ride you into hell!"

"Where's that ambulance?" shouted Harold as Pamela streamed directions down the phone.

Dottie felt the blood rush to the top of her skull. Harold tried to gently force her to lay straight, but she kept her eyes on the pale beast is it slowly moved towards them. Above it, two small circles of green fire hovered.

"She's here," screamed Dottie. "She's here. Get away from him. He's mine. I'm the mum here! You hear me? I'm the mum."

A small figure phased into being atop the horse. A little girl with green eyes and a large black hat. The kind of hat a rowdy cowboy would wear.

"Mum? Nothing's there! Mum?"

The girl pointed down at her.

Her stomach flared in agony, consuming everything.

Thirty

"Hospital toast tastes like balls," said Dottie, sitting up in her lumpy bed. "Nice of them to build the new Vic just outside the old one. Means I get that lovely view of a brick wall. Check that out. Hope someone got canned for that one. Just what a recovering patient needs. Hey, Harold? You still in there? Speak to me. Silence is making me fill it with shitting small talk."

Harold sat by the bed in a plastic chair fit for a primary school kid. "They told me it all. The cancer. How much drugs you had in your system. The lot."

"Ah. No such thing as a secret then, eh?"

"I had the right to know. You can't... You can't just..."

"I was gonna tell you. Never seemed like the right time with all this mental stuff going on. Besides, I only just found out myself. Still processing it. You gotta give me that."

"All about you, eh, Mother?"

"It's about me a wee bit. Got blue-lighted here. Special guest. Got my own room and everything. Come on. Harold? I... I tried telling you, I really did."

"What stopped you? Interfere with pill time?"

"You got stabbed, that's what happened. Don't forget who it is that hauls your ugly arse back from the brink each time. Why'd you think I tried to get you to stop it all?"

"It's not fair."

"No. No, it's not." Dottie stared at the cracks in the red brick from the building only a few feet outside the window. "I think I saw her."

"Who?"

"Barbara Streisand. Who the fuck do you think? The green demon thing on her horse."

"She chose me. You don't get to see her."

"Ah, she only for you is she? Funny how she keeps creeping up on me."

"Did she talk to you?"

"No. I just... What does it all mean, Harold? What did I get us into?"

Harold sighed and slapped the back of his neck. The noise cracked around the small, darkened room. "Can't believe you're gonna take it all away. It's what I was born to do. You see that right? I can't live without it. The rush of it all. The eyes, the—"

"I'm fucking dying, you ungrateful prick!"

"Maybe you'll get the chance to see what I mean real soon, then. See how it feels. How your soul gets squashed down real tight and pushed through a veil. Into a world of perfect feeling. Then it'll be just me and her."

"Maybe I will." She batted a tear from her cheek. "Maybe that's what you need. Me out your life for good."

"Aw, don't do that."

"What? True ain't it?"

"You should've told me, Mum. You said we were a team. Can't tell you how great that made me feel when you said it. Bought you that mask after that. Thought it was well cool, you finally taking notice of me."

"I-I've been a selfish cow all my days. Always up to no good. Your gran hated the socks off me. Your uncles were her stars, and I was horse dung. So, I did whatever I wanted. All the time. Tested her, you know? Take, take, take. That was me. It's still me. Maybe I used up all the good you get served in a lifetime. Shrivelled me up inside. I deserve this," she laid a hand over the softness of her stomach where the doctors had drained some of the fluid that had made her feel she'd pop like a red balloon, "thing eating at me."

"I don't want you to die."

"If that wee lassie is what I have to look forward to when I crossover, then I don't want to go, either. She's marked me in some way. I dunno. I can feel it."

"She chose me."

"What?"

"She. Chose. Me."

"Harold, I—"

"You don't get to take her as well as everything else. Not now."

"I don't think that's how it," the door slammed behind Harold as he stomped into the hall, "works."

Thirty-one

It was dark in the hospital room. The brick wall outside looked as if it had drawn in closer, like the window frame itself had been bricked up. Dottie slunk out of the bed, listening to the soft-padded rubber shoes of nurses skirting here and there in the otherwise quiet hallway outside her room.

Her brain was a bag of heated candy floss. She felt so scrawny that the stale air in the room seemed to move through her chest rather than flow around her skin and bones.

Slowly, she moved to the window, her bare feet slip-slapping. Dust and dirt clung to her soles. Squinting at the wall, she realised that the glass had indeed been replaced by the rough, red brick. Her hand shook like an old hag's as she reached to run her hand along its surface.

The hand journeyed through the wall.

It felt as if she'd stuck it into the gaping mouth of a slumbering beast, its fetid breath warm and moist on her fingers. She jerked her hand out, clutching it to her beating chest.

She could still feel the remnants of the drugs she'd ingested the day before. The feeling of molten joy seeped from the floor, through her calves, melting up the backs of her legs.

"How many did you take, Dots?" she said to herself, rubbing her forehead, riding the wave of plastic inertia that flooded her brain.

Her hand froze. Her breath stopped. A shadow stared at her from the skeletal chair in the corner.

"Harold?"

The dark shape was too burly to be her son. It turned its head toward her. It leaned on one thigh, its hand hanging loose, fingers held like he clutched an imaginary cigarette.

"P-Pete? Have you come back for me?"

The shape rose and burst towards her, grabbing her by both arms. Pete's desperate face came into view, phasing in and out of darkness like he swam through blackened water.

"It's not what it looks like," he said. "Don't you see? Don't you understand?"

"Ah, you're hurting me. Get—"

The thing let go of her, evaporating, leaving a taint of ozone behind.

She wrapped an arm across herself, clutching her opposite elbow. "Just a dream. Drugs fucked you up. Just a dream. Just a—"

A scuttling sounded from behind her.

On the table bedside the bed, her half-finished toast was covered in bugs as tiny as dots. They smothered the surface, eating, consuming, rising to a noise like bacon frying in a wet pan.

"Pete? Pete? Well, fuck you very much for leaving me, again, you absolute prick!"

The temperature in the room plummeted. Her lips grew tense. White plumed out her mouth.

From the centre of the room, another figure rose up as if joining her from the depths of hell. It appeared from the floor as if on some invisible elevator. Smoke swam around its legs as it stopped its ascent.

"Take it back," she said to Old Smokes. "Take it back, please. Take it all back. I should never have said yes. Is... Is it too late? I know you want to help me. I can feel it in my gut."

Old Smokes lifted its gaze from the floor. Its face was a roiling, shifting mass of fog. It cocked its head slightly, examining her. "The deal is done. My errand complete. More death at my door. Always at my door."

"Please? I'll do anything."

Old Smokes shook its head. Its smoke seemed to become thinner, less substantial. "This is what they do. Take, take, take. There's nothing left. I don't want to do this anymore. Save me? Please? They promised it would be better than this. They lie. And she the worst of all. Why won't you save me?"

"What? How can—" She darted forward, reaching out to grab him. "No! Don't go."

The scent of ancient, yellowed pages entered her mouth as she burst through him, turning him into dust.

She squinted into the mist as it hung in the air around her. The mist shifted, curled, became something like the vision of a garden.

Another figure appeared, bending over a flower bed. It was the flowerbed at the top of her garden, Dottie realised. The bluebells.

"Mum?"

The figure went on tending, getting down on all fours. And then it was gone along with the mist.

Blood pounded in her ears. Heat built in the base of her stomach. A whirlwind of pain twisted in her, making her legs fail beneath her. Black blood bubbled out of her mouth like spoiled soup. She wouldn't be around for much longer, she felt it in her bones.

It was too much. Something pulled at her, called her soul like a light had been switched on, somewhere.

How easy would it be to go to forever sleep? Find Pete. Drift away to whatever came next. No pain.

You've got something missing inside. You selfish wee cow.

"No," said Dottie, standing, pressing a hand into her side. "Bring it on, you green bitch. You can't have my boy."

Thirty-two

"Harold not coming, then?" said Dottie, sitting up in bed the next morning.

A batch of soggy toast lay uneaten on her bedside table. It had black bits on it.

"Guess not," said Pamela, fidgeting with the frayed ends of a cardigan.

"He still alive, though?"

"He wanted to go through with it. Do one show and wait for you to come save him. I begged him not to. I mean, what if you don't make it out of here? Take another bad turn? God, what is all of this? I... I..."

"Aw, pudding." Dottie leaned on the mattress to get up, but the pain stopped her. "I understand it's a lot to take in, but you've only known Harold for an hour or something. And let's be honest here, looker like you can do a lot better than Harold."

"H has this way about him, you know. He's doing something."

"He'll not be doing it for long."

"He kept going on about her, saying—" she flinched and walked over to the window. Her eyebrows lowered like she'd only now noticed the crummy view. "Doc's told me you can go home today. I'll take you. Get you sorted. Make sure you're alright."

"Seriously, doll. It's not too late to back out. This is a lot of serious stuff to be getting caught up in. I won't hate you for it, if that's what you decide is best."

"A lot has happened, right enough. Had to stop going on Insta and Twitter and all that. Crazy what people are saying. Begging for more."

"Have you heard about Dan?"

"What about him?"

Dottie's back still screamed from the effort of digging a hole by the side of the dark road. She gulped. The rough scratching of her sick-burned gullet was a fresh pain she could do without.

"Nothing," said Dottie. "Thought he'd have showed up after what happened, is all. What? What's wrong?"

"It's just... The silence. Before he'd go off on one, it's like the silence gave him energy, charged him up. He bided his time, waiting to unleash his anger, if you get me."

"I think I get you, alright. Better off without him. Better off with my Harold. He's not perfect, but he'll treat you right. He's had his moments, but he's not a complete arsehole."

The doctors gave her a stern talking to about managing her pills, making sure that she stuck to the dosage, no matter how bad the agony got. It was like they were talking about a mild toothache and not a boulder of black cancer in her belly spreading its unwelcome tendrils through her.

"D-Did they say how long?" said Pamela, driving Dottie's Land Rover through the cracked streets of Kirkcaldy.

Dottie bit her tongue, wanting to tell Pamela to smooth it with the bumps and quit hurling them around corners. Each turn, each knock was a flare in her gut. She hadn't felt this bad on the way to the hospital when she'd brought Harold into the world.

"Until I pop my clogs?" said Dottie. "Let's put it this way, it'll be my last summer. Way they're going on about it with their trippy faces, I might be lucky to make it to the other side of autumn."

"That blows so hard. I'm so fudging sorry."

The thought hadn't held much weight until now. The sun prickling her skin through the window would be among the last summer rays she'd ever feel. Never again would she run among the dandelions and their yellow smell. She'd never ride a horse under the blazing heat.

"I'm sorry, too," said Dottie. "Guess death gets us all, eventually."

Pamela was nice enough to grab some shopping while she waited in the car, then help her into the house. She must've looked a right state. The crowd that stood vigil didn't rush over. They only stared at her, open-mouthed.

"You're a good one. Marry you myself if I was younger," said Dottie, collapsing onto the couch. "Can you grab me a nip? Just a wee one. Something to take the edge off."

"Doc said you shouldn't drink as much."

"Just a wee one. Please?"

Pamela poured her one and came back, holding the glass in both hands like a candle, mulling over whether to hand it over or not.

"Do you think he loves me?" said Pamela.

"I... I think so, aye. I mean, what's not to love?"

"I get so scared, you know. What if it all falls apart? What if you die and then someone tries to kill him? What happens then, eh?"

Dottie sat up, leaned forward and grabbed the glass from Pamela's grip. She let it go easily, not seeming to notice it was gone. Dottie took a long drink, savouring its burn.

"Awfully silent up there. You should check he's alright," said Dottie. "Be the rock he needs, Pamela. I... I can't say I'll be here to support you. All I know is the look in his eyes when he sees you is the rare kind. I think I need you, too. I know that's a weird thing to say since we've only known each other a short space of time, but I believe some things were meant to be."

The temptation to tell her what she'd done to her boyfriend was strong as she caught the hurt but defiant stare of Pamela. She had strong insides, this one. Someone who wouldn't take Harold's jib.

"He needs you," said Dottie.

Pamela wiped her hands on her top and stared at the open door. She nodded to herself and walked into the hall. Dottie waited for the footsteps going up the stairs.

The front door opened, then slammed shut.

"That'll be that, then," said Dottie.

Thirty-three

The red recording light on the side of the camera burned into her vision. In the death room, Harold lay sprawled on the plastic covered bed with only a pair of black jeans on. That and the plastic bag pulled tight over his face. He'd been dead for some time, judging by the pallor of his skin. His hands were locked tight into clawed, pained shapes.

"You're a wee bastard," she mumbled, slipping her mask over her face.

He must've done this to himself not long after Pamela came to bring her home – a job Harold should've taken care of.

Despite the lack of blood on or around the body, the sharp taste of iron stuck to the roof of her mouth. She stood by the bed, feeling like some wicked mercenary's clean-up crew, only she tended the same victim again and again. Something like *déjà vu* crept over her as she leaned in close.

She considered going into the other room, loading up Harold's laptop and seeing how many people still watched the feed. How many people could see the scream of pain etched on his face beneath the tight plastic bag? His mouth was open so wide it looked as if his final scream had dislodged his jawbone.

"Sick fucks," said Dottie.

She turned, stuck her middle finger up at the camera and pushed the button to switch the camera off. She turned the other two off as well. The mask made a hollow *donk* noise as she threw it on a small cabinet in the corner of the darkened room.

Her hair made a dry sound as she ran both hands through it. She should be filling these last days with good memories with her boy. Taking him and Pamela out to lunch. Doing her best to dust away the painful regrets.

"Maybe this is the way to do that," she said to herself, stepping toward Harold.

Was she thinking about it in the wrong way? If she embraced her role as Mother Death, she could set him up for life. They could get along, have some laughs in between what he claimed was his art.

Death slept in her bones. She could feel it settling there like thick moss on a stone. One day, one day soon, she wouldn't be here. All Harold would have is what she chose to do now. How she chose to help him.

"Be an unselfish bitch for once," she said as she knelt beside her son.

The plastic crinkled beneath her as she stared into his agonised eyes. Her chest tightened, her breaths quickened. What a way to go.

She removed the bag. It caused his head to shift. An ooze of hot, rotten banana stench stung her face. She turned and spewed a globulous puddle of bile and blood onto the floor.

Her hand trembled as she held it above his forehead. Usually, she would feel the heat rise from his skin, but she felt nothing.

The soft, ethereal glow surrounded her fingers when she placed her hand down, willing him back. His eyelids trembled like he dreamed a vivid dream.

The sorting, cracking noise of him mending himself attacked her ears, made her squirm.

"Harold?"

A singular wet breath escaped him and then he was still.

"Shit."

She'd been right. There was a limit to how long he could escape from his own body without being able to return. Her eyes darted around the room. The cops sure would have a lot of questions to ask about the film cameras and their weird set up.

She pressed down on his forehead again, wishing him back. Two tears fell onto the plastic looking skin on his cheek.

"Not yet! No."

She tugged at her hair, thinking of all the news vans returning to the site of his death. One final trick too far, they'd say. And they'd point to her. The last of her days, vilified as the worst mother in the history of Scotland.

Harold gasped in a pained breath, sitting up, clawing at his throat.

"Jesus!" yelped Dottie, jumping back, hitting the bare wall.

She reached out a hand and he squeezed it until she felt her knuckles pop. "Come back to me, Harold. It's alright. Ssshh. Come on back."

He twisted and jerked about like a seizure had taken him. Saliva glistened down his chin. She held on, burying her face in his shoulder, praying that this wasn't it. That he was fighting his way out.

She gently held him in place, pushing him down onto the bed. "Take it easy. You're alright. Breathe. Breathe. That's it. In and out."

Slowly, he found his breath again, sounding more like he'd just come in from a long run. A moist, clicking sound accompanied each inhalation.

"There you are," said Dottie, gently slapping his cheek. "Back to the land of the living."

"She was right there with me." He closed his eyes. "Dainty wee thing. Showed me the real you. Home soon. Not getting you. Won't let them. So bright."

"Easy, bucko. Calm yourself."

She squeezed his clammy hand, eyeing his chest, noticing how his ribs stuck out of his skin.

When his breath returned to normal, he hauled himself up on his palms. "Why didn't you tell me?"

"About the cancer?"

"Nah, about the price of bread at the shop. Of course, about the cancer."

She opened her mouth to speak, but laughter spumed out of her, taking her words. Each contraction in her abdomen felt like it dislodged something within her. Despite the roaring pain it caused, she felt suddenly lighter.

"Can't even laugh without it lighting me up," she said. "I... I guess I was waiting for the right time. I'm sorry. I should've told you as soon as I knew something was up. Shouldn't have tried to ignore it for so long. Whole lot of stuff I should've done. Guess I'm a pretty shitty mum."

Harold pressed his finger into the back of his other hand, creating little dots of white. "I know it's been rough. And, aye, you should've told me. But guess that doesn't change things, does it? What we gonna do?" He stared into her eyes. "Do you want me to stop?"

She felt her face scrunch up. She fought against the tears, but it was no use. They tumbled down her face. She mopped them up with the sleeve of her shirt.

"I really thought that was it, this time," she said, trying to keep her voice even. "Felt like I was dying. I... I wanna leave you with as much as I can before the time comes. It might be tough, and you might have to deal with me turning into an old, withered crone, but fuck it. Let's go for it. Me and you. Let's show the world what you're made of. Literally."

A smile cracked his dimples, his eyes shining black. "That's what we hoped you'd say."

"We?"

Harold lay back on the bed, staring up at the ceiling as if watching the clouds swim by. "The sky is so different there. Like you can almost reach out and grab the stars. She walked with me. Took my hand. Oh, you should've felt it. I've never been so... so... *happy*."

The way he breathed the word made a shiver crackle up her spine. "Don't let her get to you. You hear me? You can't be taken in by her. She won't let you go. Not ever. Don't fall to her. Please?"

His eyes were dilated, black orbs in the dark room. A slow, maniacal smile ate up his face. "I know what you're made of now, Mother. I know how far you'll go. She showed me what you do to those who do me harm."

"What? Don't tell—"

"Where is Pamela, anyway?" He sat up and gave himself a shake like he'd just taken a catnap. "She down the stairs?"

How to tell him they had a heart to heart? How she told Pamela she was too good for Harold, that she could leave? And that she did?

"H?" Pamela called from the bottom of the stairs. "Mrs. Matheson? You there?"

Thirty-four

The creamy warmth of the rum and the oxy glowed inside Dottie. She leaned on the kitchen counter, watching Pamela and Harold talk in hushed tones on the couch in the living room.

She missed Pete. Could almost feel his calloused hands massaging her shoulders, his breath on the crown of her head as he leaned into her, smelling deeply of her hair. What would he say to all of this? What would he say at the sight of the dried-up person she'd become since he'd opened his own veins?

"Why did you have to leave me like that?" she whispered, taking a long drink.

Don't you see? Don't you understand? he'd said in her dream at the hospital.

A sad chuckle fell out of her. He'd probably kick her arse for being so mopey. Wrap her up in his arms. Shake her up in the best of ways.

The thought of it had her cheeks flushing. "Guess I'll be seeing you soon enough, my long, tall and handsome man."

"Mum?" Harold beckoned her through.

Pamela stared down at her purple dolly shoes. "I-I'm sorry for just bailing like that. It's all a bit much, so I—" She sighed. "Dan's officially a Missing Person now. Police are out trying to find him. No one's seen hide nor hair of him for days."

Dottie bit her bottom lip, feeling a chemical rush bound through her blood. Dan's eyes had seeped of life because of the drugs she'd ploughed him with. The way he'd flopped about, trying to get away from her was something she'd never forget. She glanced at Harold as he lowered himself on the couch beside Pamela. He folded his arms, giving her a knowing, almost sly smile.

"He'll show up somewhere, doll," said Dottie. "You gonna go back to him? Is that why you left?"

"I left to go break it off with him for good. Figured that's the best thing for me and H. Fresh start, you know. Nothing hanging over us or that."

Harold put his arm around Pamela and drew her close, kissing the top of her head.

"I'm sure he'll come out of whatever hole he's crawled into," he said.

"I let myself into his house," Pamela continued. "I keep thinking about the pile of bloody clothes I saw in the corner of his bedroom and what that meant. Him and his brothers aren't short on enemies."

Harold's blood, Dottie realised. If the cops came sniffing, how could they explain that away? Tell them he stabbed Harold? Wouldn't that give him probable cause to retaliate? Had he murdered Dan as revenge using a substance Dottie just happened to have in spades? Then what? Harold would rot behind bars while she rotted alone in the house.

"Good to see you back, love," said Dottie. "Kip here all you like." She rubbed her hands together. "Right, let's get onto the more serious business at hand. How do we make quick bags of money murdering Harold over and over?"

Thirty-five

Sleep didn't happen. She'd lain in her bed, staring out at the sky, wishing that the pain would abate for just five seconds to give her mind some breathing room. It felt like the teeth in her brain were constantly clamped shut. The ghosts of countless nights with Pete cuddled in next to her didn't help any, so she got up and poured herself a mean one, using it to chase down a handful of pills.

Pamela's raucous laughter buzzed down from the ceiling, irritating her so much her jaw muscles ached. She resisted the urge to tell the happy wee cow to shut her trap and get out.

Her hand slapped the kitchen counter as she caught herself from falling. Her vision blared at the edges like someone shone a torch in her eyes. A radiant warmth seeped up her legs, but did little to stop the claw of bloated, red agony in her gut. The cancer dug its hooves in now. She felt it coil inside her, a thing almost real, almost born.

After they'd done jotting down lists of ideas for Harold's death, he'd made a comment about her putting her feet up, letting him look after her for a change. She'd told him to fuck off. She didn't need him waiting around after her hand and foot like some worn husk in a nursing home.

She cringed at the old lady noises she made when she lowered herself onto the couch in agonising slowness, staring at the ceiling, breathing shallow breaths, praying for the sweet drugs to cradle her in their marshmallow world.

And here it came, lancing up the back of her neck and numbing her brain with its enveloping heaven. Christ. She understood now why opioids like heroin were everywhere. If she magically recovered from the black beast eating her insides, she'd find herself in the throes of a mighty bad habit.

Pamela's chirping laugh floated down to her again, sweet as a tune now that her mind was at ease. How she longed to be young and free again. To float off with the first person she fancied, not thinking of tomorrow. *Tomorrow* was the cancer.

"Oh, sweet jumping jacks, that's the stuff," she mumbled, her eyelids going all mushy and soft. "How did you die, Dottie? I melted myself into the couch. Was worth it, too, I—"

A familiar snorting sound made her sit up. Her head felt too heavy for her shoulders as she looked around the living room.

"Hello?"

The noise came from the hall. It clopped closer. The nightmare mist of a bad dream settled over her, freezing her muscles rigid.

The pale horse moved into the room.

A small girl with blazing green eyes sat on the saddle-less horse. A broken giggle spurted out of Dottie. Her first reaction had been to ask where she got the wicked hat. It looked like something a villain would wear in a western film.

The horse drew nearer, bringing with it the smell of rotten apples and buzzing flies. Its maddened pink eyes glared at her.

"You can't be here," said Dottie.

The girl appeared to be no older than eight, Dottie guessed. Its impossible green eyes flared down at her. When it spoke, its glistening teeth were backlit by green light as if her tongue was a glow-worm.

"Coming for a ride?" it said.

"You can't be in here. I-I'm dreaming."

"I assure you, you're quite awake."

Dottie brought her hands up to the side of her head, covering her ears. When the thing spoke, it itched at something in the centre of her brain. "No. No, you can't. Get out."

"I can feel the praise tapering off. Such a bad job you're doing, Mother Death. You'll never be good enough for him. I can make it easy, Dorothy. Painless even. Just do your job and then he can be mine. Cherries on the bottom and cherries on the top."

Dottie bolted past the girl and her wicked horse, out the front door, into the muggy night air. The wholesome scent of cooling pavement reached her as she made it to the end of her pathway, looking back at the house.

The horse galloped out of the front door. The girl no longer sat atop it.

Dottie took a step back. The horse's muscles stood out as it got closer, not showing any signs of slowing down. White foamed out the sides of its mouth.

She turned and ran down the street, past a couple who rigidly held hands. The teens stared down at the ground, ignoring her like she was a junky they didn't want to draw the attention of.

Each lunge forward drained her energy. A dead scream hissed out her throat. She looked behind her. The horse stood in the centre of the road, glaring at her. It worked itself up into a lather. It was here to collect her. Bring her to her death.

Her ankle wobbled as she hit the edge of the pavement. Skin scraped off in chunks on her palms when she stopped herself from hitting the concrete face first.

When she rolled over, clutching at her stomach with bloodied hands, she caught the quivering of curtains as shadowed figures watched her. It didn't matter what time of night it was, there were eyes everywhere.

She got up. The horse gained. Her legs wouldn't go fast enough. Its hot breath covered the back of her neck and then it nudged her shoulder, knocking her to the ground again. When she fell flat on her stomach, razor blades of pain ripped into her. She moaned and grabbed at her midriff, rolling around like a pathetic, injured footballer.

The white horse blocked out the stars as it leaned over her.

"Not yet," whimpered Dottie. "Not now."

The horse reared up, cycling its front legs high. Dottie covered her face as it slammed itself down, about to crush her skull with its weight.

Dottie yelped, cowering herself into a ball on the ground. "Fuck fuck fuck fuck fuck."

Death hadn't smashed her. She was alive. She opened her eyes.

The street was grey and empty.

The night air rushed to her head when she stood. A merry feeling swamped its way over her. A large moth pumped its wings inches from her face and danced on into the night, climbing a lamppost to get at the dull amber light.

What had she just seen? It all felt so real. More than a dream. The fire swarming in her gut promised she was awake. Through the two holes in her ripped-up t-shirt, she could see the bloatedness of her stomach.

"Dottie," a man's voice said.

Dottie turned, eyeing the silent street. A figure caked in shadow stood on the path beneath a thick tree that grew in an unkempt garden. The man stood with his hands in his pockets, rocking back and forth on his heels.

"Pete?"

As she moved towards him, the street seemed to shiver under her like she'd just stepped off a boat. The scent of his woody aftershave took Dottie back to times when she'd hold him close to her, desperate, safe.

"You're not really here, are you?" she said, stopping on the road before him.

She leaned closer, squinting into the dark. Her heart beat so loud it wobbled her vision.

Twisting, popping, squelching noises like branches breaking in a wet forest hit her ears as he stepped out from shadow.

"Pete," she said, "your mouth. It... You..."

The thing standing before her wore Pete's body. A flash of green flared in its eyes before the light died away. Up both sides of Pete's rugged, weathered face were lines of red like his skin had sliced open, giving him a joker's grin.

Dottie shuffled back, covering her mouth. Pete smiled. It split the scars. Red ran down his cheeks. He craned his neck, roaring at the night sky. The top of his head started tearing away like some unseen monster had its hands in his mouth, pulling the upper part of his jaw back until things started breaking. In the glow of the streetlight, Dottie was able to see Pete's black fillings and yellowed teeth.

"Stop it!" she shouted.

His jaw snapped open at an impossible angle. Inside the darkened, saliva strung cave of his mouth, something black slithered around.

"You get what you want yet?" Pete's voice gaped out of the hole. "You cold, selfish cunt. You ever think of me, eh? Give up, Dorothy. Come to me. Get what you deserve. Eat it."

She looked around for help. All she saw were lights turning on and sleepy eyes poking from gaps in curtains and blinds. They wouldn't come to save her. What did they see? Was Pete even here?

"Y-You can't have me, you hear that?" she shouted in all directions. "You little bitch. Think you can just throw Pete in my face like that and... and..."

She fell to the ground, trembling with sobs. The cracked concrete on the road looked like a dried up river.

"Come join me in the forever. You'll like it through here."

"No!" Dottie screamed, then covered her ears. "My Pete would never say that."

On the path stood the little girl, hands merrily by her side like the picture of innocence and sweeties. "He always thought you were a selfish wee cow, every miserable day of his life."

Dottie scrambled up to her feet, standing in the middle of the road. "No. No, what is this? What do you want?"

"Imagine driving a man to the private act of death just because he couldn't stand to talk to you. To look at you any longer. Makes me sick. The stench on you. You do have a stain on you." The girl closed her eyes. Beneath the brim of her hat, Dottie saw her eyelids start to glow green. "The sweet, gentle way he opened himself up. Ah, you should've seen it. Seen how happy he was in those dying moments. All because of you."

"What do you want from me?"

"What do I want?" the little girl giggled, a sound that made wet snakes slime around in Dottie's gullet. "I want through. I want Harold. Kill him. Kill him again. Kill him again. Let the world see. Build his following. Build his power. Make him mine."

"Don't you get it? I'm dying. It won't work when I'm gone. It—"

The demon flew up to her, feet hovering over the concrete. Dottie shrunk back, clutching at her chest. The air around the floating girl turned into cold, sparkling mist.

"Then hurry up and get to work. Choppy, chop, chop. Death crawls its slow shadow over you, and what are you gonna leave your precious boy with, eh? A legacy? Or nothing? What kind of brittle, useless mother are you?"

The scream of tires burning made Dottie turn her head. A car's headlights blared down on her. A rusty Ford Escort swerved and Dottie threw herself backwards, landing with an elbow-scraping thump on the path.

Dottie turned her attention back to the road. The girl had vanished.

The struggling motor burbled as the driver got out and slammed his door shut.

"Aw, here we go," said Dottie.

"The Gods sure like to put a challenge before me, to help those in need," the man said, towering over her.

"Bob. How's it going, pal? I believe I owe you a kick in the nuts or two."

"Near made me empty my dinner onto my seat, if you catch me." He leaned down, offering her a long-fingered, bony hand. "Even?"

"Even? Fuck your even." Dottie got up. She sucked in a breath and held herself perfectly still until the white strobes drizzling in her vision faded to normal. "Had quite the eventful evening, so if you don't—"

"I can help you. I've crossed paths with her before."

Thirty-six

"That vile creature took Glenda from me," said Bob. "Turned her into a skeleton day by slow, endless day. She used to be so hale, so healthy. Rosy cheeked, my wee pigeon."

Dottie stood in the middle of a cluttered living room that smelled strongly of stained wood. Tiny wooden figures of warriors, bears, griffins, and other creatures covered every surface. They all had a coating of grey dust that made it look like it had just snowed inside Bob's house.

Bob sat on a chair that faced the window, his elbows on the knees of his spread legs, swaying from side to side as if full of energy, ready to pounce. A fever seemed to plague his eyes, shining midnight black.

"Did you see what I saw?" said Dottie. "Did you see the horse?"

"Horse? No. But I know her stain. I can smell it on you. Powerful as the spells of old ruin. She cannot be allowed to walk this earth. The Book of the Black Earth states it. She comes. She comes. She—"

Dottie laid a hand on his shoulder. He jerked like she'd just tazed him with a cattle prod. "Woah, Nessie. Gonna work yourself up to a heart attack. You got a drink or something? Could use something to take the edge off."

"You'll find nothing but water in this house. Clear drink, clear mind."

"Vodka then? No? No." She ran a hand along the back of her neck. The effects of the oxy and whatever else she'd shoved in her gob started to burn away. "Guess I should say thanks for not turning me into mashed potatoes on the road out there."

Bob talked at the window as if she spoke to him from the other side of it. "Knew there was a reason the good hand guided me outside for a drive. Had an inclination I'd be needed. The Gods work like that. Pushing and pulling where they may."

She eyed the dark corners of the room. A squashed doggie bed held an orange, squishy pumpkin. "Hey, Bob? Where's Biscuit at?"

Bob looked at the corner, then looked about his feet as if expecting the dog to be there. "I... I don't know."

"Not got all your screws in, have you? You gonna apologise for smacking me one in the street the other day?"

Bob licked a glistening tongue around his lips, barely blinking. As he mumbled, the streetlight tracked over pock marks up his face like craters on the moon.

"Bob? You gonna tell me what you know about this wee demon thing? I... I could really use some help. If you know anything, please. Bob?"

He'd grown still as a statue. All that moved were the tears that flowed down his face. "I feel her on you. I could sense that little harlot anywhere."

Dottie stepped in front of him, leaning the small of her back against the windowsill. A wooden horse clattered over. She picked it up and patted the dust off on her jeans. "Who?"

Bob chortled, a scent like rancid mushroom soup floated up to her. "Let me tell you all about her. *An stoirm mharbh* – the dead storm. She's as ancient as this land."

"The dead storm." A jarring, electrical current seemed to vibrate up her back. She looked around the noisy room that was devoid of a woman's touch. The entire house felt like a shell. Like some haunted ruin. "What did she do to you?"

"I was a different man back then." He leaned back in the chair, his head against the greasy backrest. "Had me a wee lassie. Glenda was her name. Wee superstar, she was. Wasn't a single heroine in all the sacred books could match her spirit. She was gonna change this doomed world. She... She had a problem with food. Happened a couple years after the cancer took her mother from us. Stole her without much warning, so it did. I used to think cancer was a punishment laid on those who deserve it."

Dottie ran a hand over her stomach. A fiery retort burned to get out but she held her tongue. "What happened to her?"

"Happened one April, I think. When the sun gets good and bright. I remember being happy and then turning to see Glenda standing in the hallway. Looked like a cloud of wasps stung her all over and she'd had a reaction. Puffed up real big. Swollen like. Well, turns out I just hadn't been paying all that much attention. Had my own problems after Harriet went. Poor soul." He shook his head, then as quick as a snake, he grabbed a small wooden fox from a small table between the chair and the window. "Glenda hid her midnight skirmishes from me. Got to the point where I had to lock the fridge at nights. Guess she found something in the food that I wasn't able to give her. Comfort, maybe. Love."

Dottie wished she'd carried another pill to dampen the lamp of pain shining in her gut. "Must've been hard losing her mum like that. Bound to have an effect."

"I was too hard on her. Cracked the whip, as it were. She got bigger. A lot bigger. She morphed into this creature who could barely waddle down the hall to get to her bed. Worse thing about it was the shame it brought me. I can see now, the error of my ways. Back then, I saw everyone staring. *What kind of father raises a hulking walrus like that?* The failure rested with me. And then, *she* sent her minion. Heard my prayers that I would do anything to change Glenda."

"Her minion? Old Smokes?"

"It felt as if I were having a stroke just looking at him. I remember the day well. Valentine's Day. I still make a card for my wife, see. Wee hearts like she used to love. Used to make her giggle. She must hate me for what I did to our daughter."

Dottie closed her eyes. The blurry vision of Old Smokes standing outside her front door on that night felt like so long ago. She'd prayed so hard. Felt her regret in her bones as she sent out her wish to be able to protect her Harold no matter what.

"He made you a deal," she said.

"He said with my blessing, she could lose the weight. It would fall right off if I continued to believe hard enough. He'd grant me the gift. But I needed to keep it alive, be faithful to it. I always remember what he said right before he vanished into thin nothingness. 'Pray and pray, and the weight will melt right off.' That was true, right enough. Fresh place in hell for a father like me. That's where I'm going. Guess maybe that's why I wanna help you. Make up for a little part of what I've done."

"You can't blame yourself for that. These things shouldn't exist. They're evil. And I get the feeling the girl is the worst."

"What your son does is all real, isn't it? They offered you the chance to bring your boy back from the dead. And you used it for gain. For show. Money. Shame on you."

"Quit it with the judgey shite. You took the deal just like I did. How was I supposed to know Harold would turn it into this huge thing?"

"You're in mighty big trouble."

"What happened to her, Bob? What happened to your Glenda?"

"Weight fell off her. It was a miracle at first. I felt like the happiest father in the whole good Earth. She became this spritely thing, full of hope. You should've seen her wee face. Angel eyes lit up because I had helped her, been her guiding spirit. The day when she declared she could see her feet when she looked down herself was like a hundred Christmases. I could see the future. A healthy girl with nothing but the wonderful promise of the world. I strutted about like a cock on the walk. Exalted. Vindicated. The weight kept on shifting and soon, young men started eyeballing her as we passed by. Ha, I had to have been the only father in Scotland to welcome that kind of treatment after what we'd been through. Those were the good times. The times I relive every day."

"She got thinner."

"Aye, she did. Turned into a walking rake by the end of it. Size zero models had nothing on her by the time she got to her death weight. Five stone, Dorothy." He sighed deep and ran a hand through his mad hair. "Five stone. Doctors were all stunned. Ran their tests, but it picked up speed before they could get their arses in gear. You ever see a skeleton trying to walk? When she finally went, she was a bag of twigs in my arms. I held her aloft, breathing her in before the ambulance came. One of them threw up. Ever see a paramedic throw up? They've seen everything. My wee Glenda. Heart had given in, they said. My wee girl. My wee..."

"What did you do after that?"

"I prayed. The man, Old Smokes as you called him, said if I could pray hard enough, the gift would save her. So, I blamed me. I hadn't been faithful enough. I didn't love her enough. And do you know what? Every night I'd sit here and pray. Pray my eyes out. Beg." He scratched at the side of his head with a gnarled, yellow fingernail. "She was there, the little girl, floating outside my window each night. Laughing. Giggling. Her green eyes afire with malice. Gripped me until I'd go out into the night, screaming my head off at the moon. Not been the same since. My mind was stretched. I wanna kill that demon. That witch. Banish her to the below."

"You said you could help. How?"

Bob's wide eyes glared into hers. "Oh, you are a selfish one. A man sits before you broken, in need, and you jump to the part that benefits you. You'll get what you deserve. And I hope I get to watch."

"That's not what I—" Dottie held her palm against her forehead. "We both want to stop her. How do we do it?"

"It's a long shot, but all the books point me to one thing we could try."

"What's that?"

"Let me exorcise you. Cleanse you of the demon."

"Really? Have you watched any films where they do that? Doesn't end too well."

"This isn't the movies, and I beg of you to consider the bigger impact."

"Like?"

"If we hurt it, kill it, we stop anyone else succumbing to fates grim as we."

"You swallow some Shakespeare or something? Alright, let's give it a wee go. Not that I like the idea."

The image of Harold's fish-dead eyes came to her. The gasping, desperate way he clutched to life when she revived him.

"What if Harold's taken it upon his righteous self to be dead at this moment? I might need to bring him back. I can't lose that right now."

"She was five stone. As light as a dream."

Bob rose to his full height, a towering, languid shadow. The shine in his eyes looked like two stars in the dark. Madness lived there. Hate was all he had. All he had to hang onto.

He stepped nearer. "She'll take him if she has her cold heart set on him. Everything that you held dear will be taken away." He clicked his fingers. "Gone. Into the forever place."

"Maybe if I go sort things out with Harold first," she said, moving backwards into the centre of the living room. "I'll come back and we could try the whole exorcism thingy. Make sure he knows the score."

A wooden animal cracked under Bob's shoe, splintering. "I do wonder what made her seek you. How desperate you must've reeked. At least we were a righteous family. We were going places. My Glenda would've raised the whole world higher if she hadn't been robbed."

Anger pulsed in Dottie's temples. She wanted to push him in the chest, shout in his face, but she felt wafer-thin. She stepped back, eyeing the open doorway.

"Lord willing," he said, "I'll be able to haul that wee demon through and have my revenge. Cast her away."

"The good Lord, whoever the fuck that is, hasn't been here for a long time. He skipped on places like Pitlair. Doesn't care for shitebags like us. I'm gonna go. Thanks for the, ehm, hospitality."

Bob surged forward, grabbing her wrist. Fingers pressed into bone.

Warm liquid pattered up the side of her face that reeked of ammonia. He aimed a small vial at her, whipping it at her as if it were a wand and he cast a spell. Droplets of liquid continued to rain on her.

"By the glory of He who will save us all, be gone, foul demon. Monster. Creature of the blood. Roar thy tempest of evil elsewhere. Leave this cracked vessel be."

Dottie punched him in the nose.

A smile rose up his face as a line of blood glistened above his upper lip.

"This is the only way," he said. "You're not leaving until I excise the beast. She was only five stone! Don't you get that? Five stone, Dottie. Nothing. Y-You can't save your boy. He plays with forces not to be played with. A plane not to be crossed. You can't save him."

"I'll save fuck out of him, you twisted bastard. Let go!"

"You shall walk these streets no more, demon. Prepare to be extinguished."

"I'll extinguish your fucking skull."

"She takes, and she takes, and she takes. She is the force that never stops. She'll rip your heart right out your chest and make you live through the pain. The pain you created. No one should have to live through that. No one. Let me save you."

Dottie launched her foot at his balls. He let go of her wrist and jerked sideways.

She leaned forward and shoved him full in the chest, making him stumble backward, falling over the musty chair he'd sat on. When he leaned on the table to get up, animals toppled onto the carpet.

She ran for the door, the pain in her stomach a white-hot brick inside her. The air seemed to swirl like a door had been opened, letting in an autumn whirlwind that smelled of dead leaves.

The back of her knee billowed in agony. She fell to the ground, clutching it.

"You'll help me rid this world of her," said Bob, pointing at her with the walking stick he'd just whacked her with.

She spider-scurried on her hands, nearing the doorway. "Get away, you bastard. I need to check on Harold first."

"I have to try and fix it. It's all I have. The world needs to be rid of her. Then I can join my family again. My Harriet. My Glenda."

He advanced. Dottie held her hands over her face, ready for the blows.

Bob coughed out a disgusted, choked wheeze. When she looked up at him, it was like he'd been frozen to the spot, his walking stick raised above his head ready to deliver a strike.

He opened his mouth, but all that came out was a long, dry croak.

His bones popped, snapped. A sound she'd become most familiar with, but it still chilled her marrow.

The wind cycled in the musty living room, picking up. On it, she heard the giggling and roaring of the evil little girl. It was an innocent sound masking something dry and ancient.

Bob floated. He kicked his legs out as if trying to run in mid-air. His veiny hands clutched at his neck as he tried to suck in a breath, his face going purple. His eyes bulged, pleaded. "You brought her."

The invisible force stretched his arms and legs out in four directions as if he lay on a torture device. His eyes screamed at her to help.

"Bob? I—"

His head snapped to the side like a horse had reared and kicked him.

The air died out of him. The blow had broken his neck by the cracking sound of it. A pathetic, whimpering noise filled the room before she realised it was coming from her.

"Don't," said Dottie, standing, reaching out a hand as if to save him.

The bones in his limbs began crumpling into the centre of his body like shoelaces being twisted in on themselves. He looked like a long-dead, shrivelled spider stuck in its cobweb.

Bob's dead eyes seemed to accuse her, saw her selfishness. She could've tried to help him instead of cowering in the corner.

"Just leave us alone," she yelled in the cyclone wind. "Please. You've done enough. I can't... I'm not strong enough."

Thirty-seven

Indecision pulled at Dottie as she snuck back into her house. She paced the living room, wiping the sleeves of her shirt. It was like the dust from Bob's house clung to her. She could still smell its powdery mothball scent.

What now? The pain inside made it impossible to think, so she downed three pills and tanked a glass of rum. The liquor hit her empty stomach hard. She leaned over the sink, breathing slow, a cold sweat breaking out all over.

When the feeling passed, she went back to the living room. She should call the police, she knew. Bring them here, tell them about Bob.

"Tell them what, exactly?" she said to herself, running a finger over her bottom lip. "You were in the middle of it and he somehow ended up dead as an old fly? And then what? Where were you the night Dan went missing? Fuck. Might as well sign a cheeky confession now, get it done with."

The *pop, pop, pop* of Bob's bones snapping made her close her eyes and stand perfectly still. If he'd only listened to her, instead of trying to go ahead with some forced exorcism, would the demon have left him alone?

You have a stain on you.

Bob had been right. She was a stain on everything she ever loved. Harold. Pete. Jimmy. Her mum. Brothers. Everything she touched, spoiled to rot.

The full weight of her predicament seemed to press down on her shoulders. They were messing with something all powerful, ancient. Something that would do anything to get what it wanted. Build Harold up, it said. Kill him over and over. Make people praise him. And do it quick. What would it do if she just stopped?

It was messing Harold up in the head. Each time she pulled him through, the half-witted look of ecstasy was almost worse to bear than his actual death, sometimes.

She lay herself down on the couch and watched the lights of passing cars. Their amber lights looked like exclamation marks as they swayed across the ceiling.

The medicine took hold. Its driving force ballooned its way up her hamstrings, caressing the back of her neck. When she closed her eyes, sleep pounced on her.

Her dreams were vivid and fucked up. She was back in Zorbo's tent, watching Harold step up and stop the rioting crowd. When he stepped up to the lion, about to put his head down the tame beast's throat, the crowd erupted in brays and whinnies. She looked at the crowd from behind her mask. The crowd was made of horses. And they all charged at the stage, their hooves pounding a rhythm on the dirt floor and—

"Police, open up." A gruff voice said as it pounded the door.

The low morning sun hurled its light into Dottie's eyes as she attempted to sit up. She must've slept all night. And now the cops were here.

She tried to sit up again, but her stomach said a firm no. It felt as if it would burst apart, imploding, taking the life from her. The pain pressed at her eyeballs.

"Harold?" she called. "Harold, get that. Please."

Nothing. No noise from upstairs.

"Lazy cunts."

The shape of a large man appeared at her window, shielding its hand, his eyebrows raising slightly as he spotted her. The whole house seemed to vibrate under her when the pounding at the door continued.

When she opened the door, she was hunchbacked and wheezing. "In. Come in."

The two cops stood, concern on their faces. She left the door open for them and shuffled back through to the kitchen, gobbling a couple of pills, downing half a pint of crisp, cold water with them.

They joined her in the kitchen.

"I'm PC Lithgow," said the one with his thumbs tucked behind his stab vest. "This is PC Singh."

"How do?" said PC Singh, casting his eyes over the array of pill boxes on the counter.

"Just finishing my breakfast, officers. Nothing beats a bit of oxy in the morn. Legally prescribed oxy, that is."

"Mrs. Matheson, is it?" said PC Lithgow.

"Aye." She patted at the sleeve of her shirt, dusting off crumbs.

"We found a body."

Her hand froze over her wrist. Lithgow looked at her like she was getting in the way of him grabbing a cake and a bacon roll, but Singh lowered his eyebrows a wee shade, enough to put her on edge.

Who'd seen her at Bob's last night? Fucking eyes everywhere. Probably dozens of the pricks.

"Led to believe," continued Lithgow, "that Pamela is biding here with you?"

"Pamela?" said Dottie.

"Is she here? I have a few questions for her."

"What's Pamela got to do with it?"

Lithgow turned and gave Singh a *we're-dealing-with-a-fanny* look, then said, "She was his girlfriend at the time of his death."

"It's Dan," she said.

"Yes," said Singh, nudging past the other cop in the small space, "he's been missing for days and we made a discovery not far from here. Suspicious, to say the least."

"I'll, ehm, just go wake the lovebirds up then, will I?"

The cops stared at each other. Singh gave a vindicated little nod as she shuffled between them.

She clutched at the banister and called out from the bottom of the stairs. No response. With each step, her swear words grew more and more vile. When she reached the door to his room, sweat prickled on her forehead. She nudged his door open.

"Harold, you wee prick, I'm gonna kill you myself if you don't—"

He wasn't there. The curtains were drawn. The room smelled of sweat and vinegar. Harold's laptop sat open, the only source of light. She saw the feed coming from the other room.

"You did a show without me?" she said, opening the door to the death room.

"I hate it," said Pamela. "How can you stand to be this close? The smell. It's... It's all wrong."

"Maybe leave it to the pros next time, dearie."

"It was his idea. I told him to wait."

Dottie walked further into the room. Her nose tried to turn itself inside-out with the scent of puke and blood spilled into shining puddles on the plastic coated floor. Harold held something purple. Dottie thought it looked like some kind of funny sausage before her mind turned sour, realising what it was he clutched.

"They asked him to pull out his intestines and he actually did it?" said Dottie, pressing a hand down on her own stomach and the bloating pain that thrummed there. "I can't believe your nerve. Doing a show without me, I—" she pressed the bridge of her nose. "Doesn't matter. Police are downstairs looking for you, missy. Got some, ehm, news, I guess."

"Dan?"

"Get yourself a wee wash, I'll bring worm-boy back. Take care of business."

The sounds of muffled, gasped conversation between Pamela and the cops reached them as Dottie brought Harold back from the dead. His innards slurped back inside him, dragged by the grey strands that healed him up.

Dressing him was like dressing an invalid on crack. He kept on mumbling about the demon with the green eyes while she directed him. It was hard not to slap him in the chops.

"—that's when I let myself in," said Pamela as Dottie dragged Harold into the living room.

Pamela sat on the couch while Lithgow and Singh hovered over her like they'd found her drunken on the street corner, checking she was okay.

"And did you see anything when you went in?" said Lithgow. "I'm sorry, love. I know this is distressing."

Dottie noticed that Lithgow suddenly acted the concerned copper for the pretty, heartbroken girl, while he'd looked like he wanted to bunk just a few minutes ago.

She felt the heat of Singh's stare as she walked into the room, followed by Harold.

"Aw, H," said Pamela. "They found him. Dan. He's dead. Ditched by the side of the road somewhere."

"Fancy that?" said Harold, casting a playful look at Dottie before morphing his face into something bordering on concern. He took a seat next to his girlfriend, holding her hand. "You alright?"

"Where was I?" said Lithgow.

Pamela cleared her throat. "The room where—"

"Look here, officer," said Harold. "You not see she's gone through quite the shock? Hardly the time to be ploughing her with questions."

Singh stepped before Harold, staring down at him with a jaw that looked like it chewed a troop of wasps. "Got a dead body by the side of the road like someone tried to bury him and gave up halfway through. Surprised the magpies didn't have at it."

"Greedy bastards around these parts," said Lithgow, "those magpies."

"Now, we hear on yon grapevine that you and Pamela might have loyally pissed off our dear Dan, ain't that right?"

"Maybe." Pamela sunk her head in her hands. "This all wouldn't have happened if I'd just stepped up and finished it with him. But no, I had to keep it going, despite falling in love with—" Pamela sucked in a breath and looked at Harold. "I should've done the right thing. This happened because of me. Now his family. His family will want me. They... they..."

She buried herself in Harold's shoulder, bubbling away.

"Sure it wasn't a suicide, officers?" said Harold. "He seemed awfully unstable."

"Toxicology reports say he was fed enough opioids to knock out a few horses," said Singh, shifting his weight from one foot to the other. "Given the place he was dropped—"

"Arse end of Drumnagoil it was," said Lithgow.

"—looked premeditated to me. To us."

Both cops stared long and hard down at Harold and Pamela. Pamela continued to cry into Harold while he stared up at the them, challenging, defiant.

"You sure you don't wanna take a wee seat?" Dottie said to the cops. "Grab you a cuppa if you can go one?"

"Officers," said Harold, "I think I can help. Think about it. You know Dan and his brothers. They're into all sorts. Drugs, I hear. Why'd you think Pamela was so scared to break it off? Is it not just possible his bad acts," he met Dottie's eyes, smiling a smile that Dottie wanted to slap off his face, "caught up to him."

"I'll need to know your whereabouts the last few days," said Singh. "All of you."

"We can write it down, no problem," said Harold. "But we've actually just had a horrible bit of news, ourselves. Isn't that right, Mother?"

Dottie felt the burning attention of all four sets of eyes as she leaned against the cool wall. "Right. I've been given the news I've not got long to live. Cancer. Come to think if it, we've barely left the house. After all that's happened in the news with Harold and me trying to get my affairs in check, we've not had time for anything. I include Pamela in that. She's been most helpful. A member of the family."

The hearty look on Pamela's face made something lodge in Dottie's throat.

"Now, if you don't mind, officers," said Dottie. "I'm gonna have to ask you to go. Need to rest up. Is that all the questions you had?"

The two cops shared a look that said they had plenty of questions but were now wrestling over whether to ask them. Dottie oozed out a pathetic whimper and clutched at her side. It was enough to make them relent.

"All for now," said Singh, moving to the door, Lithgow behind him. Singh stopped in the doorway and looked down at Harold's feet. "That blood on your socks there?"

It pained her to see how effortlessly Harold came up with a lie. "Mum has these... episodes. Don't want to go into specifics, but her spew doesn't come out all diced carrots anymore. Just done cleaning up the bathroom."

Singh stared down at Harold for a long, heavy moment. "Something in my bones tells me we'll be seeing each other soon."

Thirty-eight

"Not felt this dead in ages," said Harold as he seethed back to life under her touch. "In a good way, I mean. Man, that zings."

He held a hand over his eyes, riding the storm of being brought back to life. It'd be her turn soon. She'd know first-hand what it felt like to crossover, be 'pulled through' as he put it. The thought made cold fingers swarm her spinal cord.

A scent like black, oily insects flowed from his mouth, clawing at the back of her throat despite the mask covering her face.

"Mind, just one or two more and we're done, alright?" said Dottie, sitting on the bed at his side, looking down on him.

Her eyes were so heavy she struggled to keep them open. The slaughterhouse taste of the dark room seemed to seep into her skin.

They'd devised a crude system where they swept the fresh blood from the plastic sheets into a turned over trough lined up against the wall. Once full, they'd tip the sloshing contents into pales. It was Pamela's job to carry them out. Since Dottie didn't want to do her back in or risk spilling it all over the carpet, they stopped taking the blood out to the spot where the bluebells sprouted. They poured it down the bathtub, rinsing it away as best they could. Soon, the very walls of the house oozed with the iron scent of Harold's unmaking.

"Next one's in," said Pamela coming back into the room, wiping her hands on her apron like a butcher at work. A line of blood glistened along her forehead. "Sicko wants you to beat the monkey while you hang yourself. Let's just say no to that one, shall we?"

"She's... She's getting closer," said Harold, still hiding from the world under his hand. "Louder, she says. Let's cover this plane in dust. You ever throw a dust ball at someone? Like a snowball, only dustier. Dust can be bones and blood. Bob was there. He—"

"Right, cowboy," said Dottie, laying a hand on his arm. The heat roiling off his skin made her flinch. "Just you calm it. Pamela? Could you tip some of that blood out? Thank you."

"Do you need to keep that mask on?" said Pamela. "Gives me the fudges. Creepy arse thing."

Dottie saw Pamela's nerve in the way she set her jaw as she got to work. The backbone in that girl would serve her well throughout her life. She was not a pushover. Just what Harold needed. Someone to tell him what's what. Keep him right. On the straight and narrow.

She watched as Pamela heaved a black bin and waddled into the hall. The cascading surf of blood sloshing in the tub crashed through the house.

"Do you need to stop?" said Dottie, looking down at Harold. "We can stop right here. No more."

Her stomach gave a blinding *thump-thump* like a large heart pounded the walls of her abdomen. She sucked in a breath through gritted teeth and pushed the mask up so it settled on the top of her head.

Just a little bit more, she pleaded with her own body. Don't give out just yet. Do these last few, get the money in. Count that as 'getting the affairs in order'. Doing the job a mother should. Providing.

The sound of Bob's cracking limbs doubling in on themselves like liquorice laces came back to her. The sound was so real inside her head that she slapped her hands over her ears.

"That's surely enough," said Pamela, pinging her blue marigolds against her wrists. "Look at the pair of you. Keel over at any moment. You're not well, Dottie. You can't be over—"

"She needs me," hissed Harold. "More. We built this together. More."

It felt as if Dottie's soul left her body, leaving her cold and insubstantial. Gone. She placed her hand on Harold's wrist, feeling the slow, steady rate of his heart. "Tell me again what it's like when you go over. Is it... Is it easy?"

Harold sighed, then pushed himself up on his palms. His knees popped as he drew them close to his chest, hugging them with both arms.

"I guess I'll go check out the weirdo-mail, then," said Pamela, marching out the room.

"Fiery one, that," said Dottie, watching her leave. "Good lass."

"It's kinda like sailing." Harold closed his eyes and swayed gently as if a small wind hit him. It sent him rocking in a slow, pendulum motion, his feet hovering just above the bed. "You feel free. Light. It all suddenly makes sense. Like we've had it wrong this whole time. Then it hits. Pulls you through, rollercoaster-fast. And that's when I see her. The colours..."

"I don't wanna go." Dottie clutched at her chest, trying to hold back the sobs. "I'm not ready for any of this."

"Tunnels. It's like tunnels, down there. Falling. Falling."

"What?"

Harold opened his eyes. The animalistic look made her let go of his wrist. "She showed me how you've fought for me. Didn't know you had it in you. She... She means business, Mum. I'm scared."

"The dead storm."

He looked up at her, eyes shiny with tears. "What?"

"Maybe we should stop this all of this, what do you say? Not give her the chance to pull through. W-What did she show you?"

"Dan. Bob. The pain you've been in. I had it all wrong. Look what you've done for me. I don't want you to go. I don't want her to get me. We're just getting to the point we should've... We should've..."

Dottie wrapped her arms around him and drew him close, not caring for the roiling fire in her gut demanding she stay as still as possible. "Listen to me, alright? I've been a shit mum. I know I have. I just wanted to set you up for when I'm gone. You can understand that, right? Thought it might go some way to making up for being as selfish as I've been." She rested her chin on the top of Harold's head. "What kind of mother does this to her kid, eh? Let him brutalise himself for the kicks of everyone else."

"I'm glad you did it. You know that, right? Taught me things. Weird to say, but dying's taught me all about living, if that makes any sense at all."

She thought about the cancer coiling its way round her insides. "It does. It really does. Well, let's just call it a day then, eh? Convert this death room into a library or something. I'm done watching you die."

His boyish smile tugged at her heart. She'd have been happy to fade away, have this be her final memory.

"Right," huffed Pamela, stepping into the room, "seems I've found chief sicko. How about this?" She read from a scrap of paper. "*Mother Death to stab yon Harold until he can't stand up straight. When Harold collapses, turn cameras to floor and show us Mother*

Death stomping on his skull until bone splits and brain spills out. Break him." Her hand slapped her side as she turned her gaze on Harold. "Believe this shit? How long until one of these bastards sees you on the street and has their own fun? This isn't safe, H."

Dottie stared down at her hands. She remembered the searing pain on Harold's face when Dan had stabbed him in the gut.

Harold's reputation was turning into something like religious fervour. Just what the girl wanted – to ride that wave of praise and breach through to their world.

"No," said Dottie. "We've decided to—"

"Offering a hundred big ones. Six figures. More money you have, the sicker you get, it seems."

"We're not doing that," said Harold.

Dottie had a hard time thinking straight. The room spun around her as she closed her eyes. That much money was a ticket of sorts. The last stop to set Harold up for life.

"Let's do it." Dottie put her mask back on, straightened it.

"Mum?"

"One last ride."

"You serious?" said Pamela, folding her arms.

Dottie moved her head from side to side, the old bones cracking in her neck. "Find me a good knife."

Thirty-nine

Dottie stood under the roasting water, scrubbing at her fingers until she almost drew blood. The air in the bathroom had long since turned to steam. There wasn't enough water in the world to wash off the stain of what she'd just done. She looked down at herself, watching water sluice lines around the lump of her stomach. Hot puke rivered out of her mouth, covering her feet. The chunks of what looked like mushed carrots and globs of hardened blood caught in the drain.

"You sick fuck," she coughed up another thick line of blood. "You sick, selfish, selfish fuck."

It didn't help that Harold seemed to take it all as a challenge, standing for as long as possible before his body collapsed after the countless stab wounds she'd given him. She'd stabbed him slow and unsure the first time, which caused the veins to balloon up the centre of his forehead. He only stood there and nodded at her, willing her to go on. Put on a show. She did.

"Show the world how Mother Death does it," he'd said.

What happened after that was a hazy, bloody memory. The muscles in her forearm ached by the time he finally keeled over. When he'd slumped to the floor, she'd actually gone down after him like an angry, punch-drunk boxer on the kill, still swinging the knife.

She could smell the salt of her own tears and the blood that had spattered over her mask as she stood over him, watching him go.

"His head," Pamela had called from the other room. "Head."

She'd closed her eyes and stomped at her boy, giving all she had, wanting it to be over. The dull *thud* of her kicks became a dry *crack*, and then she was through. She wasn't kicking a solid rock anymore, she was kicking through the centre of a watermelon. At least that's what it sounded like as she sent her boot crashing through into softness.

She leaned on her thighs, gagging on dry nothingness. Her empty stomach had nothing left to give, but that didn't stop her body from trying to wrench it out.

"Straight to hell for you, Dots," she said. "Signed, sealed, delivered. Postage and packaging paid for. The works."

Her face was gleaming like she'd spent all day in a sauna by the time she got out, made her shaky way downstairs, and slapped some more oxy into her gob. The agony screamed on the inside and the out.

Someone had left an NHS flyer on the kitchen counter. *How to deal with what's coming,* blared over the drawing of a sad blob person. No one could teach her about what was coming next. She had an idea it was filled with otherworldly things, such as a wee girl and her pale horse.

The beer scratched an itch at the back of her throat as she lowered herself onto the step at the back door, looking out at the unkempt garden. The bluebells danced over weeds, taking their hold at the top of the garden like some underwater thing. The sun shone on them, but the flowers seemed less vital, less vibrant.

She leaned her head back, welcoming the sun's touch. Another scorcher of a day. Why couldn't all of this happened during a typical, torrential Scottish summer? Instead, they had themselves a summer so hot it felt almost tropical.

"A day meant for riding," she said, taking a swig.

To roll her jeans over her calves, sitting atop Jimmy, Queen of all she surveyed, would be heaven. Just one more time. She could almost feel the slalom of the horse as it walked, its muscular body shifting beneath her saddle.

She rubbed her nail on the glass bottle, peeling a corner of the label off, while she stared into the nothingness of the moving bluebells. She blinked, catching herself from falling asleep. The whole world seemed to pause around her, like it was holding this moment, just for her.

The soles through her socked feet complained at the heat soaked up by the uneven slabs as she walked towards the pale blue flowers.

A magpie fluttered to a stop on the fence. It hopped along the wood, pitying her with its black little eyes. It leaned forward, opened its beak, and let out a shrill shriek that cracked around the gardens. Then it flew away into the sky in a dance of black and white.

The tang of copper met her as she stood before the entity of bluebells. How long until they took over the whole garden? A vision of the flowers bursting through the walls of her house, cracking through the floorboards, invading everything, took her.

She stared up at the blue sky, sucking in a lungful of moist earth and pollen. The clouds seemed to hang in the sky, unmoving.

The cup of a bluebell reached over and pawed at her hand. Despite the listless afternoon, the flowers flowed as if a strong wind rattled through them.

They protect, you know, her mum had said. *They wash away the dark.*

She smiled as she traced a finger along the stem of one of the flowers, becoming aware of a weight in her other hand.

Without a thought, she punched the knife into her wrist.

She pressed the blade in from the top of her forearm to the point where her wrist met her hand. The wound opened, gushing. She fed the bluebells her blood.

"What the—"

She flinched, clutching at her wrist, blinking.

There was no blood.

No knife.

No gaping wound.

Just the ghost of the imaginary pain.

The tiny puffs of cloud moved once more in the sky, released from frozen time.

The wind sighed through the bluebells.

Their dry, pale blue colour sang in the sun.

Forty

"Losing your mind, Dots." Dottie shook her head, turned, walked away from the bluebells, through the back door and into the enveloping cool of the kitchen.

Dorothy...

As she crossed the threshold, she could've sworn she heard someone whisper her name. She turned and gulped in an acid-laden breath. She could almost see the ghostly outline of her mother on her knees by the bluebells, digging and tutting away to herself.

She strode into the kitchen, fished a fifth of dark rum from the cupboard. Her mouth went dry on seeing the liquid slosh around inside.

She couldn't open it. The skin on her palms went red with the effort of it, promising to split. It was so pathetic that she broke down in tears, hugging the bottle tight as if it were a broken dolly.

The tears seemed to shake something loose inside of her. It made her feel light-headed, as giddy as a fresh-born colt. She shimmied her way out of the kitchen to stand at the bottom of the stairs, the unopened rum in her hand sloshing in her grip.

"*Giddy up, my horsey,*" she sang. "*Giddy-up, sugar-pie. Giddy-up, my lassie. You're all gonna die.*"

Her laugh cut off short as she recalled the vision of the pale horse bearing down on her. She held up the bottle of dark rum, looking into its thick caramel reflection. Did she really need to go upstairs and beg for help to open up a bottle of sauce? What had Harold and Pamela been doing all day anyways?

"Probably boinking fuck out each other, cooking me up a gran—" her arm fell to her side, the bottle hitting her thigh.

She was about to set her foot on the first step when Pamela marched out of Harold's room. As Dottie climbed her slow way up to her, Pamela paced the corridor, turning away when she laid eyes on her. How many tears had this lassie shed in the short time they'd known each other?

"What's happened?" said Dottie, hating the ragged, exhausted sound of her voice.

Pamela spun to face her, cheeks puffy. "He's not right."

"You only figuring that out now?"

"Not that." Pamela sniffed, a small laugh falling off her face as quick as it appeared. "He's been quivering like a limp pancake since the last time. After you... you know."

"What, stabbed him to death and staved his skull in? I remember." The memory of cracking bone made a tense heat jolt its way around the back of her neck. "Not gonna forget that one any time soon."

Pamela hugged herself tight, staring down at her bare feet and her painted pink toenails. "It's like he's still trapped in between. Like he's still here and there. Wherever *there* is."

"He'll shake loose from it, love. Don't worry."

"I just keep trying to get him out of bed, you know. Do something. Maybe even take a walk. Weirdos seem to have stopped gathering outside."

"Aye, just gathering online to watch him off himself in style."

Pamela sighed and itched beneath her ear. The scratching noise of nail on skin seemed to tremble inside Dottie's ears.

"You alright after that last one?" said Pamela. "Went a bit far. Sickos."

Dottie held up the unopened rum. "Nothing a little drink won't sort." And the happy pills, she almost added. She held the bottle towards Pamela. "Fancy opening that? Old crone fingers don't work like they used to."

"I need him out of this death business."

"Don't we all."

"I mean it. That time was the final one. If he goes again, he can say bye-bye to us."

Dottie lowered the hand with the bottle clutched in it. "I think that's for the best. Why don't we corner him now? While he's bedridden and useless?"

"No, just you. He'll listen to you."

Dottie couldn't help but walk a bit straighter as she entered her son's darkened room. The sun blazed on the other side of the thick curtain, not cutting through. The bed was empty. She placed a hand on it. Still warm.

In the corner, the sliding mirrored door of a walk-in wardrobe lay half opened, clothes spilling out. Something sniffled from inside the dark space. The smell got more like the inside of a musty running shoe as she crawled over the mound of dirty clothes. She felt the heat baking off of him before she saw him and sat next to him, their shoulders touching in the dark.

"Surprised you can keep a looker like Pamela around. Smells like tomato cupcakes in here."

When her eyes adjusted, she saw how large her son's pupils were. He gently moved his head back and forward as if listening to the world's slowest heavy metal song.

"She'll leave me, too," he whispered. "And then you'll be gone. I'll be here on my own. Just like I deserve."

"Where's this coming from? Talk to me."

He buried his face into his knees. "I'm all hollowed out, Mum. Can't do it anymore. I'm sorry to disappoint you, but I just... I can't. The things she says... I can't, I—"

"You don't have to do anything. I'm not gonna be disappointed. In fact, me and pretty features out there were just about to gang up on you and tell you it's time. Just like we agreed before that sicko gave us so much money. You're set up, now. You don't have to do this, okay? It's done."

He tried to speak, but all that came out was an excruciating sob that tugged at something deep inside her. She put her arm around him and he leaned his head against her shoulder. The sweat caked into his unwashed hair drifted around them in the small confines.

"I was doing it for you, Mum."

"Don't lie to me like that. You don't need to—"

"Mean it. It was like you saw me for the first time when I killed myself. When we both didn't know what was gonna happen. You begged me not to, but your eyes... They told me you wanted to see. And so I showed you. Don't make me die, Mum. I can't do this. It's not fair. I don't know if I can just stop. It's got me now. Got me. Got me—"

"Where's all this coming from, eh? Could've said this at any point."

"She's... She's not playing nice now. The girl. The... thing. She's almost here."

"We don't let her get through, then." She closed her eyes, the nightmare of Bob's contorted, floating form coming to her. "That little witch can't have you. I won't let her."

Forty-one

I, Dorothy, hereby duly leave my worldly possessions, meek as they are, to my son, the righteous bastard Harold. These include this house and all the useless shite in it, including the one thing my mother left me, those creepy bluebells. I ask that the mountain of painkillers be sold – they could probably pay for my funeral! It is my wish to have a small, private service, with no freaky little girls in attendance. And that Bruce Springsteen's Sad Eyes is what is played when they cart me to my grave.

Sincerely, and of (half) sound mind,
Dorothy Matheson
Mother Death
She who sees.

"She who sees?" said Dottie, putting the cap back on the stripy yellow pen. "Where the fuck that pour out from?"

The crisping scent of bacon filled her nostrils as she scribbled away at a practise version of her will, sitting on the living room couch. A bar of sun lit her hand. She looked out the window at another languid, hazy day. Perfect for getting her affairs in order.

She scratched a line through the last words on the lined paper, almost stabbing through.

With everything in order, she could choose her time. Take the pills. Sleep. Be gone. Hit the big sky. When she did it, Harold would be free from all that tormented him. He'd be forced to live a life of splendour and richness with his stacks of dough along with the mortgage-free house she'd leave him. She couldn't really ask for more, except to fly back in time and fill in the void where the memories of raising her son should be. She couldn't even remember much of what he looked like when he was a baby.

Pamela did a happy wee jive in the kitchen as she poked at the bacon smoking in the pan. The smell danced around Dottie, drawing the hunger from its deep slumber. She couldn't remember the last time her stomach welcomed a meal.

"Harold better?" said Dottie, joining Pamela in the kitchen.

"Think so." The bacon popped, making her jerk her hand away from the stove. "Wouldn't settle at all last night. Said the weirdest things."

"What he say?"

"'She's almost over the bridge.' Kept saying it over and over, his eyes open, but not seeing shit. Ain't that a kettle full of weird?"

Dottie stared into the sizzling depths of the frying pan. She had the sudden urge to pick it up and throw the contents down her own throat.

"All that dying has went to his brain," said Dottie, drumming her fingers on the counter. "You feeling alright about Dan? Must've come as a bit of a shock."

"I knew it was gonna end badly. Who'd do such a thing? Crass as it sounds, I just wanna move on, you know?"

"I get that. That mean you're moving on to my Harold? You gonna look after him for me?"

Pamela paused, dripping bacon held in a pair of tongs over the pan. She shifted the bacon to a waiting plate. "What you mean?"

"Not asking you to marry the weirdo, but I see that way you look at him. See the way he looks at you. All googly and sickening."

"I... I guess we'll see how things go."

"Take the good things while you can, love. Don't let the things you should've done pass you by."

"Mrs. Matheson, you're scaring me."

"Well, maybe we should be scared. This thing's got its claws in me and it's not letting go. Seems maybe it's helping me think clearly for the first time in my life."

"Harold seems to think he can do something about that."

"The cancer?" Dottie giggled. "I'm not for the saving."

"He sleepwalks sometimes. Just in the room. Stares at the walls. Stares at the mirror – that's the worst. Like he sees someone inside himself. Doesn't snap out of it no matter how I shake him. Said something about all things being reversible, that he'll do what's needed. I dunno. Sounded like they were talking about you." She clamped the tongs together twice and did a wee bounce on her tiptoes. "Space to breathe is all he needs. Get away from all that. Fresh start. Live for the life bit instead of the death bit."

"You gonna send some of that bacon my way, or do I have to tweeze your beak off with those tongs?"

Pamela set a plateful of baconly heaven in front of her, brown sauce dripping down the sides of a stacked sandwich. "Would you change anything?"

"No, that looks perfect, hen. Crispy, just the way I like. Could go a side of Irn Bru, though."

"About life, I meant."

Pamela grabbed a can of juice from the fridge and set it down in front of her. Dottie bit a gobful of sandwich, chasing it with the frigid fizzy juice. Her stomach gave a long, strangled growl which she ignored and took another chomp.

"When you're young and supple, the world is there for the taking," said Dottie. "Take it. Drink up. Fill your nights with the fire of it. But there'll come a time when the fire is taken from you. You might wanna chase that fire over and over, drink harder, or whatever, until you feel the memory of what those young nights were like. It'll never be the same. Don't kid yourself. Don't chase the high. I... I wish I lived more for other people, you know? Specially my Harold. Never did right by that boy. Hope I didn't fuck him up too bad."

"Looks mighty alright, far as I'm concerned."

Dottie gobbled down a chunk of sandwich to hide the emotion welling up inside. When she was done, she ran the back of her hand along her mouth. "You're alright, Pamela. Good head on your shoulders. Glad we suckered you into our hellish wee circus act."

Pamela slapped her forehead. "God, that circus. What a shit show. Feels like forever ago now when—"

The front door slammed open, hitting the wall. Dottie stood, her heart galloping in her chest. Heavy footsteps pounded through the hall.

"Where's the cunt at, eh? Where?" a man yelled.

Dottie held her palms up at Pamela, urging her to stay put. When she stepped into the living room, three masked men swarmed her. The frostbite of a nightmare settled in her legs. All three wore white hockey masks like cheap plastic versions of Mike Myers.

"Gents—" Dottie croaked then tried again. "You look like the worst rap group ever. Get yourselves to fuck before I show you a real mask."

"Shut it, you old boot."

She stepped up to the one who'd said it, catching the strong, green scent of weed. "Beat it before I—"

He shoved his face forward, his mask touching her forehead. The maddened, bloodshot eyes glared at her. Under the stench of weed, the black stink of motor oil hit her, settling on her tongue.

"Don't wanna hurt no fragile old hag," he hissed in her face. "But I will. Where's the cunt at? Gonna mash him up like... like mashed potatoes on Sunday."

"Good one," she said.

They stood around her, one to each side and one in front. The one on her right itched at his nose under his mask. "Yo, Don? We gonna—"

"Ssshh!" said the one in front, reaching over and slapping the back of his head. "Stupid, stupid prick." He turned back to Dottie. "Where is he? Where's Harold?"

"Oh, Harold the Impossible," mocked the one on her left with a high pitched voice. He flapped his gloved hands beneath his chin, raising his voice. "Welcome to the stage the magical bastard and his fake death shite. Whoop whoop."

"Mum?" called Harold.

The three men turned. Dottie's spine zinged with warning at the sound of the smile in the leader's voice. "Put him in the car."

"Donald?" said Pamela, bracketing her reddened face with clamping hands. "He didn't have anything to do with it, you bell-end. Let him go. Stop!"

"Cunt deserves a taste of his own medicine," said Donald, turning to face the other two who struggled to hold Harold still. "You like to die, eh? I'll show you dying. I'll show you all the dying you can get."

She watched as her son raked his fingers underneath one of the masks, making the guy yell out. When the mask slipped off, Dottie saw the resemblance to Dan. His brothers. Pamela had warned them they'd show up. Exact their revenge.

Dottie lunged, but Donald held a palm up, stiff-arming her, shoving her back, his hand lingering on her chest a bit too long. She wished she had something to brain him with. A knife. Anything.

Pamela joined the fray, aiming a kick at his stones, but he turned to the side and lamped her across the jaw with a balled fist. She flopped to the ground, landing on her rear-end, staring up at the events like a confused child.

Donald still held his large palm over Dottie's chest as she swiped at him to little avail. He held her there without much effort, shouting down at Pamela.

"That you all lovey-dovey, aye? Shagging here while our Dan's gone? Not gonna fly. We know it was you. Always wasn't good for him. You're gonna find out vengeance is a bastard."

Dottie looked past the man. The two others had lifted Harold, taking a side each, hauling him to the front door. "Take three of you to take on one? Pathetic. Absolutely pathe—"

Donald punched her square in the gut. Agony folded her up, making her collapse to the floor. She sucked in a long, groaning breath, her face starting to glow red. The only part of her she could move was her jaw that opened and closed over and over.

"Mum!" yelled Harold. "Muuum!"

Pulses of light strobed before her, filling up her vision.

The front door slammed against the wall again as the intruders dragged her boy out to the car and to who knew where. A vehicle started and roared off into the distance.

"No!" Dottie fought through the pain, army-crawling her way to the open door, her knuckles going white as she tugged at the carpet.

Pamela sat with her legs splayed, hunched so far forward the ridges of her spine lumped up her top. "*Gonna find me a mister, gonna find me a mister.*" The offkey singing made the bile creep up the back of Dottie's throat. "*Gonna find him a-waiting, waiting at the top of the stairs.*"

The taste of summer breeze flowed over Dottie as she crawled her way to the hallway, the brilliance of the light almost blinding. She dug her hands into the carpet like she scaled a tall skyscraper. Pain seized her every joint, making her stop her pathetic progress. What was she gonna do like this? Crawl and beg her way after them? Should she phone the cops?

"Too much worms for those buzzards," she said to herself. "I'll end up in the jail counting the hours."

She felt Pamela's thumping footsteps through the floor. She was about to try sit up to talk when Pamela leapt over her, running out into the sun and gone.

A noise like a hurt pig crept out of Dottie's gullet as another wave of agony threatened to burst her stomach apart. Each breath, each movement made fire. She set her forehead against the grey carpet, trying to breathe evenly, unmoving.

This was all her fault. She knew it in her bones that some evil fucker would come along and test Harold's ability. What would they do? Would they regret killing him when they saw his dead body? How would they do it?

The open door and its wafting taste of grass and sun-baked concrete seemed to call to her as if through another portal, welcoming her to rest her head, give herself up. She had nothing left. It was all for nought.

You selfish wee cow.

"No!" Screaming in defiance, she hauled herself up, leaning on the banister, sweat dripping down her temples. "Enough of that shite, Dots. Do right for once in your stinking life. You—"

The girl stood at the top of the stairs – the dead storm.

A taste like a bed of dry autumn leaves drifted down to her. Little arms crossed over her stomach, she furrowed her brow under the dark hat. Her eyes were aflame with emerald light.

Dottie's mouth hung open, her jaw bobbing up and down as she fought to speak. "H-Help him. Help."

The girl turned her eyes on Dottie. It felt as if a torch of flame passed through her. The demon lifted a dainty hand, pointing at the door. From somewhere outside, a horse whinnied a long and lonely note.

Dottie's world turned sideways. Her head banged against the floor, bringing darkness.

Forty-two

"She's after them, she'll rip their fucking heads clean off their—" yelled Dottie, breaking out of the dark, sitting up on the couch.

"Thank goodness," said Pamela next to her. "Thought you were done. Swore your heart stopped and everything."

Dottie winced as a lump of pain on the side of her head throbbed, reminding her of her fall. "Harold?"

Pamela sighed out her nose, staring down at her hands. "Ran after them. Didn't do much good by the time I came back to myself. Clocked me pretty good. It's all on me, Mrs. Matheson. Should never have dragged Harold into it all. Dan's brothers are all so twisted. Do nothing but sit in their garage and plot like they're some kinda gang lords. Wimps, all of them, but banded together, they... well, you saw what they did."

"We're gonna need to get after them. I— argh!" She tried to sit up, but the pain inside stopped her. It had her gagging on her own breath. She turned to the side and coughed up a line of blood. "Fuck. Not gonna be any good like this. Fuck, fuck, fuck!"

"C-Can I help? Should I call an ambulance?"

"Nah, just grab me some pills."

"What ones?"

"All of them." The swirling pain made it hard to focus. Her memory and her words felt like cumbersome, foreign things. "Back of the cupboard. Patches. Fentanyl. Slap me with one."

"That's some serious stuff, isn't—"

"Just bring me it!"

As soon as Pamela gently placed the patch on her upper arm, someone chapped at the door. Her instant reaction was that the girl had come for them on her white horse.

"Good, they're here," said Pamela, getting up to let whoever it was in.

"So," said PC Lithgow, holding his tiny notepad close to his face as he leaned forward in the chair, "Harold was kidnapped by three masked men. Did you manage to get more details than that?"

"Aye," Pamela sat beside Dottie on the couch, manically clawing a hand through her hair. "One of them slipped up. He called—"

"We don't know anything, officers," said Dottie. "Honestly, they came in, clapped both of us out, then Harold was taken. Were wearing a bunch of creepy masks over their stinking faces. Got in a car and zoomed off." She turned and gave Pamela a meaningful stare. "That's all we know."

"Can you describe what Harold was wearing, at least?" said Lithgow.

Dottie grit her teeth, feeling the pressure of it in her gums. "Ripped black jeans. A t-shirt I bought him of a dragon riding a motorbike."

"Colour?"

"It was blue."

"And what were you two doing exactly, before all this happened? Making tea? Having a chit-chat? Fawning over the latest—"

PC Singh leaned over and nudged the other cops shoulder, gave him a hard stare, then turned a pitied eye toward Dottie. "Enough. You remember the delicate situation this family finds itself in."

"We're really worried, officers," said Pamela. "Find him. Please? Time's an—"

"Would you shift your arse and get my son back," said Dottie, "you pair of lazy bastards!"

They left in a huff, promising to track him down.

"Why'd you lie like that?" hissed Pamela.

"Just trust me."

She thought about the demon girl's raging eyes and the sound of the horse. Did it mean she had some otherworldly plan to help? The closer the cops got, the closer she would get to having to spill the truth to Pamela and possibly break up the relationship. Pamela could never know that she was the last person Dan saw before his heavy eyes shut for the last time.

After tending to her until the pain abated, Pamela hid herself in Harold's room. This was it. She had to do something.

In her bones, she could feel the ticking away of her essence. Truth was, she welcomed it. Her days were getting long with agony. How long until she couldn't move? How long before she could no longer save her son? The letters said she could die in a hospital when it got 'really difficult' but she didn't want that.

"Harold does not travel the road," said a familiar, chilling voice.

Dottie forced herself to sit up. Her eyes felt as dry as dead leaves. "He's alive? What are they doing to him?"

Dottie hadn't seen the demon up this close. She stood at the side of the couch, meeting Dottie's eyes. Her skin glowed with faint green light on the inside.

The voice crackled like a scratchy record.

"You and I have business," it said. "Will you ride with me?"

"He doesn't want you. Leave us be, you wee... you wee boot."

The girl, the dead storm, stepped forward, a slow rising smile spreading up her face, making her skin look like dry leather. Emerald light seemed to glow brighter through the cracks. "This started with you. You are the one who begged with everything in your bones, as I recall. You build power here. Power that tastes like the honey of sweet, sweet death."

Dottie tried to blink away the sluggy feeling enveloping her brain. She felt the nightmare thing's stare rooting her to the ground like she was trapped in the midst of a cold dream. "What do you want?"

"To be part of your world again. Draw breath. Sink my teeth in. Was rather creative, how you both used your gift. Never thought anyone up here had the stones to challenge death directly. The adulation your boy now draws is powerful in all veils."

"Y-You want through? To do what?"

"To suck on bones like fried chicken wings and speak in tongues ancient and mind-blowing. People need to see death for what it is. They need to fear it. They need to fear me." The girl leaned forward and inhaled, closing her eyes like she smelled a baking cake. "Oh, seems you'll be finding out all about death soon enough. It grows black within you, touching everything. Before you take that bad trip, come with me. We need to collect our prince. His work cannot go unfinished."

"You're evil." Dottie stood up straight, towering over the girl, but feeling none the stronger for it. "What if I say no?"

The girl held up her hand. The fingers looked like crooked things that belonged to an ancient witch. She pointed at Dottie's stomach. Blazing pain shot through her and up her spine, lighting up every synapse in her brain.

Dottie jellied to the floor. Sickness spumed out her mouth. She heaved on all fours, tears dripping out her eyes.

"You don't want to be saying no to me," the dead storm said. "You don't wanna see what's behind that door, missy. Nut-uh. Don't take the selfish cow option."

As Dottie stared up into the circling, fiery eyes, she heard the clopping of a distant horse, its thumping hooves deep as a bell tolling her name.

"Do not mess with the plan, Dottie. What we set in motion."

"I-I can't do anything. Can't you see that? Can barely move."

"We can assist you with that, for a small time."

The pain. It floated out of her like a ghost. She could still feel its promise in the pit of her stomach, waiting to erupt.

Dottie felt the muggy clouds in her head dissipate. She almost laughed with glee. "What are you?"

"More than you could ever know."

"Dan's brothers have a garage not far away. Do you know if he's alright? Safe?"

"Safe? Ha, that's rich. His song is of great suffering. They toy with him. They flay his soul. They might send him over."

Outside in the bright daytime, the impossible horse whinnied, stomping a leg on the path. The little girl turned her attention to the direction of the sound.

"Your chariot awaits. Bring him back, Mother Death."

Forty-three

The white horse waited on the path outside Dottie's home, its pale, pink eyes on the cusp of madness. She stepped her way toward it, feeling light and nimble. The sun hung high in the sky. Two magpies shrieked at her from a neighbour's roof, then broke into the air in a panic of black and white feathers.

A tingle of electricity passed through her fingertips as she ran her hand along the horse's side. She could feel its abrupt, pounding heart beat through her palm. It turned its alien eyes on her. Her hand froze its soothing motion. Everything inside her told her to bolt, get away from this thing.

"She who rides the pale horse," she whispered.

She set her foot in the stirrup, then hoisted herself over in one smooth motion just like she used to when riding long and carefree with Jimmy.

"Where to, yon steed?" she chuckled. "Shall we burst into the garage where the fuckers who took Harold might be? Stomp their heads into mush. What do you say?"

The horse clomped forward. She tried to use her feet to guide it, but it ignored her like it was being pulled along an unseen track. Ahead of them, the demon girl stood with her back to them. It stood as still as a statue, casting no shadow, feet not moving, yet it never got any closer. The horse followed the shape like a beacon.

Dottie reached down and pet the side of the horse's face out of habit. It shook her off, white foam spitting into the air.

Was the horse real? Did people see her floating past, her legs akimbo? Or did they see nothing at all?

"Let's give them something to see. What you say, pal?"

She dug her heels into the horse's sides and grabbed the reins. The horse took off at a pace she'd never experienced before. The summer breeze tunnelled around her. A bee slapped her cheek, leaving its pollen stinging her nose. They rumbled on after the frozen marker of the little girl as if they played some video game.

Being on the back of a horse was freedom. It ached something inside of her. She'd missed it so much, the thundering of hooves, the way she felt like a giant. The motion took her into a meditative state. There was only her and the horse and the air and the sun. Freedom. Uncaring. No tomorrow.

It was only when she saw the tattered *Welcome to Drumnagoil* sign that she came back to herself. Cars swerved around them on the country road. The drivers didn't cast them a glance. It was like they sensed they had to move, rather than see them.

The horse turned onto the long dirt road where she'd half-buried Dan. The dirt was so dry and sun-baked it was almost red. She tasted it in her mouth, it mingled with the sweat of the horse. The sun splashed over them then flashed away again as they clopped past the rows of planted trees that lined both sides of the road.

A cold breeze waved over her. The horse slowed to a walk. For a time, they didn't seem to make any progress on the long straight road. It seemed to her that the road turned under them like a treadmill, until a mound of darker earth appeared at the side of the road.

"Shit," she said. "Shit and double shit."

The memory of Donald's punch to her stomach made itself known. Her eyes felt suddenly heavy. Her shoulders dropped. Energy sagged.

The grave was shaped like a pill. She stared down at it from her spot atop the horse, clutching at her stomach. She fished around inside the pocket of her red and blue chequered shirt and came up with two pills that she shoved into her mouth. She chewed them into powder, savouring the tart, eye-watering taste of them that flooded her mouth with saliva.

Around the grave, multiple sets of boot prints were marked everywhere. A blue t-shirt with a maddened dragon riding a motorbike hung on the limb of the tree next to the grave. It was the t-shirt Harold had been wearing.

The brothers must've all chipped in. Was Harold alive when they buried him? Close to where she'd buried Dan? The thought of strangling on packed dirt almost made her cough her pills out, but she covered her mouth and forced herself to swallow.

The horse dipped its head toward the mound.

"Alright, Whitey," she said. "I get the picture."

She dismounted with the grace of a misshapen potato, nearly falling on her arse. Leaning against a tree was a spade, its speckled orange rust shining in the sun.

"*Grave digger me, grave digger we,*" she hummed to herself as she shoved the spade into the earth. "*We must be brave, we dig the grave.*"

The sun blazed its heat along her back, almost singeing the hair at the back of her head. Moist, purple things wriggled under the violence of the spade. How long had Harold been under here? How far down? She already felt her triceps spasming with effort. A full six feet down would be impossible for her.

Sweat pierced her eye. A swirl of pain galloped through her innards. She fell to her knees, yelling out. The spade fell into the loose dirt beside her. She'd hardly made a dent.

Her phone's screen blurred before her face as she thumbed a message to Pamela, telling her to come quick, to help dig him out. She groaned, deleted the message, put the phone away.

"Pathetic," she wheezed. "You can do this."

Red thoughts circled her mind as she picked up the spade, its metal handle warm and moist in her grip. She'd find the fuckers who did this. Show them what Mother Death was all about.

"Fruits of your own labour, hen," she said to herself as the spade made its *scoot* noise in dry earth.

The flood of soggy numbness from the pills made the work easier. Soon, she entered a rhythm, losing herself in her thoughts.

Little Harold creeping into her room when he was six, holding out a shiny book to her as the thunder rumbled outside. The fear only a child could know was written all over his wee face. She'd turned him away.

Her mum tending bluebells on all fours. Dottie standing in the kitchen watching, something inside her telling her to march to her mum and give her a hug – take this moment. She'd ignored it and went to grab herself another beer.

Anger seethed out of her as the spade dug into the earth. Her knee wobbled, her leg muscles gave in. She launched the spade across the road. It landed by the horse who glared at her, willing her to continue.

She wiped the back of her hand along a forehead covered with sweat. The sky had turned a shade darker, the sun lower in the sky. When she stared down at her reddened, irritated hands, they seemed very far away, like she viewed them through a wonky telescope.

MOTHER DEATH

Burning sick burst out her mouth. She turned her head and coughed up all she had, feeling like a lung would come out next. She lay down on the grave, laying her forehead against it.

The sun hid itself behind a large cloud, making her skin drop a few welcome degrees. Whitey moaned and stomped on the ground, willing her on.

She lifted her head from the dirt and reached for the spade. It was an effort just to stand and raise it again, but she pierced the earth, stomped on the blade, then threw the dirt on the growing pile beside the grave. Slowly and again, over and over. She'd be here for days at this rate.

"Do you require assistance?" said a man's voice.

Old Smokes stood on the lip of the hole she'd dug. He stared at her, wisps of black material flowing from behind him like a comic book hero staring down on a dark metropolis. His face was a bank of clouds turning in on themselves. You could get hypnotised searching for a face in that void.

"Need more than assistance, big guy," said Dottie. "Don't suppose a do-over is in the works? Start again?"

The horse had disappeared from the road. He noticed her stare. "She cannot be in all places at once. She has... other seeds to sow."

"So, you come to help, while she wasn't looking?"

"Something like that."

"Good," she stepped over, her legs unsure and knackered beneath her. She handed the spade over, handle first. "Be a gent and get cracking. Never been so happy to see your... face."

She parked her arse on the dirt and leaned her back against a tree. Her insides and her very soul seemed to sigh with relief. The wind was much cooler now, soothing. Old Smokes got straight to work, digging at a rate that made her feeble attempt laughable. Grains of sand-like dirt hit her, but she made no attempt to shield herself.

"Let me guess," said Dottie. "You've done this before."

"My masters sends me many tasks. Some are less savoury than others."

"How does this rate on the savoury scale?"

"About a five out of ten."

"What's a ten?"

He froze, the spade inches from the dirt. From here, she could see the vague suggestion of his hands that had fog rolling off them, fading into nothing.

"That bad, aye?" she said.

"Some things you should never have to see." He shoved the metal blade into the dirt. "If I could kill myself, I'd have done it a million times over. Hell seems like a good alternative."

"Well, I'll reserve you a seat. Maybe one day you'll make it. We could do lunch."

Old Smokes straightened. She felt the heat of his attention. "For one so small, so fragile, you sure have a strong spine. Many a person I've seen would go mad by this point. Throw in the towel, as it were. Why does she have to pick people like you?"

"You didn't have to help me."

"I am here of my own volition. Always get mocked for taking an interest, caring. They lost their souls a very long time ago. They can't have mine. They've got everything else, but they can't have that. I won't let them."

His shoulders bulged as he attacked the soil. His arms were a blur as he brought it down again and again. Little puffs of cloud swam into the air from where his face should've been, his breaths jerky.

"Are you—" Dottie stood, going to him, holding a palm up. "Are you crying?"

"It'll never be enough. It'll never be over. My Michael... My Abigail... I can't..."

He pushed the spade into the ground. Something snapped below the surface. Dottie moved slowly forward as he folded himself over, leaning on the spade. The grey clouds continued to mist off his face, vanishing into the air above him.

She laid a hand on his shoulder. The trembling, rolling mass of him vibrated through her hand.

"You have to find a way," he said, his voice cut up with emotion. "Fight it. Fight her."

"I..."

"She's not as strong as she seems. You have to. She respects you. She doesn't respect anyone. That can only mean she's scared of you, right? That you can do something. Please?"

She opened her mouth, a gulletful of emotion promising to tumble out. What was she supposed to do? Tickle-fight the little witch to death? She had nothing. She could barely swing a spade.

She looked down. Resting against the toe of her cowboy boot was a severed finger.

Forty-four

Harold's grave was three feet deep. She excavated around him, scooping the dirt away from his bruised and pummelled face. He looked like he floated in water on his back, his face the only thing breaking the surface. There was something dreadfully peaceful about the look on his face like he'd welcomed his death when it finally came.

Old Smokes and the pale horse fled her. She sat beside her son's grave alone, waiting on Pamela bringing the Land Rover. She told Pamela to keep it quiet, not tell the cops. She needed a plan. Pamela needed to be kept from making the connection to Dan's death.

Fury melted around the base of her stomach like a phoenix waiting to be unleashed at the sky. She'd make toast out of the bastards that did this to her Harold. Her boy, buried alive, his mouth clogged with packed dirt. She placed her hand over the bottom of her throat. She couldn't imagine anything worse.

The sky darkened with cloud. Wind licked at her hair, heavy with promised rain. A giggle sprouted out of her at the thought of a random car crawling down this road, stopping to check what was up.

The stilted movement of her laughter lit her up inside. She doubled over and clutched at the ground. She felt the energy run through her, down her arm and into the soil.

"Shite. Harold?"

She'd touched his forehead by accident when she reached for something to steady herself with. Even through the packed earth, she heard his body being worked on by the grey things that pieced him back together.

"There's my boy. Wakey, wakey. It's alright. It's—"

His face turned beetroot. He flicked his gaze to the side, his panicked eyes screaming for help. The dirt held him in place.

Dry, sputtering sounds erupted from him. He coughed up a glob of dirt, but started choking on it again. He struggled for air, but had no way to turn his head.

His death was slow. His face was a picture of twisted, bloodshot pain by the time he went.

Pamela showed up in the Land Rover and they dug Harold's dead body from its grave, dumping it across the back seats. He looked like they'd hauled him out of the mines. His skin was caked with dirt, hair matted with it.

Dottie scooped as much dirt from his mouth as she could reach, slapped at his back to dislodge it from his innards. What if it was in his lungs? They wouldn't be able to get it out. He'd be done for, no matter how often she revived him.

They set off for Pitlair. Pamela drove. Dottie sat in the back beside the cold body of her boy. How much damage could one soul take? She shifted beside him, combing her fingers through his tangled black hair.

"Here goes," she said, and placed her hand on his forehead.

After a few minutes of desperate, exploding coughs, he was finally able to settle down and get his breath back to normal.

She handed him his t-shirt. "Wanna talk us through what happened?"

"I died. Again." Harold's voice was marshmallow thick, like he had trouble moving his mouth to make the words. "Hurt. Hurt good. They gave me their best."

"I'll give them my best. Those wankers."

"It's beautiful. The feeling... It's a river. It's not. Och, you'll never understand."

Dottie looked at the rear-view mirror. She caught the rabbit-in-headlights look in Pamela's eyes.

"Strapped me to a chair," he continued. "Tore my fingernails off. One by one. Pop, pop, pop. They laughed about it. Filmed it. They... did things. And you know what?" The look of fever in Harold's eyes as he turned to face her made Dottie's bowels turn cold. "I loved every intense second of it. In pain is life in all its glory."

Dottie opened her mouth to speak, her words drying up in her mouth, shrivelling away. The force of Pamela whipping round bends brought her own pain singing back to her. Her pain didn't feel glorious. It felt like waiting death.

"H?" said Pamela. "If they took a video, the world will go crazy if you turn up alive somewhere. And do you think the cops will charge them with anything if you're cutting about like nothing happened? They'll think Dan's brothers were all in on it. It was some act. And you know what? They'll do it again. And again. Someone else will try their luck. Maybe wee Tonya's family, who still blame you for her death, will pay a wee visit. And how long until your mother can't pull you out? That'll be it. Done. Dusted. No coming back. And I can't... I can't watch you put yourself through this each time."

Harold slumped in his seat, arms folded across his chest like he experienced mid-winter. He rested his head on the door, gazing into the green world rushing by.

"You have no idea," he said. "I've never felt so... so... alive."

Dottie burst out in a dry, croaking laugh. The sound was as high-pitched as an annoyed crow. It surprised Pamela so much that her hand jerked down on the wheel, pulling them hard left before she straightened the vehicle.

"Alive?" said Dottie. "Look at you. Alive. Seen road-killed hedgehogs with more zest than you."

"It's in my blood, now. It's wonderful, Mother. I hope you never feel it."

"We said we were done with all this death, remember? We agreed to stop. Got a million things to be looking forward to. Pamela needs you." She let out a sharp sigh. "I need you."

"Whatever," he huffed, staring out the window.

There seemed no end to Pamela's silent tears. She cried like someone who'd been taught at a very early age to hide it or she'd be given a reason to cry.

They got home and Harold stumbled his way upstairs, leaving his girlfriend to fall apart in the kitchen. Dottie consoled her, feeding Pamela a large glass of wine that looked more cereal bowl than drinking implement. Dottie gulped more pills and was soon cushioned in empty brilliance. The world was becoming unmanageable without her little white friends.

Dottie's heart filled as she watched Pamela make her a sandwich while wiping the tears off her cheeks. The plate shook as Pamela handed it to her, a small token of gratitude despite the spilling emotions.

Pamela went upstairs to mend the cracks with Harold but came screaming straight back down, begging Dottie to come save him.

He'd hung himself in the bathroom. His sightless eyes held a sickly tinge of contentment as his body spun in creaking semi-circles.

Pamela hacked at the rope with short, angry slashes with a long knife, then Dottie brought him back to the world.

"Leave me there!" he roared as he came to, sucking in breath. He blinked and ran a hand absently along his throat. The red rope marks dissolved to smooth skin. "Don't you see, Mother? It's no good here. Shallow. Useless. I'm useless here."

What followed was a night of death and heated arguments. Dottie was tempted to strap the wee bastard to his bed until he snapped out of his funk.

He slit his wrists. He stabbed himself in the heart. He took a batch of pills he'd squirreled from Dottie's supply. Each time he re-emerged, a blazing argument followed. He didn't want brought back. Her son wanted to stay dead. It was in his eyes. Still, she wouldn't let the girl with the vile green eyes have her boy.

Dottie swigged a mouthful of rum, going through the events of the last day. The sun had set, midnight come and gone. Her nerves were jacked in. Each time she hauled Harold back to the real world, it sapped something within her, leaving her hollowed out.

Finally, there was silence. She revelled in it, looking up at the stars. With a chemical buzz crawling its way through her bloodstream and up the back of her neck, she sat on the back step, taking in the quiet night. The muggy summer air wafted over her. She welcomed its touch.

The song of the rustling bluebells drifted to her. She squinted at them. Someone was on the ground beside them, hunched on all fours. They seemed to be examining the plants, snipping, digging with all the frantic care her mum had shown on the rare occasions she visited. Those visits, she knew, were more to check up on the flowers than check up on Dottie and Harold.

The garden had been silent, she was sure. She'd had that soothing feeling of being utterly alone, no eyes on her for once. No one had been here. She scratched at the side of her head. "Keep it together."

The feeling of sludgy nightmare gripped her by the shoulders and made her walk forward. The figure started ripping up the plants with bare hands.

"M-Mum?" said Dottie.

The person on all fours seemed to morph before her eyes. The familiar, doughy shape of her mother replaced by the deathly shape of her son.

"Harold?"

He flinched and hissed an animalistic snarl at her. Dirt smothered his hands. He picked up a clump of soil and shoved it into his mouth, chewing, swallowing deep.

She stopped a few paces from him. He'd ripped up a good section of the flowers. Beside him, stacks of ripped out bluebells shone in the moonlight, their cups weak and withered.

"What the hell you playing at?" said Dottie.

"You're not tending to these like she told you to. Now they must go. They must go. You don't deserve any of this. Didn't she tell you? Do you understand? Do you see? You selfish wee cow."

He turned back to the flowers and punched both hands into the dirt, ripping up bulbs, throwing them on the pile. To Dottie, the bulbs looked like white onions that sprouted long grass. Dirt hit her socks as she watched the muscles in his back work through his t-shirt – the ripped one they'd buried him in.

"Your gran left me them," she said. "It was the only thing she ever gave me. You get away from them. Harold? You hear me through those thick lugs of yours?"

The wet, ripping sounds of each unearthed plant plucked at something in her gut.

What a selfish trollop you turned out to be. Bet you haven't been keeping my bluebells going in that scummy garden of yours.

"Harold? Listen to me. This isn't you." Dottie sprung forward and pulled at his shoulders. "Dunno what she's got going in your head, but you have to fight her. Come on, you wee prick."

She pulled with all her might, straining. It didn't make a lick of difference. She might as well have been a ghost trying to make contact in the real world. The air tasted of the chocolatey soil. His hands moved with blurring speed like he was a human combine harvester, destroying the crop. The toothy, maddened smile across his face filled her with hate.

She picked up a chunk of broken slab and brained him with it. It made a dense *thud*, then he toppled face first into the flower bed.

It was as if she couldn't draw a proper breath. Dots swam in her vision as she clutched at the piece of rock with Harold's blood on it. He lay with his face down on the ground, whimpering like he was having a nightmare.

How dare he go on killing himself just for the thrill of it? Didn't he know how much it took from her each time? How much it took from Pamela? What had her raging from her very core was just how much Harold had sounded like her own mother. If only she loved Dottie as much as she cared for her gardening and those stinking bluebells.

She stepped forward, raised the block, brought it down on the back of Harold's head. She done it again. And again.

She was sobbing uncontrollably by the time she came back to herself. A stiff ache tensed her forearms as she took three steps back. The rock dropped by her feet, covered in thick blood.

"What have you done, Dots?" she said to herself, holding her hands over her mouth.

The dry, crackling sound of the bluebells was all she could hear as she sunk to her knees. Harold's blood seeped from his cracked skull, over the white of his brain and bone, being sucked into the earth. A noise like someone taking slurping sips sounded in the quiet air.

The cups of the flowers and their pale blue seemed to glow, an iridescent image of their movement burned into her vision. The stalks shivered.

"What have I done?"

Forty-five

Dottie left him there, face down in the flowerbed.

She paced the kitchen, sipping at the fifth of vodka she'd fished out the back of the cupboard. Vodka was Pete's drink, something she'd always mocked him for, but right now, she'd take whatever she could to feel close to him.

The oily tinge of the clump of bluebells she'd scooped up and placed on the counter filled the air. Already the small, curly petals started to dry off and tumble to the floor.

"You can't leave him out there, Dots," she said to herself, continuing her pacing.

How long before some random arsehole saw Harold from their own back door? She needed no more attention from PCs Singh and Lithgow. And yet, she only stared out the window at the sight of her dead boy.

The sky had the taint of the coming sunrise. She sighed, something heavy inside pulling at her core.

She needed sleep. To rest. For it all to be over. Tears stung her eyes as she wellied more vodka. In that moment, with her mother's beloved bluebells next to her, Dottie realised she was ready. Ready to go. Say goodbye. It would all be so easy.

Her head shook violently at the thought of leaving Harold as he was. She couldn't. He'd meet with her in whatever afterlife there was, always hating her. She couldn't bear the thought of that hate for all eternity. But yet, she stayed away.

Pain engulfed her. It felt as if someone's hand was inside her stomach, twisting moist fingers with sharp, gnarly fingernails. She gripped the counter, staring at the flowers, her vision going blurry.

"A promise unfulfilled is yucky."

Dottie turned. "You. You're not welcome here."

The girl with the green eyes giggled. "Harold begs me here every chance he gets."

"He doesn't want you here. Doesn't need you here."

"Is that why your little boy runs to me every chance he gets? Just the suggestion of me is enough to make him break out in hives. You hold him back. Naughty, naughty, Mother Death."

The little girl moved forward. Her feet made no sound on the floor. Looking into the two burning eyes made Dottie's brain slip. The soul inside her wanted to float away.

The closer the girl got, the wider her agony seemed to become.

"Stop!" begged Dottie, clutching to the counter, her legs nearly giving out. "Please. Leave."

"Bring him back, bring him back, back from black."

"Why do you go around like a wee lassie when you're anything but? D-Dead storm."

"Since we're friends, you can use my real name. Olca."

The name seemed to vibrate itself in Dottie's skull. Cold prickled down her legs. "You killed Bob. You sick fuck. No one deserves what you did to his family."

The air changed in the room as if a window opened. Olca rose into the air. "We all have our regrets. Isn't that right, you selfish wee cow?"

Dottie's hand slipped. She slapped the countertop, caught herself from falling. The crushed flower of a bluebell left its moisture on her palm.

She turned to stare up at the impossible demon. "If you think I won't rip that smile off your face, you've got another thing coming."

"Oh, my." Olca floated back to the floor. For a brief flash, the girl's eyes dimmed their emerald light. "So feisty. As for my appearance – little girls get what they want. Isn't that right, Dorothy? You never let anything stop you. Buried your mother in the process. She still calls your name in hate. It's delicious."

"What did you say?"

"Imagine being left to rot. *Worms in your guts, snails in your eyes, my, my, my.* She died because of you. Everything gone in the world, yet she wanted to see you. You left her alone. You killed her."

The petals made a soft crackling sound in Dottie's palm as she squeezed. "No. The dementia. And her fall. I had nothing to—"

"Don't you see? That's what killed her. Drove her mad. Ended her." The demon stepped forward, a flash of midnight green hiding behind her teeth. When Olca spoke, it was her mother's dry voice that came out. "*Your brothers wouldn't have treated me this way. You never had a motherly bone in your body. We're all waiting on you, Dottie. We'll see you packed to hell for what you did. Take. take, take. And how we'll laugh, and laugh, and—*"

"Stop it!" Dottie roared.

Her heart gave a sickening lurch. Its heavy beat seemed to flash in the shadows of her vision. Upstairs, she heard Pamela mumble as she got out of bed.

MOTHER DEATH

"My mum gave me plenty," said Dottie, forcing herself to stand straighter, puff out her meagre chest. "I will kill you. You hear me?"

Olca smiled. A scent like purpled, rotten things heated the space between them. Dottie shrunk back at the sight of the rows of tombstone teeth. Beneath the facade of a little girl, something ancient smiled up at her.

"Harold will be collected," said Olca. "He will be mine. I will ride the wave of adoration straight into your world. And I—"

"No!"

Dottie pounced forward, aiming a pathetic slap at the girl. As she drew near, she thought she saw Olca flinch. The girl's face started to slip, dribbling into something like molten custard. Olca shrieked, started to cover her face, then vanished into nothingness.

Dottie's hand moved through that nothing. The follow-through of the blow sent her off-balance. Her knee protested as she hit the ground, kneeling.

Although she hadn't hit anything, it felt like she'd just slapped five shades out of someone.

Her palm stung. When she raised it, the perfumed scent of the bluebells drifted up to her.

"I'll be your Mother Death, you wee witch."

Forty-six

"Harold?" said Dottie at the bottom of the stairs early the next day. "What you doing?"

Her son swayed as if pushed by a heavy wind. He glared down at her, menace and malice rising up his features. His dank hair hung loose over half his face. "Mother? Oh, Mother? Is that you dearest? Remember me?"

It had taken all of Pamela's pleading to agree to bring him back to life after staving in his skull. As she'd turned him over, touching his forehead, Pamela's eyes cast the blame that seemed stuck in her throat. *How could you kill him and leave him for so long?*

The merry, giggling way Harold held himself made ants crawl over Dottie's gums. His voice was different. He hadn't stopped killing himself since she'd brought him back. The look on his face each time he died was of pure elation.

"Do you remember your wee boy?" he said, swaying from side to side at the top of the stairs.

"How could I ever forget a face like that?" said Dottie. "Just, come down. Have a chat."

"One, two, buckle my shoe," chimed Harold as he flung his body forward, arms folded behind his back. "Three, four, knock at the—"

The smile on his face remained as his head got stuck between two spars in the banister, his neck cracking as his head stayed one way and his body twisted the other.

She sighed at the image of her dead-again boy, rolling up the sleeves of her shirt. The thinness of her forearms held her attention. It was as if two sets of bones poked out her clothes. She was wasting away into nothingness.

Harold's neck snapped further when she pulled at his limp legs. Sweat began to seep from the pores on her face as she hauled him down the stairs. The clown-mask smile made her pause. It was as if he'd been having the time of his life when the death moment came.

Green fire seemed to flutter in his unseeing eyes. His feet thudded on the stairs when she let go.

"W-What the actual fuck?" said Dottie.

The fire was gone. She was just jumpy, that was it. Seeing that little girl, that Olca, in everything. Had she really scared her away so easily?

She brought Harold back and lay a hand against his cheek, staring into his eyes as he slowly became himself again. "You're playing into her hands."

"There's no place I'd rather be."

"Well," she said, standing up, doing her best not to jerk about with the pain roaming free inside her, "I can't help you, then."

"You... You can help me. You need to help me. I wish I could make you see. Be a good mother. Be Mother Death." He closed his eyes and breathed deep. "It won't be long now."

Forty-seven

Dottie and Pamela hovered around Harold, keeping a death watch. The day dragged on in a vulgar silence, her and Pamela on edge. He wasn't even allowed to go to the toilet by himself.

A bright morning gave way to driving gale force winds that pressed at the window. It moaned through the window frame as they hunkered at the foldaway kitchen table, eating lunch.

Dottie chewed at her chicken mayo wrap, turning it over in her mouth until it was nothing but white paste. Her distended stomach didn't thank her for it. It seemed to bloat more with each bite, expanding pain.

Harold stared at his girlfriend, his jaw hung loose like he'd just had a lobotomy. The change in him these last weeks dragged at Dottie. She just wanted to drink herself stupid, forget that this was all her doing, her wish.

She should tell them. Tell them her plan. Make the pain stop for good. It was overriding everything.

Three sharp knocks thudded from the front door.

"Mrs. Matheson," said the gruff voice of PC Lithgow through the letterbox, "we need you to come with us."

Dottie looked around the table. Harold continued his vacant stare. Pamela gazed at the roll on her plate as if it held all of life's magic secrets.

"You phoned the police?" Dottie asked her.

"Look, I'm sorry, I—"

"Save it. Why?"

"Dan's brothers need to be taught a lesson. They can't just get away with it. I... I was pissed off. I'm sorry. I thought it would be a way to snap Harold out of it all, you know? I shouldn't have."

"Aye, you shouldn't have. What were you playing at?"

Dottie gulped a couple of pills before being escorted to the station. They didn't talk to her all the way there. Soon, she sat in a windowless room, a cup of hot, rancid coffee held between her hands. The room smelled of the sharpness of cold metal and cigarettes.

Singh and Lithgow sauntered into the room, scraping out cheap wooden chairs before they each took a seat.

"Am I under arrest or something? Getting the whole TV drama experience here."

Lithgow turned to Singh who nodded for him to continue.

"No. Not yet," said Lithgow, scribbling away at a thick pad on the table.

"Then, why am I here? Time's a-ticking, boys. Not got time for this shite."

"No. No, I don't suppose you do. And for that we are extremely sorry."

"So..."

"Pamela gave us a very unusual phone call. Up in arms about what happened to Harold, obviously. Now, let me be very clear, Mrs. Matheson." He stopped scribbling and looked her dead in the eye.

"The story she told me kinda goes against what you said when we first spoke. Might be enough to book you on obstruction."

"I'll obstruct you, you can of tuna. Do I look like I've got much time left to hang about for a trial?"

"Listen, here—"

Singh held up his hand, palm up. He recrossed his legs, taking his time, surveying her. In his other hand, he held a small brown envelope which he tapped a slow rhythm on. "First of all, is everything okay? Can I get you anything? Fresh coffee?"

"No, this shite is still clinging to the roof of my mouth, thank you very much."

"Harold okay after what happened?"

"Guess so."

"You know," Lithgow leaned in, his foul, almost flatulent breath rolled across to her, "we visited the grave."

Singh reached into the brown envelope and casually threw three photos onto the table as if he slammed down a winning poker hand.

Dottie shifted in her seat, leaning over to examine them. From somewhere on the old, dusty road, someone had taken photos of her and Pamela dragging Harold's corpse from his grave.

"Funny how it was close to the exact same spot as where Dan was buried," said Lithgow.

"You've been tracking us."

"Biggest question we have right now, Dorothy," said Singh, "is the reason these masked people are roaming about killing folks. If what Pamela says is true, and it is Dan's brothers doing the killing, surely they wouldn't have offed Dan first. Someone else is in the game. And we intend to find out exactly who that is."

Dottie felt her skin go clammy all over. The fluorescent tubes running the length of the ceiling suddenly hurt her eyes with their harsh light.

"So, why am I here?" said Dottie, trying her best to sound pissed off.

"Pamela said something... interesting. A real headscratcher," said Lithgow, itching at his scalp. "Told us what Harold does is real. Real magic. Like Santa or the Easter Bunny."

"What do you make of this claim?" said Singh.

It felt as if they'd inched their chairs closer. An itch on her forearm demanded to be scratched, but she held her hands still, fidgeting on her lap under the table. Acid rubbed its thin claws at the back of her throat, tasting of last night's vodka.

"You were snapped while dragging his dead body out of the ground," continued Singh. "And now, he's somehow alive. Full of life."

"Well, I wouldn't go that far, officers," said Dottie.

"So, you admit it, there is something *else* going on here? Something... *other*?"

She imagined Harold strapped to a hospital bed somewhere while the government ran tests on him, seeking to find the answers to his gift. Wires ran in and out of his skin. Various machines beeped.

"Cat got your tongue?" said Lithgow.

"Look at me," she said, holding her arms above the table, showing them her thin wrists. "You really think I could kill him? It was enough to just..."

"Just what, Mrs. Matheson?"

She stared up at the tube on the ceiling. The light flickered, making a small *ting* sound each time. "T-They came back for me."

Singh's eyes narrowed. "Who?"

"The Chuckle Brothers. Who you think? The arseholes who took my boy. T-They bundled me up, just like they did to Harold and took me out there. Told me they'd finished burying him, and that I'd have to dig fast."

The silent, sterile air seemed to increase in pressure. She could almost see the slow cogs turning in Lithgow's stupid head. Singh on the other hand chewed it over, examining her, looking for signs.

"It's surprising what a mother will do to save her boy," said Dottie, staring down at her hands. "Can barely lift my dinner, but when he was in that hole, something just came over me. You ever lost everything? Watched it slip away slowly, but surely? I was nothing in that moment. I clawed at the earth with that spade, and I managed to get to him while he was still breathing. Wasn't buried deep, thank the magpies. Was a close one." She held Singh's searching gaze. "Got lucky. I called Pamela to come get us. Once the men in the masks left us."

"They left you alone?" said Singh. "All that and they left you?"

"Guess so."

Lithgow smacked his lips like he'd just finished a bacon roll, his lips oily and wet. "Thank Scooby Doo for that. Wasn't ready to believe in any voodoo shite. Have us up with the loonies at Stratheden."

Some excitement seemed to leech from Singh's eyes. He stood to his full height, the chair almost toppling over. "I suppose our search continues for these masked men, in that case."

"Anything you can tell us about them, Mrs. Matheson?" said Lithgow.

"Did Pamela—" she dug a fingernail into her thigh.

"What?"

"Never mind. Please find the sick fucks in those masks. Get them done for assaulting an old maid nearly on her death bed."

MOTHER DEATH

Singh drove her home. The wind rocked the car as it turned bends, zooming past stottering druggies who wore their habits loud and proud in front of the police station that was charged with stopping that sort of thing.

"I'm really sorry to hear about your cancer," he said, navigating a small roundabout.

"Thanks. It's no cake walk, I'll tell you that."

"I bet not. Throat cancer buried my dad. Took him. One day he was fine, the next he complained of a sore throat and what he said felt like a grape stuck in his gullet. Three weeks. Gone. Just like that. I guess you don't know what you have until you watch it get taken from you."

"No. No, you don't."

They rode in a hefty silence all the way to her house. She thanked him and set her hand on the black door handle.

"You know, a lot of weird shit happens around these parts," said Singh, his intelligent eyes focusing on her in the rear-view mirror.

"I bet weird shit happens everywhere."

"Did you know Robert Hagerty?"

"Robert? Wait, Bob?"

He nodded, waiting.

She thought of Bob lying in his house, alone, the reek of decomposing flesh fluttering around the figurines that dotted his living room.

"He was a right nosy bastard, aye," she said. "Why'd you ask me that?"

Singh squinted his eyes at her, then pushed a button on the centre console. The locks clicked open.

"You take care of yourself, Mrs. Matheson. I'll be in touch."

Forty-eight

"Holy fuck, you're actually not dead," said Dottie as she did her best to walk straight and not like an old, withered crone. "Well done, matey. Blue Peter badge for you. Such a good wee boy, yes you are."

Harold lounged on the living room couch. The soles of his feet were almost black like he'd been walking around in the mud. He shot her a sideways look like she smelled like a barrel full of shite.

"Why you being weird?" he said.

She slumped next to him on the couch, forcing him to move his yucky feet. "Trip to the station will do that to you. Where's Pamela?"

"She's hella sorry for getting the cops in. Don't go through her, alright? We're kind of a team now."

She went to draw her knee up to her chest, hug it close, but the fire inside said no, so she set it down again. Harold pretended not to notice.

"Guess I don't have a lot of time left to be mad, eh?" she said.

"You don't know that. It could work out. Haven't you been at them to try chemo or whatever? Surgery?"

"Too late. Straight to stage four. Do not pass Go. I'm opting for the stay home option. Fuck going out in a hospital bed. I'll be pilled to the nines. I... I guess if you see me passing out or that you should get ready to call the ambulance. Get ready to—"

"I made you something."

Harold took out a small, beat-up looking box from his pocket. His hand trembled as he opened it, holding it out to her.

The breath caught in Dottie's throat. On a slim, gold chain was a large heart-shaped pendant, see-through as if made of glass. Inside the plastic heart were dried petals, some pale blue, some verging on purple.

"My mum's bluebells," said Dottie, holding it.

"I can barely remember what happened out there." He nodded in the direction of the back garden. "Alls I know is that I ripped up a heck of a lot of plants. I... I think it was her. The girl."

"Olca." She squeezed the pendant in her warm palm, thankful that it seemed thick enough, sturdy enough to handle the pressure. "That's the wee witch's name. Olca."

He stared at the gift, sighing, fidgeting with his thumbs. "It's stupid. I know. I just thought—"

"I love it." Dottie put her hands around the back of her neck and fastened the thin chain together. The pendant settled right where she imagined her own heart was. "It's perfect."

"I know I've put you through a lot."

"Ditto."

She wanted to throw her arms around him, give him the hugs she never gave him as a child. She stared down at her thin wrists, tracking the blue, protruding veins with a forefinger.

"Guess I better check on Pamela," said Harold, standing.

"Tell her it's all cool, aye?"

"Aye. All cool."

He gave her a peaceful smile and sauntered out the room. That smile filled her with hope. It was all over. Olca's hold on him was done.

She drank herself to tears, flicking through old photos on her phone. Pete creasing himself laughing after Jimmy had turned and whipped him in the face with his tail. Her leaning against the entrance of a pub she couldn't remember the name of, her skin browned, her hair lush, eyes afire with the things she wanted to do to her husband.

Back she went in time. The wedding. Harold looking awkward stuffed into a kilt, the promise of the handsome yet gangly man he'd become.

Everything was here for her and she didn't take the time to enjoy it fully, make sure she appreciated them. She downed her drink and let the glass drop to the floor as a spasm of pain took her.

By the time the sun had set, she was well on her way. The alcohol fuzzed its warmth with the four pills she'd taken, plus the patch of Fentanyl. It made her feel all rubbery, like she could just melt through the fabric of the couch forever.

The only thing that seemed to bring her any comfort was the feeling of running the pendant slowly back and forth, the motion tugging at the chain, tickling her neck.

Something smacked the front door with a loud *bang* that wavered in her eardrums. She stood and tiptoed to the window. A tall, white shape waited, its tail rigid and straight, pointed at the ground. The pale horse whinnied.

"You calling on me again, are you?" said Dottie.

She knew fine well that Olca could summon the horse in the confines of the house, drag her skinny arse out and do whatever. But the horse simply waited, looking like the automaton version of a real horse. The way it held itself was too still, too dead.

The room swirled around her, the edges of her vision swayed. The air held a chill like the promise of autumn as she stepped outside, standing beside the horse. Heat radiated from it, prickling her skin.

It whinnied again, a loud noise that she knew would normally have every neighbour darting for their curtains.

"Am I even really here?" said Dottie, staring into its deadened eyes. "Are we real anymore?"

It stomped at the ground, sending a small stone into Dottie's shin.

"Alright, alright," said Dottie. "Point taken. Let's ride. Where you taking me, stud?"

She hauled herself up onto the horse's aged saddle. Its hooves made no sound as it moved up the path and onto the dark, silent road. The moon lay bright in the sky, its dark craters staring down at her as she rode along on the pale horse.

"Wait? Wasn't the sun just setting two seconds ago? What's happening to my head?"

She closed her eyes, let the gentle sway of the beast take her far away.

How she longed to pace beside Pete and Sundance. It didn't matter that she could never keep up, it was the thrill of the chase. Tallying up her whole life, she'd never felt happier, more at peace than she did atop her black horse, the world eaten up under his hooves as they thundered along. She was certain there were memories of Harold as a baby that should've made her feel the same way. Truth was, she hardly remembered any of the milestones, took hardly any photos.

"You never should've been a mum, Dots," she whispered to herself.

She carried on, dream-like, toward some pre-destined place. Through some decrepit back streets, past rows of sheds, a large stone garage loomed, light spilling out an open door. To Dottie, it looked like a bomb shelter. A long piece of wood nailed along the top of its rusty shutters was weather-beaten, its wording lost to the wind and rain.

"And where have you brought me?" said Dottie, running her hand along the horse's neck.

Muffled sounds came out from the open door. The horse bowed its head and Dottie slunk off. The stench of motor oil caked everything, stains of it splotched on the thin concrete path she crept. Heavy-looking plastic barrels were set against the wall. She peered into the building, moving slowly, quietly.

Three men sat around a small wooden table, grunting, laughing, swigging from bottles as they played cards. Curls of blue cigar smoke played in the air above them. Just inside the door was a toolbox of sharp looking screwdrivers.

She turned back to the horse. It simply nodded, urging her on.

"What the fuck you expect me to do here?" she mouthed.

The horse shook its head as if to say, *You stupid, dumb bitch.* Its hooves made no sound as it moved closer. The mushroomy smell of its breath made her gag. She swallowed the sick back, careful not to give herself away. The thought of these three men burying her alive made her throat constrict. She massaged her throat, touched the heart pendent on its chain.

Moonlight glinted off something in the horse's mouth. She held out her hand and the horse dropped it into her palm.

A lighter.

It was hot in her hand, almost burning, like it was ready to go. She looked back into the large space where the three men went on cursing, scratching their balls, slapping each other on the back of the head. The scent of petrol and oil was so strong she could almost see the air wavering with its chemicals. Her eyes stung with it.

"You wee firebug," she whispered.

Grab some of the newspapers that sat at the door, light them, chuck them in and bolt. Half of Pitlair would probably go up with it.

She turned, looking up into the horse's eyes. A warped reflection of herself shone back at her as the horse nodded again, waiting, beckoning her to start the fire.

"It's all one big show to you," she said, patting the horse's side. "You'll never stop. Want to watch everyone suffer. That's your game, eh?"

The horse flashed its tail from side to side. Heat vibrated out of its sweaty coat – a smell that always transported her to better times.

"So, what will it be?" she said. "Barbequed mechanics? Watch them char? Smell them burn? Would you like that?"

The horse quivered under her touch.

"Tough."

She leaned inside the door, grabbed a screwdriver from the toolbox, pushed it into the horse's neck.

Cold blood swarmed over her hand. The horse bucked, shrieking at the sky. She watched the players continue at their poker, not hearing the eye-splitting noises the horse made. It turned its head, trying to bite her.

"You can't have him," she whispered. She took the tool out and stabbed the horse over and over until she felt her hand go useless. "You hear me, you little bitch?"

A pang of sadness hit her as she stepped back, clutching the blood blackened screwdriver to her chest. The horse fell, tried to stand, fell again, its eyes furious with pain.

"Now you know how I feel. Die. Die you little bitch. You can't have him. I won't let you."

The horse set its head on the path, curling up into a ball before its side stopped moving.

The creature flaked away, dispersing into the air.

Forty-nine

Pamela greeted her at the door, her eyebrows shooting up at the sight of the caked blood on Dottie's white t-shirt.

"Sight for sore eyes, eh?" said Dottie, kicking boots off, her feet screaming with relief.

It had been a long walk back to the house. As she walked under the twilight sky, she'd expected Olca to spring out at her, make her pay for killing the pale horse.

Dottie stared at Pamela, noticing her bloodshot eyes and reddened cheeks. Pamela wore an oversized black jumper with peach coloured splotches all over it like someone had lobbed bleach at her. The deep, swimming pool smell of chlorine hit Dottie in the nostrils.

"H-He won't stop," said Pamela. "He won't. No matter how much we beg. She won't let him stop. Like she has a hold of him, controlling him. Bleach. Fucking bleach. Upended a whole bottle before I could stop him. It was awful. Worse than anything we've done."

"Show me."

He lay on his back in his bed. A dried river of curdled bile and crimson streaked down his chin, pooling on his stomach. The stench was enough to make her turn her head and add her own puke to the floor.

His glazed doll's eyes were the worst sight of all. He hadn't passed over like a contented wee bunny this time. The yellow of his skin and his thin frame made him look like a skeleton twisted in agony.

Dottie leaned in closer. Despite the chemicals and the puke, she could still smell the horse blood that had covered her hand and stained her t-shirt.

She traced her forefinger in a gentle figure eight along his forehead, the skin cold to the touch. The golden glow that fuzzed out of the end of the finger made her giggle. "E.T. phone home."

Behind her, Pamela chuffed and shook her head.

As Harold came back from the land of the dead, his insides mended by the grey things that stitched him up, she thought of the dying horse and the vengeance the little demon girl would take. More of the chemical stink spewed out of Harold's mouth as he came back to life. He shifted, spewing a puddle of it by Dottie's feet.

"Och, you'll ruin my socks," said Dottie, stepping back, covering her stinging eyes. "Come on, big dude. Cough it all out. There you go."

"W-What have you done?" said Harold, his voice straining between gasps.

"What you mean?"

His face scrunched up and he sobbed. "What did you do, Mum? What did you do?"

"I may have pissed her off. Why? What happened?"

"She was not pleased, let's just say. Or maybe you could say she strung me up and flayed my skin off. Killed my soul off, piece by slow piece then started all over again. Nothing's hurt so much my whole life. Y-You're not supposed to feel pain when you die. It's supposed to stop."

"Maybe then, you shouldn't kill yourself every chance you get? If she'd turned on you and—"

He exploded up into a sitting position. "You will not take that away from me! I need it. It's all I have."

"God," said Pamela, leaning in the doorway, "make this all stop."

He glanced at her then turned the full power of his anger on Dottie. "See what you've done, Mother? See what you've turned me into?"

"Me? You done this, remember. I was just supposed to protect you. It's you who's dragged out the fucking demons from their games of scrabble to give you their full attention. You who turned it all into an act for money. Don't go blaming me just because I enabled it all. You're the one—"

"Shut it!" Pamela roared, stamping her foot on the floor. Her shoulders heaved up and down, tremored. "Just stop, alright? I can't take this anymore, H, look at you. Can you honestly say this is a way to live?" She straightened and closed her eyes, seeming to come to a decision. "It's me or her, H. Me or death. I can't watch you do this to yourself anymore. Decide."

"I..." Harold shook his head, then groaned. He clawed at the sides of his head. "Don't you think I know how stupid it all is? I swear each time is the last, but I can't stop myself. I need it. That empty, beautiful space. Draws me in. It melts me away like nothing else."

"Wish I made you feel that way."

"Oh, don't be like that. That's not what I mean. You'd do it, too, if you could."

"Are you actually saying you'd draw me into this if you could make it happen? Lay me down on the bed next to you while we share a bleach daiquiri? Hold hands so sweetly while our insides rot? You're sick."

"One dead bastard at a time, please," said Dottie. She stared down at her bloated stomach, blinking. She could've sworn something moved around in there like a baby kicking.

"Can you take this seriously?" shouted Pamela, stepping up to her.

"Calm down, hen. No need to get in my face."

"No? Don't you see it? You're the one that keeps saving him. Why do you do it? If he didn't have you, he wouldn't be in this mess to start with. Maybe it'll be better when you curl up and die."

Dottie swirled her tongue along the sharp ridges of her teeth, staring into Pamela's eyes. She could see panic and regret coming to their surface. Something inside Dottie threatened to boil over. She turned her attention to Harold who watched with a pleased, half-lidded grin.

"Listen to me, Harold," said Dottie. "People have died because of this. That wee Tonya. Bob. Dan. You know all about that. Olca showed you."

"Dan?" whispered Pamela.

"I can't stop it," said Harold. "I can't. I won't."

"I'm not the one who's gonna take it away." Dottie reached over and took Harold's clammy hand. "Sweet bitch cancer is taking care of that." She shot Pamela a cold look and returned to Harold. "One fine day you'll wake up and I'll be dead as a doorknob."

Harold itched at his neck. The sound of his rough nails scraping skin made something crawl about on Dottie's skin.

"You?" said Pamela. "It was you? You murdered Dan? The drugs. That random trip you took that night. I see it all, now. Telling me to shut my trap when the cops were here."

Silence spread its heavy cloth over them, turning them all into statues. Dottie felt Pamela glaring at the side of her head. She kept a stiff neck, not turning to meet that stare. "Hate me all you want, but—"

Pamela stomped out the room, slamming the bedroom door closed. Her feet pounded down the stairs and then she was out the front door and gone.

"I had high hopes for that one," said Dottie.

"She'll be back."

Dottie ran her tongue along the dry roof of her mouth. The white, powdery taste of pills came to her, making her heart beat a little harder.

"We need to beat this thing, Harold. She's coming for us."

"Gran was wrong about you."

"What?"

He lay back down, setting a limp hand over his chest, staring at the ceiling. "Funny stuff to tell a bairn, come to think of it. She used to sit me on her knee. Told me... Well, let's just say she wasn't your biggest fan."

"Kinda knew that already."

"She was wrong. All this is because you tried to do your best."

"I—" Tears welled in the corners of her eyes, the emotion taking her words away.

"You sounded like a right handful when you were wee."

"Still am."

"Aye, I guess so. Never had you down as someone who'd kill a horse."

The memory of the horse's blood chilling her hand as she'd ended its life made her skin break out in goosebumps. "That thing wasn't a horse."

"Nothing is what it seems."

She clasped the heart pendant, staring down at her boy all grown. A boy who'd have to navigate life on his own and soon. "I'm so fucking sorry. I'm sorry. I'm such a cow. A selfish cow."

"Aye, but you're my selfish cow, though."

Dottie wiped a tear off her cheek, a little giggle worming its way out of her, releasing some of the pain she felt. The smile fell away from Harold's face.

"What is it?" she said.

"The answer is over there. Maybe there's a deal to be struck. Some way to—"

"No. I won't have it. We're done."

"What's to stop her from being able to fix all of this?"

"It's not just about us, Harold. People have died. More people will die if she gets her way and breaks into the real world. She nearly had me blow up that garage where Dan and his brothers work. We just need to stop you from dying. Cut her off. I know it'll be hard, but we can fix it."

"No one can fix this. It's all fucked." He sighed. The smell of rancid swimming pool drifted in the space between them. "Either way, she's coming. You wanna wait around to see what she'll do? Or do we take the fight to her?"

Fifty

As the quiet morning light seeped its way across the living room, Dottie soaked into the couch. She'd tried to sleep, but there wasn't a position she could get into where the cramped ball of agony didn't jab her with its spikes.

Upstairs, Pamela and Harold roared it out, arguing about everything in the fierce way only fresh lovers can. Pamela had swanned back into the house in the wee hours. Their eyes had met, then she slunk up the stairs in silence.

Dottie sipped at a rum, savouring the taste, but unable to gulp the thing down – nothing stayed down for very long.

She made her slow way to the kitchen, going into her cupboard. Two white pills sat cradled in her palm.

Pamela was back. Harold was fine, would always be fine. If they could make it through this they could make it through anything.

The two pills turned to ashy chalk as she crunched them in her mouth. Her tongue protested at the sharp medicinal taste. As she bit into them, turning the pills to dust, she stared at the packets of pills remaining.

Tears burst from her, starting in her chest. She leaned on the kitchen counter, head in hands. The image of her Pete hovering behind her, placing a calloused hand on her shoulder, breathing of her hair, made her ache inside. The loneliness was a physical thing.

"Why'd you do it, babe?" she said, her voice hitching through her sobs.

Life had been perfect until she found him before that Christmas day. She could still remember how cold it had been. How she crept into the bathroom to join him, get him to satisfy an itch in the way only he could. And then kneeling by the bath, breaking apart.

Pamela's voice streamed to her from upstairs. "I love you, you big dopey bastard. Stop this shite. You're killing all of us."

Dottie craned her ear up at the ceiling, but could hear only distant mumbles as the fight seemed to simmer down.

Don't you see? Don't you understand? Pete had said to her in her delirium when she'd spent the night alone at the hospital.

Pamela's scream burst through her thoughts. Dottie could almost feel it through the soles of her feet.

"Harold?" Pamela yelled, sounding like someone backing away from a fight, palms up. "Don't. Argh!"

They struggled about, tipping things over. Dottie wrestled with herself whether to go up and put an end to it before it got out of hand. Would Harold hit a girl? She'd never seen him hit anything before.

The flow of chemicals seemed to swirl inside her, heavy with numbing, eye-closing fire. She concentrated on the noises upstairs.

Something hit the floor, crashing through what sounded like a wooden table that splintered. Then all was quiet.

"Harold?" Dottie yelled. "Everything alright?"

The offbeat *shuffle, thud* of footsteps made her back straighten. Harold made his slow way down the stairs. The breeze outside ceased its press on the windows. The fridge buzzed its incessant noise. The whole world seemed to hold its breath, waiting.

"H-Harold? That you?"

Her heart bumped loud in her chest in weak, uneven pulses. Her vision clouded in a red film. She tried to blink it away. Her heavy eyelids wanted to shut up shop, bid her go to sleep one last time.

She felt Olca's green presence. It was her, somehow, coming to get her.

Take the fight to her, Harold had said last night.

"How?" she whispered, holding her hand over her mouth.

No matter how loud she could scream or kick or claw, nothing could stop death's train from stopping at her station. She was done. Ready to crumble. No fight left in this empty carriage.

Harold stood in the doorway, swaying on the balls of his feet. His long, baggy t-shirt reminded her of a mental patient, the way it seemed to sway around his knees.

"Stop with the freak act, Harold. Quit looking at me like that. Harold?"

His mouth moved, bobbing up and down. Scattered words hissed out of him as he stared at the floor, hauling his legs forward as if they were alien appendages.

"*There,*" his meek voice shuffled out of his loose mouth, "*there we go. Onwards and onwards, flow by flow. To the kitchen we go. Eatery of pleasant bliss and white things missed.*"

"What in the fuck are you gibbering about?" said Dottie, pushing herself away from the counter, placing her legs apart to make it look like she wouldn't back down.

He continued onward, his head bowed low, dangling. He stared at the floor. Fluorescent light bounced off his black, oily hair. He smelled of purple worms and ancient, dusty books.

She gulped and stepped forward, placing a hand on his chest, forcing him to stand straighter, meeting her eye. In his irises, green light flickered and dimmed like flame struggling to find fuel.

He shoved by her without an effort, like she was nothing but a ghost.

When he spoke, it sounded like squirming maggots multiplied inside his throat. "*Through the door open, into the world. Come my boys, come my girls. Up and up the stairs we go. Up and up to find the glow.*"

Something in her marrow told her to bolt. Run out into the pre-dawn light, find help.

Harold stood before the kitchen counter, swaying from foot to foot, a ring of sweat staining the back of his t-shirt with a dark semi-circle like an upside-down grin.

"We want the same thing, your Harold and I."

"Get the fuck out my son's body."

It giggled, sending a shiver of ice down Dottie's spine as it turned to face her. "You don't see it yet, do you? You can't stop it. No matter the game, death forever wins. It levels all beneath its hooves."

"Shame you haven't got any hooves after what I—"

Harold grabbed her by the throat, lifting her into the air. She kicked feebly as the pressure built behind her eyeballs. She strained for air, choked.

"You will pay for taking my steed," said Olca, small voice rumbling through Harold's throat, alien and multiple.

Dottie stared down into the fiery eyes as she flailed at the iron grip that closed around her neck. Sparks of emerald green sputtered out, returning to Harold's familiar grey eyes before it started again, trying to catch hold, take him over.

Dottie felt her face going thick with trapped blood. Her voice struggled out. "Hope losing the horse hurt, you wee bitch."

It let her go. Her arse thumped to the floor, sending a jolt of pain through her coccyx, gripping her abdomen.

"You can't hurt me," said the Harold-thing. "Silly toy."

Dottie rubbed at her throat, shuffling herself back until she rested against the doorframe. Vibrant dots and lines slashed about in her vision. She closed her eyes, the strobing lights making her head spin. Her throat burned for air as she sucked in lungfuls.

"You need me," said Dottie, glaring up at her possessed son.

Harold's face morphed into angry, sharp lines. He kicked a cupboard, putting a dent into its middle. "Not for long. My time is soon. I'm so close, I can almost taste it. I will show you what death can do."

"Bring it on, you evil cunt."

She expected the Harold-thing to take a run at her, to football kick her between the eyes. She almost wished for it. Maybe that would bring about the end. She could say she gave it a good shot.

Olca leered down at her, a smile vexing up the side of Harold's face like a kid thumbing Playdough into a grin. It turned, opened the cupboard door, reached in, brought out her boxes of pills and the secret baggy Martin had given her.

"W-What you doing?" said Dottie, hauling herself up.

"I feel the rush of chemical numbness deep in your blood. Free yourself, Dorothy. Free yourself of its hold of you. And maybe, just maybe, you'll be able to see things from my point of view."

"No!"

With his back turned, Harold emptied the pill bottles, popped all the pills loose from their casings until the counter was littered with them. Dottie ran at him, slapping at his back, trying to get him to stop, but he was a tree rooted to the ground. She picked up a pot and whacked him on the back of the head, smashed a bottle of rum over him, nothing.

He put the pills down the sink.

She recoiled at the sound of them rolling about in the pipes like loosened teeth. When he was done, he tore up the Fentanyl patches and covered them with water, before ripping them up, sending them down the sink as well.

"Let's see if your courage came from your heart or from your desperate doctor friend. *Round and round the drain it goes, drag it down the drain you know, pulled each way and split apart, now broken without white, white heart.*"

"Why?"

"Because you deserve it, that's why."

"Don't take him from me. He doesn't deserve this. He's the only good thing I've ever done. And I fucked it up."

The thing blinked and bobbed its head like it struggled to keep itself from falling asleep. "M-Mum? I—"

Dottie stepped forward and wrapped her arms around him. "You're back."

"I... I'm sorry." His cold hands rubbed at her back as he wrapped his arms around her, hugging her tight to his chest. "I tried to stop her. She shut me out like she was pushing my soul away. I had to cling on. I saw everything. My hand around your..."

Dottie turned her head, looking at the drain where all her miracle friends had been washed down. The pain was already blossoming back, firing up.

"Ssshh, you're back now, that's all that matters." Dottie pulled him closer. "That's all that matters."

Fifty-one

The world around Dottie bleached of all colour. The solid presence of Harold phased away, leaving her alone, cold. It was as if she'd taken a picture on an old camera and was now looking out at a negative world. A wind played through her hair. Bat-like creatures glowing blue trails snaked their way through the air around her.

"You're not in Pitlair anymore, Doto," said Dottie.

It felt as if she walked through space, out in the open. The place tasted like smoky charcoal.

Was this it? Had she died in her boy's arms?

"Not a bad way to bow out," she said, hugging herself, stepping silent steps, going nowhere.

At the edges of the world, the blaring white images of leafless trees swayed in the wind. This was it. She was being taken. Blissful end. She welcomed it. Closed her eyes and imagined being a young, lithe version of herself. A wee filly prancing across this field of nothingness.

"Harold..."

She opened her eyes.

The dull kitchen stared back at her, judging her. Pain throbbed in her gut, doubling her over.

In sweaty desperation, she bent over the sink licking at it, hoping that some part of the pills or the Fentanyl had stuck to the stainless steel.

She straightened, only coming away with a taste of metal and a fresh spark of shame. Sink licker. A new low.

Harold wasn't in the kitchen with her. How much time had passed during her wee voyage? Had she really stepped out of this world and into another or was her brain just fried?

As she made her way into the living room, the negative world imposed on her vision again, flashing before her. One second she was in the living room, the sun blindingly bright through the open curtains, the next it was black with creatures glowing in the sky around her like zooming fireworks.

A figure stood before her, reaching out a hand. Despite the light radiating off of him, she'd recognise her Pete anywhere.

She threw herself at him. When she tried to wrap her arms around his broad frame, she phased right through, almost falling.

He flashed her a wide, brilliant smile, setting a ghost hand against her cheek. She felt it there like she'd walked through a fine mist.

"There's my man," she said, leaning into it, feeling the hand fuzz through her skin. "You here to collect me, stud?"

Pete motioned with his hands, frantic, saying something in a stream that never met her ears. She'd never seen him in such a state. He was Mr. Unflappable, her rock when she was in a state. Her silent, steady shoulder.

He pointed at her chest, his eyes going wide, desperate words tumbling silently out of his mouth. She could see his teeth and tongue like the images of an x-ray.

"Why did you cut yourself up like that?" said Dottie. "Left me to find you in that state."

Pete's hand paused, a finger still pointing at her chest. His face trembled, the dimple on his chin quivering as he tried to hold himself together. His lips moved again.

"Hey, cowboy, I can't hear you. Pete? Pete? Look at me?" She stepped forward, placing her palm on his cheek. The hand phased through, finding no warmth. She groaned. "I need you."

He whipped his head around as if thunder cracked the sky, shaking his bones. When he turned back to face her, she could see a sheen of jumpy nightmare in his normally calm eyes despite the blaring reversal of colour.

He leapt at her, throwing his arms around her. Dottie felt the shiver run through all of her. For an instant, it took the pain away. The worry. Everything.

And then he was gone.

Alone, she stood in the hallway of her house, hugging herself, tears cooling on her cheek. The whiff of sweaty shoes at the front door reached her. "Why did you have to leave me the way you did? Take me back. Take me. Don't you see I'm ready?"

Heat filled her world, building from her core. She slumped to the floor, curling herself into a ball. She still rode the reserves of the pills she'd chewed not so long ago, but the unguarded pain that was coming would write her off, she knew.

Feeling like her end was coming, she hauled herself up, needing to see Harold.

The world blinked out of existence. Another figure stood before her.

"H-Harold?"

The sickly green glow coming off his negative image made her step back. He came closer with slow, graceful steps, stared into her eyes, mouthing the words slow.

Come get us.

"What?"

We're here.

Dottie stood at the bottom of the stairs, back in the real world. When she blinked, the flashes of colour burned into her vision. A frustrated noise growled out of her, rumbling in her throat. Eyeing the stairs, they seemed an impossible mountain to climb.

She gripped the banister. By the time she set her shaky foot on the landing at the top, sweat poured off her in cold drops.

"Harold?" she said, her voice like dry twigs rubbing together. "Pamela?"

They both lay on the bed like a couple of discarded dolls, glassy eyes staring at the ceiling. Both their mouths were agape, yawning wide with pain.

The sight of her dead son never got any easier to witness. Seeing him clasp hands with his dead sweetheart stung something new within her. The familiar tang of iron was on the air again, stuck to the roof of her mouth.

Dottie collapsed to her knees, clawing at her sallow cheeks. Congealed blood marked the side of the duvet, puddled on the carpet in a crimson ring.

Harold had called to her from the other world, hadn't he? *Come get us.*

"You stupid, stupid bastard. What did you do? What did you do?"

She moved closer to the bed. The sun warmed the drawn curtains, blazing red around their edges. Large splinters of wood lay across the floor from the broken desk where Harold normally hunched over his laptop. She remembered the crashing sound from earlier and the silence that had followed.

On the bed, Pamela's neck was lumpy, her head twisted at an unnatural angle. It looked like he'd knocked her out then slit her wrists before coming down the stairs. The blood still trickled out of his wrists, fresh and coppery.

Silence pressed down on her like a physical hand on her shoulders. She thought about going downstairs and calling the ambulance, stating that he killed himself with his girlfriend, confining him to the land of the dead forever. She'd visit him soon. Real soon. And they could be a family again.

She slapped her own face, the *smack* resonating in the dark room. "You selfish arsehole."

She would not deny Harold the life he was meant to lead, no matter how tempting it was to let him die so she could be with him.

Dottie reached over and closed Pamela's eyelids. They made a dry, *click* noise that she felt in her bones. "I'm sorry, doll. You were far too good for the likes of us." She kissed Pamela's cool forehead. "Love you, lass."

Anger pulsed within her when she pressed her hand against Harold's warm forehead, drawing him back to life, back from the negative world. Each time her eyes were drawn to the sleeping beauty next to him, she wanted to reverse the process, leave him in there.

Harold coughed, the bed creaking under him when he shifted about. He clamped his eyes shut as the life seemed to thunder through him like a shot to the arm.

"Go on, then," he said, sitting up on his elbows, nodding at Pamela's still body. "Bring her back."

"What?"

"Bring her back. Just like you do with me. She promised."

Dottie's breath was so hot it felt like a furnace billowed with each indrawn breath. "Who promised?"

"You know... *her*. Olca."

"What did she promise you, Harold?"

"Made her a deal."

Dottie closed her eyes. "Are you completely gone?"

"Och, don't act like I ate your last bag of crisps, I did this for you. For us. She said that if I crossed over with Pamela, you'd be free to go, and—"

"We're still in the shit from the last deal we made."

"Last deal *you* made."

Everything suddenly seemed so far away, like she was being dragged up to the clouds, staring down on everything. She reached out to touch the covers on the bed, her thin wrist elongating, stretching, finally touching.

"She made you think I could bring Pamela back?" said Dottie. "You killed her, Harold. The one good thing in your whole fucking life! Dead."

"I'm trying to find our way out of this hell – the hell you made, Mother. Just bring her back, for fuck's sake. Hurry."

"She was the sweetest wee lamb, and you thought you'd help her slice her wrists open, that it? How did that feel? That how you show your love?"

"That's how Pete showed you, isn't—"

She slapped his face with about as much strength as an idle breeze. His face didn't even move. Her anger flashed into cackled, maddened laughter, which gave way to molten stabs of fresh agony.

Harold sneered up at her, then his own pain fell across his features as he turned his attention to Pamela. "Olca promised you'd be able to save her."

MOTHER DEATH

Dottie nodded, her side twitching fire as she shuffled around the other side of the bed, stepping in a thick pool of blood. Cold seeped through her socks as she leaned over the dead body.

This girl had been a light when they needed it the most. She'd shared in their secret. Dottie prayed to the heavens and whoever listened to desperate souls that she could save Pamela, bring her back from the clutches of the girl with the green eyes. Back from death.

Her fingers seemed like gnarled twigs as she reached out, beckoning all of her energy as she hovered over Pamela's forehead.

"I can't be without her," said Harold. "Bring her back. You have to bring her back."

Dottie lightly pressed Pamela's forehead with her index finger, waiting, holding her breath.

Nothing.

No spark of energy. No promise of a golden glow.

"Mum?"

She closed her eyes and summoned the last of her strength. Nothing.

"Won't work," said Dottie, slumping down on the edge of the bed.

Harold held both hands over his mouth. "No! She said you had the power. Try harder."

"She played you, son."

"No. No, it can't—"

Dottie reached over and squeezed his hand. "This is what she does. Pamela's gone. She's gone. You hear me? And... And the cops will see it was you who did it. Your marks all over her. You need to go bury her. Bury her now."

The slight light buzzing in through the curtain reflected in the two tracks of tears streaming down his face. He looked up at her. "What?"

"You need to get rid of the body. I'll clean up everything else. Make it look like she split with you."

"That little witch. She lies. She lies so bad. What we gonna do?"

"Drive. Find a spot. Bury her. Bury her deep. Say your goodbyes. I know it sucks, but you need to take her."

"Alone?"

The sight of his lost little boy eyes cut her deep. "I can barely move, never mind sling a spade or drive a car."

"And when I'm done, what will we do? How do we stop her?"

Find that little bitch, drag her into the real world and set her on fire, is what she wanted to say. The anger made her head pulse in time with her heartbeat. She placed her hand around the heart pendant and slowly moved it back and forth, placing its iron-tasting necklace in her mouth.

"I don't know, yet," said Dottie, "but I know we're not finished with her."

Fifty-two

The pain bared its fangs, making a fresh meal out of her. Just when she thought it had peaked, a fresh fire would sizzle and froth to life. She writhed on the couch, unable to move, unable to sit still, in an agony of in between.

Time took on a marshmallowy quality. By the time Harold came back, it had grown dark outside. He paced the living room, his words barely registering. A sweat trickled down his temples like he was in the clutches of some tropical fever. The room filled with the stench of moist dirt. She hoped it covered the shameful stink of her own urine.

Harold stomped towards the open door, slapping at the tears falling down his face.

"Don't do anything stupid," she pleaded though her voice came out a pathetic moan. "She's close. Can feel it in my bones."

"Don't you tell me what to do," he turned back, yelling down at her so hard she felt dots of spit on her face. "Just one more. One more, then I'll quit. Argh! This is all your doing. How does it feel, eh? Bringing all this death."

"You..."

"What? What is it?"

"You. It was only ever for you."

"No, it fucking wasn't. You can't just—" he groaned then marched up the stairs.

She felt each of his steps vibrate in her swollen belly. She felt she'd give birth to black death any moment now. Drip her guts all over this old couch. Her time was very close. Death's cold wisp played at the back of her neck.

"Saddle up Jimmy for me," she said, thinking of Pete. "I'm coming."

She closed her eyes, wishing that the room would stop spinning. The last few weeks played themselves out in her mind. Old Smokes and his regretful offer. Harold playing superstar, building a cult following. Jimmy. Tonya. Bob. Pamela. Gone. So much needless death. So much blood.

"You showed them all, son," she said to herself, remembering the awe of the crowds. "Showed them something they'll never forget."

At least he had his stack of dough to set him up for life.

Floorboards creaked above her as Harold paced and paced, mumbling to himself. She could almost feel his raw emotion phase down to her.

"Don't do it, son," she said, her voice all croaky and pathetic. "Fight it."

His steps quickened. He punched things, knocked things over, yelled notes of anguish until his throat gave up.

"Stay away!" Harold screamed so loud it made Dottie's eyelids quiver. "No. Get out. You can't have me. It's too late. No. No!"

Dottie forced herself to roll off the couch. Pain fizzled in the corners of her vision. She breathed, kneeled on one knee, willing herself to stand, go help Harold fight off the demon thing trying to claim him.

"*What's the time, Mother Wolf?*" chimed Harold, standing in the hallway.

His eyes were circlets of green fire, his voice a duality of his and the demon's. The sound of it grated at her brain like an electric buzz saw. His plastic grin looked like it would split open his face in a red, pumpkin smile.

"Shit." Dottie slapped at the floor, forcing herself up. "Get out of him, you filthy wee bitch."

"Bitch?" Harold turned, a dainty hand clutched to his heart. "Is that how you treat a guest in your own house? After all the glory I've fed you."

"Given us nothing but death, you wretch."

It moved forward with a smooth, feminine grace. The streetlight glowed on the beads of sweat on Harold's bare chest.

"Death was already here," said Olca. "It's in the walls. Such a pity, you know? All that power. Potential. Harold was building something that legends will speak of in echoes. It could've been so much more. I will make it so much more."

"W-What are you gonna do?"

"Once Harold's soul quits with its grip on this vessel, I will take over. I'll make the world bleed. And they'll pray to death. My time is soon. His spirit wanes."

Her son stood a few paces away, leering down at her. Somehow, the tips of his fingers seemed like claws, his hair like a nest of snakes.

Olca raised a finger, pointing at Dottie's stomach.

White pain rushed through her and she collapsed into a ball on the floor, heaving red lines of blood into the carpet.

"Please. Stop." Dottie wrapped her arms around her stomach as the pain climbed. "Leave him. Let us go."

"No." Olca stomped Harold's foot like a rebellious kid. The two voices made Dottie's head want to implode. "*The suffering, the suffering, all a merry offering. The suffering, the suffering, flays away the mothering.*"

Dottie opened her mouth to scream her anger, tell the unholy thing to cease its singing, but all that came from her was a rumbling wail followed by another globulous line of pink saliva.

"Y-Your horse suffered," hissed Dottie, staring up into the emerald fires. "Shrieked like a wee banshee. If I wasn't laid up like this, I'd make you scream that way, too."

"You creatures. All the same. Each time, I give you a chance to be gods among the riff-raff that squander their lives here. This place," Olca closed its eyes and breathed in deep through its nose, "reeks of such desperation. Home. That's why I bide here. But why can't you ever learn to accept what you wish for, eh? Why do you have to break down and claim it's all my fault? Silly rats." Olca waved her hand to the side and the pain in Dottie's stomach eased a shade. "Almost wasn't worth drawing Pete to his death in the first place."

Dottie raised her head. "What?"

"I watched him beg for you as I made him cut those red lines across his wrists."

"Pete? You killed my Pete? No. No. Why?"

"The stink of desperation was on this house. Sometimes people just need that last little *push* before calling out for help. Before they stop caring who heeds their call. I needed that to be you. To make you that desperate. It was beautiful."

Guilt swarmed inside. Dottie set her forehead on the carpet and roared, tasting dust on her tongue, inhaling it as she sobbed.

Pete hadn't deserved the blame she placed at his door. Since last Christmas, she'd harboured a secret hate towards him for choosing to quit like he did. But he hadn't.

"He... He didn't want to leave," said Dottie. "He still loved me."

"It's enough to make you sick." The thing took on the rough baritone of Pete's voice. Hearing it made Dottie feel the world was swallowing her, pulling her down.

"Stop!" said Olca in Pete's voice. "You can't make me. No. I won't. No. Tell Dottie... Tell Dottie... No. Shit, argh! What are you? Stop. Arrrgggh!"

Dottie pushed herself up. She glared up into the demon's eyes. "You don't have a soul. You're nothing. You hear me? Nothing!"

Olca clapped its hands and jumped up and down on the spot like a cheering kid. "*Make them dance, make them squirm, make them beg, make them burn.*" The thing's face changed from merriment to stone-cold serious with no transition. "Hey? Wanna see something cool?"

It head-butted the wall.

The sound Harold's forehead made had Dottie's nerves jumping into her mouth. It did it again and again until it split the skin, showing white bone beneath.

Olca turned to face her, a jolly smile strolling up Harold's face as the blood trickled down, staining his teeth that glowed with a faint green light.

Webs of grey shot between the wound, drawing it tighter, patching back together until the skin was smoothed over.

"Y-You can heal him?" said Dottie.

"No. I can heal *me*. Once I drive him out, there'll be nothing but me. Party time!"

"I'll give you what you want."

"Oh, will you now?"

"Just tell me what it'll take to send you back to hell."

"Hell?" The Harold-thing smiled. "You've got it all wrong, dearie. I'm an angel, see?" It held Harold's arms up high. "*Soar, soar, high, high, sky, sky, die, die!*"

Olca took a small gun from Harold's back pocket and placed the grey barrel in his mouth. Dottie darted forward, holding her palms up. The green in his eyes faded.

"Mum?" he muffled over the metal, voice back to normal.

"Don't—"

The gun went off. It splattered red and purple gunk up the wall. Harold crumpled to the floor, the gun dropping out of his hand. Gunsmoke curled in front of her, tasting of spent lead.

"You fucking bitch," she screamed.

Dottie fell next to him, hugging him tight. The skin was ice-cold to the touch. He shook in her grip, coming back to life without her touching his forehead.

Thick blood slipped under her palm as she used the wall to haul herself up. The hole in the back of his mouth stitched itself back up and the demon stood, clapping its hands.

"Oh, this is going to be ever so much fun," said Olca. "I wonder what else I can make this body do. I'll make them chant my name, join in."

"You're not fit to wear that skin. My boy is so much more than you'll ever be."

Olca's nostrils flared as it stepped forward, placing its forehead against hers, spitting into her face when it spoke its two conjoined voices. "I walk the veils. *Achmacalla* sings my name. You have no idea what I am."

"I know you reek like a wet mushroom. Get out my boy."

Olca gave a rumbling, ogrish cackle. It held its hands before its face, turning them slowly, spidering the fingers as if testing them out. "I'm done with games. Time to go night-night, Dorothy. Done well to last this long with the black snakes in your belly."

The room went dark around the edges of her vision. It raised its hand up, fingers splayed.

Dottie rested her hands by her side, welcoming whatever came next. She couldn't fight this otherworldly thing any more. Her time was up.

Smoke sprayed over her feet.

For a second, Dottie thought she was back at the side of the stage watching smoke machines eat Harold's legs. Olca froze, its eyes going wide, looking down into the rising fog.

Old Smokes burst from the floor, grabbing Olca by the wrist and pushing the thing backwards.

"I've done my time," yelled Old Smokes. "We don't want you here."

He left a trail of grey behind him like a lit cigarette as he struggled with Olca. Dottie watched, clutching at her heart pendant, unsure whether to dive in or call for help.

The two impossible demons attacked one another, growling. Olca's maddened voice screeched between Dottie's ears. "I'll confine you and your family's souls back to the box! You want that? You ungrateful scum."

"You can't be allowed to live," Old Smokes roared. "Be gone. Be gone. Be gone. No!"

Olca dug its fingers into his forearms, drawing him closer. A fierce wind flowed through Dottie's hair as she stepped forward, wanting to join the fight. She froze.

Olca's green eyes flared, spitting out shoots of emerald lightning. It opened Harold's jaw, cracking bone and popping muscle as it leaned back, mouth open at an impossible angle. The strong taste of ozone filled the room as Olca sucked in a deep breath.

Dottie stumbled forward, drawn in by a sharp tug caused by Olca's inhalation. She grabbed hold of the couch. "Stop. He only wants to be free!"

"Oh, I'll give him freedom," said Olca in Dottie's mind, not moving Harold's lips. "Come to me, papa."

Olca stomped at the floor, leaned back, put all her strength into sucking in air. Old Smokes started to drift apart. Olca drew him into her, into the open maw. Drips of silver saliva fell from Olca's chin as the smoky form of Old Smokes came undone.

Old Smokes turned his head towards Dottie, the roiling cloud of his features almost gone. He nodded, then his black clothes collapsed into a pile by Olca's feet.

"My, my," said Olca, seeming to stand taller than Harold ever did in the body, "how noble. Seems you have all the guys just tripping over themselves to die for you. How lucky you are."

Dottie ran forward, aiming a slap at her son's fevered face. He wasn't there. She fell to the ground in a heap, tripping over the clothes Old Smokes left behind.

Olca appeared behind her, giggling away, dancing from foot to foot. "Now it is time to leave this place, Dorothy. Any last words?"

This was it. She'd failed. Failed to protect her boy. Failed to set him up for a future without her. A selfish mother, through and through. A lifetime of me-me-me.

"About what you deserve, Dots," she whispered to herself.

Olca leaned over her. "What's that now?"

In these last moments, she found herself thinking about her own mother. How lonely she must've been in that home, drifting away, knowing that no one loved her enough to visit.

You've got something missing inside. You selfish wee cow. That was right enough. Some lessons you learn too late. If she could only go back to that day when she'd sat on her back stoop, watching her mother tend the garden, let flow the sudden urge to tell her mother she loved her, that she was sorry. Instead, her mother had gone on sorting the bluebells while Dottie drank herself numb.

They protect, you know. They wash away the dark, her mum had said.

"They wash away the dark..."

Dottie rose, clutching her side as she glared up into the malice-filled eyes of Olca. Did her son still live inside that skin? Did his soul cling on?

She could almost feel the contours of her Mother Death mask sit over her face, turning her into something else. Olca took a step back, its green eyes dimming as it squinted at her.

"My," it said, "don't we have a spine?"

"More than you'll ever have."

Dottie darted forward, tugged the chain from her neck, and shoved the pendant into Olca's mouth. The thing panicked, stumbled backwards, hands flapping about. Dottie leapt at it, clamped both hands over her son's mouth as they both fell to the ground.

She used all her weight to smother Olca's head as the demon tried to spit the pendant out. It made desperate, maddened sounds as it flailed under her, clawing red welts into Dottie's back.

She wouldn't let go. Couldn't let go. This would be the last thing she would do. She closed her eyes and let the monster beat at her back, pull her hair, but she was stone, immovable.

The thing gulped, swallowing the pendant and the bluebells inside.

Dottie rolled off, getting to her feet, the world lurching around her.

The demon thing got up, leaning forward, its eyes bulging like they were about to explode. The buzzsaw of its voice doubled between her ears, a shrieking banshee noise that felt like angry wasps tried to dig their way out of her ear canals.

"What magic is this? What have you done?" it screamed.

"I'm sorry for what I did, Harold." Dottie stepped forward.

"No, don't—" Olca shuffled back, hands raised to its chest like a terrified night creature slinking away. The green in her son's eyes faded. "M-Mum? I felt everything. Make her stop. I-I love you."

"Harold? Don't let go. She's dying. You hear that, you bitch? Eat the damn bluebells, you sick fuck. Get outta here. March on."

"Mum?"

Emerald light burned in his eyes again. The demon lurched forward, jerking about in a twisted world of agony, cracking Harold's bones as it convulsed. Oil-black blood swam out of its mouth. The air whipped around them, kicking up, making a shiver run up Dottie's spine.

Olca's voice was distressed, angry. "I'll haunt him for a thousand forevers. Think this is the last you'll see of me? I'll be waiting. I'll be—"

The storm inside the room intensified. The smell of dusty, ancient books and chocolaty soil was strong in Dottie's nostrils. She watched the thing in her boy's skin twist and turn, trying to escape.

"Die," said Dottie. "Just die, already."

Olca turned its full attention on her. Something inside Dottie squirmed around. Razor hot flashes shot along the top of her skull, making her eyes blink.

The demon reached behind its back, pointing the gun at Dottie with a shaking fist. When it spoke, it sounded weak, almost defeated. "If I can't have him, you can't either. I'll be waiting. Toodles."

"What? No!" Dottie held her palms up.

The pain in her abdomen sliced through all thought. It froze everything around her.

Silence blanketed everything, ringing in her ears.

She stared down at the small bullet hole and the growing circle of crimson staining her white t-shirt. It grew and grew as she struggled to draw breath. The air tasted of gunpowder.

"You... You..." said Dottie, dropping to her knees.

"This party is over," said Olca, raising the gun to Harold's temple.

"Don't—"

The force of the gun going off changed the air around them. The flash of the muzzle burned in her vision. The sound of her son's head cracking to the side then the weight of him collapsing to the floor pulled at something deep inside her.

Dottie coughed up blood, staring down at the mess of her dead son. "Harold?"

A chill spread through her. Her eyes wanted to close, to welcome sleep for the last time.

She blinked. Two green circlets of fire drifted from her son's body like the soul of Olca left him. It glared at her. A sound like thunder ripped through Dottie and then the presence vanished. Olca was gone. The stormy pressure lifted.

The floor came up to meet her. The slap of her stomach on the carpet made her shriek in pain.

Not long now. Gut shot. The blood trickled out of her, seeping into her jeans.

Harold lay in a crumpled mess a few feet away.

"Come on, Dots," she said to herself. "We're not going out like this."

She army crawled forward, clawing at the carpet, nails and fingers breaking as she hauled herself along. The world blinked in and out. She crawled among the slimy things in the negative world, then she was back, still too far from her son. She felt warm. Cosy. Stop here. You've done enough. Can't go any further. Death draws near. It's your time.

You selfish cow, her mother's voice in her head. *Save that boy. Nothing else matters.*

Dottie roared in defiance of encroaching death. Get over to him. Reach. One more nail-ripping pull towards him. Pull. Again. "Ar-rrgh!"

She screamed as she threw her hand forward, touching Harold's cold forehead.

"I... I did the right thing," she said, laying her head on his shoulder. "I did it. I did—"

Golden light glowed out of her fingertips, working its magic.

Then the darkness came for her.

Epilogue

The summer wind fawned through Dottie's hair as the sun beat its force down on her, making her shield her eyes. A black form stood before her, inching closer. Its hot breath hit her, its sweet scent lighting up her nostrils, taking her back to happy days spent outside.

"There's my Jimmy," she said, placing her forehead against his nose, sniffing up his wholesome smell. "I would never scare you off. Forgive me?"

She ran a gentle hand under Jimmy's chin. He snorted a greeting at her, turning slightly as if to say, *Hop on you old git.*

The stirrups jangled as she hauled herself up. The pain in her stomach was gone. Sitting atop the horse, each intake of breath melted the years away, made her feel vital in a way she hadn't felt in years.

"What you say we give those legs a wee stretch? Been a while. Let's go, buddy."

She kicked Jimmy into a gallop, and he thundered to life under her, eating up the green field.

Was this the place Harold was pulled through to each time he died? She tried to remember what it had felt like in the moment of her death, but she couldn't remember anything save the relief of reaching

Harold and bringing him back to life. She had made it in time, hadn't she?

The field was sunlit slopes speckled with yellow dandelions. Tall trees lined the edges of her vision in every direction, like the field was penned in. She peered at those trees, noticing how thick and wild they were, knowing that she'd struggle to get Jimmy through the dense forest.

At the top of a small rise just ahead, a brown horse reared and gave a loud whinny. Pete held the reins with one hand, taking off his hat with the other, waving at her like a rider showing off at a rodeo.

She couldn't stop the cheesy grin spreading up her face. It took all of her to stop from collapsing off the horse and running up to him, arms flailing like a fool, tears streaming.

"Stay cool," she said to herself.

Her heart pounded so hard she felt it in her eardrums.

Sundance walked down the slope, chuffing at Jimmy as if to say, *You slow wee prick, hate having to stop and wait all the time.*

"Hey, cowboy," said Dottie, her voice tight with emotion.

He reached over and took her hand, the familiar callouses singing of long touches in the night.

"I didn't do it, Dorothy. I didn't," said Pete. "I-I've waited so long."

"I know." Dottie sniffed, giving his hand a squeeze to make sure he was real, that he was actually here. "I was so mad at you for the longest time. Called you all sorts. It wasn't fair of me. I thought you weren't happy. That you wanted to get away from me."

"Never. Not in a thousand years." He dropped her hand and took Sundance's reins. The sun's rays lit the grey bristles on his unshaven jaw. "She forced me here. Under her watch. She—"

A white horse shrieked nearby, appearing at the top of the hill. Dottie felt her eyes go wide, her skin want to turn itself inside-out. The horse glared at them with its pink, bloodshot eyes. She thought she could almost see the steam rise from its flaring nostrils.

"I guess that's Harold's ride," said Pete. "For when he gets here. Finally teach that boy how to sit a horse, eh?"

"Boy's got some living to do first." She tugged at Jimmy's reins and they edged out of view of the pale horse. "Did we make it? Did it turn out alright?"

"Look around. He isn't here, is he?"

A sob bubbled out of her. "There was so much death. So much blood. I... I left the cops a note. Guess I knew my clock was ticking. Said I did it all. Pamela, Dan, the whole business."

"You did the best a mother could do."

Dottie kicked Jimmy in the sides and the horse roared to life under her, catapulting away from the white horse and its dead, dead eyes.

They roamed the fringes of the field, in the shade of the trees. Sundance drew alongside, and together they churned grass behind them as they thundered by.

She raised her head, breathing in the summer smells of horse and dirt and sweat.

Within the gathered darkness of the thick trees, two green eyes watched them ride on.

THE END

Afterword

There you have it – my first novel. Well, my first *finished* novel at any rate. I have a rather disgusting pile of broken, half-finished ones laying around, gathering dust and ghosts.

Did you enjoy *Mother Death*? Writing Dottie's story was one of the best things I've done in my short writerly career. She helped me through some stuff. The best stories always do.

I'd fried my brain going over whether to publish this or not. Then my world shrunk, so I thought, fuck it, it's time to go 100% on this writing business thing. Life's too short and never is nightmare. Whether I finish another novel or not is anyone's guess though, I'm really more of a short story guy.

How has my world shrunk, you may be asking? My vestibular migraines currently has me confined to a three mile radius as travelling is vertigo-inducing hell. I'm praying by the time you read this that my physiotherapy has paid off. Or maybe I'm still stuck in my small world. Nonetheless, I shall forge on. More stories are on the way, that's the only thing I can be really sure of right now.

If you liked this book, it would mean the world to me if you left me a short review on Amazon. Every review goes a long way to helping other people find me. Thank you!

And if Olca creeped you out, why not check out my short story collection, *With Dust Shall Cover*? She features heavily in the title story and is up to her creepy tricks, and this time, it's all about drugs.

I sincerely thank you for reading my tale of horror, death and regret.

Until next time.

May your shadow never grow less,

Paul O'Neill

January 2022 - January 2024

Into the Drinking Dark – Bonus Short Story

This story placed second in Creative Ink's annual short story contest. It is set well before the events of Mother Death.

Ten beers and unknown amounts of vodka made the world around Dottie a bit blurry. Her cheeks ached from laughing so hard. Springsteen pumped out the hi-fi in her living room. Bodies leaned against walls, sprawled on couches, filled every available space. The party was good. Life was good.

She slalomed her way into the kitchen – a good party always ended in the kitchen. Where the booze was. She poured herself another. The sharp taste of vodka made her suck in a breath through her teeth.

"You partying without me, my cowboy man?" said Dottie.

Her boyfriend, Pete, leaned on the counter. He scooched over and let her in. When he put his arm around her, the smell of his manly sweat had her tracing the muscles in his back with her fingernail.

"Tell you something," a man called Eric who lived down the street said, "been here for over twenty years now and never drunked myself so hard as you drinked me. Never, never, Dottie. Trust me. Wha...

What was I saying? Aye, that was the cookie. I'm so blasting sorry about what happened to your brother, Dots. I—"

"Can it with that chat," said Dottie, closing her eyes, trying to block out the green *beep, beep, beep* in her mind. "Live for here. Live for now. That's what Trevor would've said."

"Sounds like a mighty fine toast to me," said Pete, clinking his glass against hers.

They all laughed, drank, talked about how bairns didn't know how to have a good time these days. Someone passed round a baggie with some pills. Without a pause, Dottie took one, playfully nibbled it between her front teeth, then chased it down by finishing her glass.

Pete dutifully took it and poured her another. He was always doing things like that. Such a gentleman. She couldn't wait for tomorrow when they'd nurse their hangover by visiting the two horses they owned. They'd ride across a field and chase each other. Not a care in the world. Not a—

"What was that?" she said, squinting at a small shape darting about the living room.

She excused herself and pushed her way past a couple nearly humping against her living room wall. The shadow appeared in the corner of her vision. She followed it to the hallway.

"Chasing faeries again," she whispered to herself, seeing the nimble shape scamper to the bottom of the stairs. "Chasing wee faeries again and again. Away, away, away, aw—"

It was a child. A sullen, almost skeletal thing. It turned to face her, its head down. A mop of tangled, raven-black hair covered most of its face.

"Where did you..." said Dottie, the words almost dripping off her tongue that felt two sizes to big all of a sudden.

"M-Mummy?" the boy said. "Your eyes look funny. Like big shiny pennies."

"Mum? I'm not—" She ran a hand through her straw dry hair. The walls of the narrow hallway seemed to be crushing in on her, making it harder and harder to draw breath. The warble of Springsteen thrummed up her calves. "H-Harold?"

"Y-Yes, Mum. I couldn't sleep. Too many musics go thump, thump in my covers."

"Harold," she repeated, hand covering her mouth.

She'd forgotten him. Easy as that. Her wee boy who slept up the stairs. Her wee boy who always slept up the stairs while she invited everybody into her home which she'd turned into good times central. How could she forget she was a mother? The answer touched an icy finger at the bottom of her stomach. Because she wanted to forget him, that's why. She never wanted to fall pregnant with the man who fled town straight after.

"I'm sorry, my wee guy. Up to bed with you. Go on."

"I need a cuddles in. I can't hear my brain switching off. Why's it have to be so loudy?"

She could sense the eyeballs crawling over her back. She grabbed Harold by his bony shoulders, twisted him around, then placed a palm on his lower back, guiding him up. "There's my boy. Here we go. Up to bed. Forget about us below. Drown us out."

What sick fate gave her responsibility for another life? Months from her brother's crash when he'd fallen off his motorbike, the only things she felt she cared for were the mixers for the drinks. The feeling of being alive in the moment.

"Life is short," he'd said, almost crushing her hand as he lay on the hospital bed, tubes, wires sticking out of him. Beeping machines. "Live for here. Live for now."

She'd nodded, her tears taking away her ability to speak. Little did he know that Harold was quickening in her stomach. She remembered feeling sick to her bones when he'd said it, but she forced a smile.

"But you need to come in with me," said Harold, snapping her out of the vivid memory.

She blinked away her thoughts. The boy before her came back into her vision like a creeping shadow. Like a ghost that had no business haunting her.

"In we go," she sighed. "Come on. In bed now. That's a good wee guy. Covers up. Tuck them in to your chinny, chin, chin."

She leaned in, went to kiss his forehead, mistimed it and ended up clattering her teeth against him, drawing a yelped *ow* that stung at something deep within her.

"Okay," she said, rubbing her front two teeth, unable to feel them. "Bye."

"Wait!"

"What, Harold? What is it? Can't you see I'm busy?"

"My cuddles. You said cuddles."

"Och, alright."

She darted forward, slung her arms around him, let go, straightened. "Better?"

"Kinda."

"I'm trying my best here, kiddo. I—"

"Story. Do Gruffalo story. Gruffalo!"

"A story? You want a fu... A story? You kidding me on? Place is rocking downstairs. No chance."

"Aw, you never read me story."

"Just you close your eyes and get yourself to sleep. Tell yourself your own story. That's the best way. Not always gonna be here to do everything for you, you know."

"You're barely here now."

She watched as he turned away from her. When she turned and took a few steps toward the door, his sniffles made her stop. She could feel her heart thumping in her ears. He was crying. Sobbing in a way that only little boys and girls know how. What a wee selfish bugger. Trying to make her give up the party to read a damned story.

She took the last few steps and closed the door behind her, making no effort to be quiet about it. The door cooled her back as she leaned her back against it, resting a hand on the golden doorknob. The world swam before her. Her blood screamed for more. More drink. More dance. More Pete. More anything.

The sobs. They drifted through the door, itching at her thoughts. She turned and set her forehead against the door. It wouldn't be hard to read a story. Sit with him. Be there.

"Yo, Dottie. You coming down?" said a voice she didn't even recognise. "It's banging down here."

She traced finger eights around her stomach, staring at the painted white door.

"Live for here," she said. "Live for now."

She turned and ran down the stairs toward the music, toward the party.

About the Author

Paul O'Neill is an award-winning short story writer from Fife, Scotland. As an Internal Communications professional, he fights the demon of corporate-speak on a daily basis.

His works have been published by the NoSleep podcast, Crystal Lake, Sinister Smile Press, Scare Street, Vanishing Point Magazine, Fifth Di Magazine, HellBound Books, Eerie River, Grinning Skull Press, and many other publications.

If you're in the mood for a scare, check out his previous short story collections, *The Nightmare Tree* and *With Dust Shall Cover.*

You can find him sharing his love of short stories on Instagram or Threads (paul.on1984).

Printed in Great Britain
by Amazon